I0597967

elemental

a novel in stories

Tara Mantel

Livingston Press
The University of West Alabama

ISBN 13: 978-1-60489-133-1, trade paper

Library of Congress Control Number 2014932126

Hardcover binding by: Heckman Bindery
Typesetting and page layout: Emily Edwards & Amanda Joy Nolin
Proofreading: Breanna Black, Tricia Taylor, Keneshia Cook,
Amanda Joy Nolin
Cover art, design, and layout: DiMarzo Design

"These Woods" first appeared, in a slightly different form, in *Harpur Palate* and was a finalist for the John Gardner Memorial Prize for Fiction. "Confessions" first appeared in *The Gettysburg Review* and was a Pushcart Prize honorable mention. "Trespassers" first appeared in *Quarterly West*. "Finding Women" first appeared in *Alaska Quarterly Review*. "Walking on Water" first appeared in *TriQuarterly*. "Navigations" first appeared in *The Evansville Review*. "Lake Effect" first appeared in *The Southern Women's Review*.

elemental

To all those who are haunted.

Table of Contents

Part I: Earth
(1950–1971)
Burials
These Woods
Bethany Writes Letters

Part II: Air
(1971–1986)
Funerals
The Runaway
Confessions

Part III: Fire
(1986–1988)
Smoke Signals
Checkmate
Trespassers
Navigations

Part IV: Water
(1994–2008)
Finding Women
Lake Effect
Walking on Water

Come now, hear how fire as it was separated raised up the nocturnal shoots of men and pitiable women: it is no erring nor ignorant tale. Whole-nature shapes first sprang up from the earth, having a portion of both water and heat. These fire sent up, wishing to come to its like: they did not yet display the desireable form of limbs nor voice, which is the part proper to men.

—Empedocles, *On Nature*

Part I: Earth

Burials

In 1950, Dorrie, a farmer's wife, had an unusual visitor.
She felt him downstairs on the couch waiting for her, so she went.
She lifted herself out of bed, put on slippers (a habit; it was a hundred
degrees in the old farmhouse), and let herself be called.

She felt The Chief in the lengths of her arms, especially the upper arms, and in front, along the biceps. She felt him at her breast,
already, a hot hovering just an inch in front of her, a magnetic mass
catching her exhale, the core of her sending out deep purple rhythms.
All for him.

The stairs creaked but no one would wake. Henry and the kids
slept like drugged devils.

She went to the couch and let the dawn invade her. Her light
brown curls clung to her temples. Her groin was damp and swollen
with anticipation.

She lay down and let him swirl her torso with his windy appen-
diges, pour a fury tongue inside her mouth.

These were the times when he told her about himself, about his
friendship with her grandfather, James Banach, nearly a century ago,
about how James swarmed into the reservation with ideas about re-
forming the Natives but ended up a convert and their trusted ally. He
told her of how, when he was a young man, he had a vision of her,
a solid woman with a wandering spirit, a woman, *wakan,* born into
the healing traditions of the ancients, a woman who must be guarded
and raised in the proper manner. He was here, now, to see that this
happened.

Her body opened to him, and she felt his weight upon her, a specific form and slide, a brush against her calf. He lay like the cosmos, all and one, light and heavy, all along her spine and her scalp, her hair smoothed back by his massive palm. Her legs opened and he entered her, a great wash, ripples of a magnificent consecration. He filled her with the kindness of a protector; she felt his holiness trickle down her chin and pool between her breasts.

Henry creates space, disrupting the visitor.

He admired the way the plains took the sound of a hammer pounding nails and turned it into an infinite vibration, clear but impossible to pinpoint. He pounded, then stopped, waiting nearly two whole seconds for the reply.

It used to be that he could estimate how much more time a task would take by how many nails were left in their boxes. But he'd gone rusty, just like the nails he found in the shed—jars of them, forgotton. There was a lot more to forget, though, these days—the way the foreman of the dam crew kept him and the others every day until dark, the way the project threatened to burn up millions of dollars that senators promised but never delivered, the young woman he saw the other day climbing up and into the edge of the woods. The way the noise of his family changed over the past year, the heavier steps of his two daughters, Angela and Bethany, who never stopped fighting, and the early morning steps of his wife as she left the bed. If she wanted to lie naked on the couch (this was a woman who never disrobed until the second before bathing), who was he to stop her? There was a shift taking place in the household's strata, and something told him, every morning when he left for the dam site, that there was dynamite here, too, and a fuse that's been lit.

Finishing this porch would be the end of his third summer project. The barn loft was first, then the small bathroom—inside, with plumbing—and now a shaded place in which his family could play or rest or huddle.

The nails went in every four inches. The wood had been cut precisely, all of the two-by-fours placed perfectly, the whole structure a mass of right angles and borders, like the state lines he himself mapped when he was younger and just out of school.

Ives and Bethany—his oldest and youngest—were out playing

on the tire swing. He heard their voices now that they carried on the wind just right. Parents were not supposed to have favorites, but he did. Ives was a good boy, but Bethany was clear-headed and sharp-tongued, even at five years old, and she had a mysterious way of bringing out the best or the worst in people. Henry called her "peace-dove." *Sleep now, peace-dove, I'll sing you a song anon.*

Dorrie had struggled through Bethany's delivery, which involved a cord prolapse, a rare and dangerous situation. One midwife kept Dorrie conscious and the other raised her pelvis with pillows, hoping the cord would sink past the baby's head. The strategy worked. Dorrie, however, lost consciousness, swearing upon waking that she saw visions of destruction, of fires and disintegrating homes and frozen bodies. After it was all over, the midwife said that both the baby and the mother would be fine, but that a strange coldness permeated the room as the baby slid out, and there was no crying—just a newborn resting in the blanket as if she had already lived a hundred years.

In the following months, Henry built this child a rocking horse complete with a mane and a tail made out of real horse hair. He painted on the brown eyes, each eyelash, and realistic nostrils, for which he consulted pictures. Angela, the middle child, became jealous, once even cutting off the mane and tail, and this was where things seemed to stay with his two girls, no matter how many years went by.

Lie still, peace-dove, I'll sing you a song anon.

When the last nail was pounded into the frame, Henry looked toward the swing. There were no children there.

Now that the floor and frame were complete, Henry went to get his telescope. He set it up on the tripod and placed it at the center of the porch. He got a chair from the kitchen and brought it over. He had high hopes for his stargazing; he needed the stars, needed to know that out there, they burned forever.

That night, the sky was clear. He again wandered into the half-finished porch. He sat at the telescope. He turned his astronomy textbook to the page depicting Cygnus, the swan, marked by Deneb, the young and blue supergiant star. He memorized again its pattern, its brightness, its notable neighbor stars. He sat in the chair, among the crazy cicada songs, and leaned in.

But through the lens, he saw not the distant ether or fiery nebulae but rather a luminous outline of a face flashing in front of him, like the imprint that a bright object leaves on the retina, and the face was that of a young woman.

The visitor comes for lemonade.

These fields, these acres of pod and husk—desert land, really, minus the dunes and sidewinder tracks but with that same wind: thrusting as if out of a fire's belly, a raging midsummer heat, an old heat. So hot the steam from the pot of water sanitizing the canning jars barely registered on Dorrie's forehead as she leaned over the stove to pull out what felt like the hundredth one. Most of the windows were open, but for no good reason she could think of except to remind her of life somewhere outside the farmhouse walls. Which was a pretty good reason, now that she thought about it.

Jar, rind, pack, brine. She screwed the rings on tight, using a rubber grip. They'd eat these spiced watermelon rinds through winter, with a little cream. She had been saving rind for a week, pounds and pounds of it. She cut the last rind off the last of the fruit—well, not the last; she still would have a load of watermelon to sell—just this morning. By now, though, she had iron wrists, the tendons in them as taut as fiddle strings. She had felt not even a twinge in their veiney hollows. The older she got, the more she believed that her wrists were what held her entire body together.

Jar, rind, pack, brine. Lid, ring, seal. She looked out at her vegetable garden, the leaves of the summer squash already wilted. She would go out soon to the well and to the nearby storage barrels to get water. She still liked to use the well water for the vegetables and often swore that they grew better from it.

Well water, nothing, she thought. This land was fortified with the tear-salt of dismayed immigrants, their bones shocked into silence. Their letters home said don't bother with the cast iron and the oak; there's no use for anything here besides what you might be lucky enough to assemble from bark and leather and tar paper. Dorrie understood. Here, the earth swallowed you whole, and the prairie moon shadowed mind and memory. Leave all picture frames, ceramic, and mirrors, she would add; bring only your resolve and your imagination.

Henry had recently given her the gift of a tiny indoor bathroom—a sink and a flush toilet and, in the kitchen, the miracle of refrigeration. But the little unit cost so much to use, she'd have to unplug it in October and revert to cold storage in the cellar.

They moved into the farmhouse four years ago, a house at the end of the earth, no neighbors for a mile, nothing but semi-arid suffocation and that bold and bewildering orange dust spinning into miniature cyclones and traveling down the dirt road at the speed of a man's run. Only the Farmers' Union wives came by once in a while to pick her up and take her to town for a meeting.

She transferred the batch of hot jars to a pantry shelf, which took long enough for the haze outside to clear and for the sun to send rays directly into her kitchen. When she turned, the glare off the cleaver's blade blinded her and split her forehead down the middle. Already her afternoon headache was coming—she could feel it setting in, two inches or so behind her forehead—and her eyesight was beginning to blur.

She moved the cleaver out of the sun and looked in on Ives. He sat on the braided rug, sorting his rocks. He had eight distinct piles set around him.

"Everything okay?" asked Dorrie.

Ives nodded.

She had never seen a child so meticulous. The rock sorting would continue for months as he added to and detracted from his piles. Later, Henry would help him identify them and make tags for their containers. All Henry had to do was point to a rock and Ives would be there, studying it, struggling to place it in the right pile. Henry would correct him occasionally as he rolled a rock between his fingers, pointing out a strip of mica or white feldspar.

Suddenly, the air grew electric; Dorrie felt the familiar cold pressure on her lower back. The Chief now sat calmly in the living room, on the rocker—its original cushion stitched up and then covered with a rust-colored cloth with yellow polka dots on it.

She turned back into the kitchen to make The Chief his lemonade. Fishing around in a cabinet, she retrieved the green-glass juicer, then got nine lemons from a basket on the counter. She halved them and pressed each half over the juicer's protruding middle. When she was finished with a lemon half, she gave it a few light pounds with a hammer. Nothing much ever got done properly without a hammer, not in territory like this. She was rewarded, each time, by the thinist slip of juice coating the glass and flowing into the catch. *Waste not, want not,* she thought, *and Lord knows nothing should ever be wasted in a goddamned desert.*

She paused, shocked. She had used the Lord's name in vain. And the headache coming strong.

The Chief wouldn't mind the slandering of a god. He had a sense of humor. What he disapproved of was the porch being renovated.

She called to Ives to open The Chief's window.

"It's stuck, Mama," Ives said.

Dorrie set the last lemon down, threw the soiled dishtowel over her shoulder, and went to the living room. She wrenched the window open.

"There, now, that's better," she said. "How about we have some lemonade?"

The smallest smile emerged on her son's face.

She liked to think of The Chief with his red *chanunpa*, its long stem hooked with feathers and its bowl shaped like a sphere held by an eagle's claw. She liked to think of him as having a singing voice that could penetrate mountains and the arctic winter wind swirling on the plains. She liked to think of his magic, of his triumphs over ailments and afflictions, of his access to realms most people can only imagine.

In other words, she imagined him to be part and parcel of a great kindness, a powerful and courageous benevolence.

But then, why is he not at rest? Some nights, when The Chief was agitated, she'd come downstairs and sit with him. Sometimes she thought she saw him—a whitish or blueish mass, hardly anything at all, wisping through the dining room.

She poured the last of the juice from the catch into the pitcher, added water and sugar, and stirred, then tested it and added a little more sugar, but only a little bit because she knew The Chief did not like his lemonade too sweet.

Dorrie thought she caught something in Henry's eye one day when she mentioned The Chief. It didn't matter that she had pulled out the book that her grandfather wrote about the time he spent on the reservation. There were a handful of white men like James back then. His account was rich with the details required for academia but lacked specifics about any one person. Had her mother, a midwife who watched mothers die and then raised the orphans, lived past the age of thirty, there would be more for Dorrie to know, but for now all she had was this book.

Well, and the birth log, which tracked all the deliveries her mother performed along with any complications, remedies, or procedures her mother experienced or learned. Names—pages of names. Names of dead women and of towns that have since disappeared.

On one electric night that spooked even Dorrie, the agitated Chief threw the window open. A sudden breeze flowed in and caught the log's pages, which were only loosely bound at this point because of time and wear. The log opened to page sixty-eight. Names and more names, but one that stood out:

> *November 26, 1919: Baby Rose, delivered by rail tracks approx. 1 mi. from Bismarck station. Risk of hemorrhage and freezing too great. Traveled to hospital, severe bleeding, baby born fast enough, no lasting damage. Mother dehydrated. Later dreamed of a white bison calf born at bank of river. There was mist. I saw a woman in white fur skins and there was a pile of black sticks at her feet.*
>
> *In the morning, Rose's mother was gone. Baby stayed with me.*

Buried secrets, then. And there was something buried, too, under the new porch. After all, The Chief hadn't arrived until Henry started to build it. Now that the frame was up, the visits were more frequent. But Dorrie knew better than to tell Henry this. Instead, she tried to make The Chief more comfortable and sometimes communicate with him.

And if he wanted to touch her, why shouldn't she let him? This country was vast and harsh and neverending, and someone like The Chief was an important ally.

Henry is mesmerized.

There were three ways that the earth in this territory moved: initially, when the Upper Missouri River ate away at the silt, initiating its original curves; centuries later, when the water carved out the rock, sliced under its edges, and forced debris out into a fan-shaped bed, drowning the surrounding fields; and now, a decade after the world went to war for the second time, the biggest machinery the country had would push the river back onto itself—the blockage would prevent the downriver flooding that periodically destroyed crops and farms. The legislation was passed while Henry was still in college, and now his finances dictated that he find a job on one of the crews.

It was while on this crew that he first saw the woman. She wandered down the wooded slope, still a great distance from the canyon-like valley cleared and dug for the purpose of erection. He might not have noticed her except that she moved suddenly—probably slipped—and caught his eye. Binoculars revealed that she was young, that she was a Native woman.

Weeks passed, and day after day, the woman sat. She descended in the morning and left by three. She carried nothing with her.

Technically, she shouldn't be here, Henry thought, but soon he found himself not only looking for her, but looking out for her, thinking about her, coming up with stories for her.

This area was going to change so much—she was just one human being in a woods.

Still, she sat.

The story about the incipient dam had broken about seven years earlier—someone spotted the red surveyors' flags marking the reclamation land. Now, there were entire towns built for and stocked with workers for the Garrison Dam. The flooding downriver destroyed too much, too often, and the farmers were happy to get protection.

She sat.

And hadn't Congress determined that the downriver destruction, if let to its own devices, would spell economic ruin? The river hurt, not helped, post-war prosperity, all of which could be wiped out in a single rainy season, or even a single flash flood.

She sat.

Henry looked around the canyon. The magnitude of the project was the talk of the nation, its scope the envy of ambitious engineers, its promise nothing less than centuries of growth and prosperity. Every day, the scene set men's joints into action. Any man could make a name for himself here, feed his family twelve times over, and still have a downpayment on a house. Here, Henry could keep himself and the farm afloat.

She sat. Every day, she sat.

He took the long way up the slope so as not to scare her off. He would act surprised when he came upon her; he would raise his hands, bow his head slightly, turn to leave but then have second thoughts. He would sit near her, make some comment about the project, ask her what interest she had in it. Then he would excuse himself and leave.

There was no path to speak of, so his attempts at stealth and silence went unfulfilled. At last, as he approached the precipice, he saw her, down and to the left. She sat cross-legged, facing away from him. Her straight hair flowed all the way to the ground—the shine of it was remarkable. Up close, he could see she was petite, or possibly much younger than he thought.

"May I borrow your binoculars?" the woman said.

Henry flinched.

The woman turned her head slightly. "Your binoculars. If you have them, I'd like to borrow them."

Henry took a few steps toward her.

"I don't have them with me, sorry." He was shocked at this apology, at his clumsiness, at his sudden regret at not having brought them along.

"You are the one who knows I'm here," she said.

Henry approached her, glimpsing her profile. Her face was indeed young-looking, but she was not a kid.

"May I sit next to you?" he asked.

"Yes."

Henry cleared a spot next to her. He looked out at the dam site as if at a distant planet.

"It's possible that you're trespassing," he said.

Now she looked at him. His chest constricted; he nearly looked away.

"You have a funny definition of trespassing," she said.

"I wouldn't want you to get in trouble, is all."

"You have a funny idea of trouble."

"Look, I came up here to warn you. Someone less sympathetic than I am might see you."

"Then let me be seen."

She looked away. Again, he studied her profile. He closed his eyes, trying to re-create the face he saw through the lens of his telescope the other night. Had this woman been trying to talk to him? Had he known of her before becoming conscious of her? And now, in meeting her, all of his speech flowed off of her, pooling at her base. Even now, she barely moved; he reached out to touch her arm but stopped.

"You sit here often," Henry said.

"I grieve."

Henry paused. "I see."

"No, you don't see."

"It's an expression. It just means 'I understand.'"

"But you do not."

Her ground slipped from under him. They sat under the sun now, her hair shining, his hand burning and ready to stroke it.

"You don't think I understand why you come here to sit?"

"You think the river kills. Technically, this is true."

"Where do you come from?"

"What?"

"How far away do you live?"

"You ask unimportant questions."

He felt the anger travel to his shoulders. She was in danger, and she needed help. He clenched his fists. He decided to begin again.

"I'm Henry," he said. "Who are you?"

"My name is Rose."

The noise of the surrounding machinery faded, then became louder: the wind and its tricks.

"Surely you have a home," he said.

She laughed. "Now I know that not only are you not funny, but you are also cold-hearted. Your dam will create orphans. Babies will cry. There will be long and severe addictions."

"Many of us on the crew also have families. We have drought and either too many children or not enough. We go crazy out here."

"Yes, crazy. This happens. I was raised briefly by a white woman who was killed. Tell me, who would do this? I will tell you. People who don't have enough of life. People who go wrong because they cannot find their own feet in the mud."

Henry said, "I want to show you a place."

The visitor has a gift.

She knew there would be a message waiting for her. The last time she went to the well to pump water for the vegetables, there was nothing, but that was because The Chief had to rest. This time, there would be something for her.

The headache was the first sign: this one cracked her vision in two and sent her roaming.

This is why she had to turn away Shirley, the head wife in the Union Wives, when she appeared at the door. Sacred time is sacred time. Still, she did not appreciate it when Shirley went on about how lonely it can get out here in "this type of situation," how they all struggled with "it" to some extent, and how there was "no shame" in bringing "it" up even in polite conversation.

One thing about Shirley: she would never understand about The Chief.

The Chief was so upset about the porch that he could no longer stand to be around the house. Perhaps he had moved to the well. Maybe that's what awaited her.

Dorrie went to the window: a slight breeze, the air tinged slightly yellow, the sky a bright white.

"Mom," Ives said. His voice pulled her out of her trance. He sat where he'd been most of the morning—on the chair, reading. Angela and Bethany sat on the floor.

"What is it," she said.

"Is it going to rain?"

"I hope so," Bethany said. She had a pencil balanced on one finger, her other fingers curling awkwardly around it.

"You always want rain," Angela said.

"No, I don't," Bethany said.

It was bad enough that The Chief stopped visiting her. Now her children were going to bicker? And now Bethany—she just now noticed—had one of Henry's drafting pencils in her left hand and was drawing small circles on some scrap paper.

Dorrie went to Bethany, then yanked away the paper she was

drawing on. Then she yanked away the pencil and put it into Bethany's right hand.

"I always knew you were a devil baby," she said. "You will use the correct hand."

"Yeah," said Angela. "Everyone else does."

Bethany transferred the pencil to her left hand.

"Go to your room," Dorrie said. "You're a horrible, disobedient child."

"Mom," Ives said. "Is it going to rain?"

The atmosphere had indeed changed. They were under a kind of shadow. Outside, a dark-gray front quickly blocked out the light. Even from this distance, Dorrie could see the wisps of moisture between the clouds and the earth. There would be hail like no other.

"Ives, get the chickens in," Dorrie said. She started closing the windows. Angela and Bethany watched her. "When Ives gets back," she said, "I have something to take care of."

The Chief was angry, angry, angry, and she needed to go to him immediately.

They heard the roar before any hail fell.

The sound was that of wind through a tunnel, except softer.

Dorrie didn't bother with the porch. The Chief had his own plans for it.

The wind picked up, making the farmhouse creak in its deepest joints. When the first ball of ice hit the window, Bethany cried. Even Angela huddled closer to her.

Dorrie pulled on her galoshes. She had been summoned.

Halfway to the well, the hail began in earnest. Dorrie had only the hood of her light jacket to pull over her head, and she realized that it provided little protection.

She started up the long slope. The hail fell crossways over the landscape. Ice balls bounced five inches up after hitting the ground; at rest, they gathered under Dorrie's every step, crowding out her feet, sliding her legs out from under her. She looked back at the house— gray in a scorched-yellow field, everything tunneling farther away. The next step brought her ankle down on itself, pushing her knee forward, forcing it to take all the weight of her as she came down. She had lost sight of the well, but not of The Chief: no one said getting to him would be easy, but his message would be worth it.

When she tried to get up, the pain shot through her thigh. Also, the ground seemed softer now, but that was because the hail had turned into rain, which was making the ground spongy. She limped her way forward, but her shoes were already soaked, already useless.

Another hail ball under her foot sent her down on her left side, the jolt causing the pressure in her head to spread, to fan out across her eye sockets and forehead. Another collision, and then there was nothing but the ground. Lightning? Had a bolt found its way to her? Perhaps The Chief blamed her for the porch, for containing something that needed air, for disturbing a burial ground. She told Henry to stop building it, but he wouldn't.

Her scalp grew cold from the inside. She thought she felt it dislodge and shift slowly downward, the exposed tissue jumping around. She propped herself up on one elbow but could barely lift her head. When she did, she saw the ends of her hair wadded and clumped in the mud. The whole thing seemed so familiar. *I was mud before, mud before, mud before*, she thought. She listened past the rain for The Chief's words. Then her hair turned silver; she thought of melted metal, of mercury beaded up. Then all was silent and dark. She sank and sank.

Later—hours maybe—she felt a whisper of a touch on her cheek, like that of a cat's whiskers. She knew it was her Ives, her distrusting son, her savior. She knew that his big eyes inspected her. He would know what to do.

Henry goes underground.
The hail sealed them in the cave. Henry could not believe how fast the storm moved in. Some of the crew would be caught in it, for sure. But here, under the earth, was a rhythm of its own—tunneling animals, radon seeping out of rock, sprawling ant colonies—the hum of a vast and buried life.

The cave walls pulsed as Rose touched them. Or perhaps this was an illusion, a trick produced by the lantern's imperfect glow. Rose held the lantern up to the wall, searching. Then she backed away. "Less light seems to help," she said. "Ah, there." She pointed. On the wall were vague images—chalky-brown scrapings faded in places to gray, even black. Henry had to look for a few minutes before anything emerged for him.

"I don't know what these are," Rose said. "And sometimes I think my eyes are playing tricks on me."

"But I see them, too," Henry said.

"Maybe your eyes are playing tricks."

It occurred to him that they were alone. Not alone solely in the sense of there being only the two of them, but alone as in removed from their respective environments. Henry hadn't longed for home for many years.

"My wife is not well," Henry said.

"I know," Rose said. "That is why you are here with me."

"I suppose you're right." Her youth made him crazy, a strange woman in a cave filled with distortions and harsh clarity, with all of his unacknowledged need.

"What I mean is," Henry said, "she's not right. Her mind is slipping."

Something caught Rose's eye. Henry followed her gaze but couldn't identify anything in the weak light. Rose walked a few steps toward the back of the cave and bent to pick something up. A locket. She opened it. "No picture," she said.

"More unknowns," Henry said.

She stepped closer to him. "In a couple of years, maybe less, all of this will be underwater. Fish will swim through it. Everything will start over."

She was more alive than he could bear. Again, he reached to touch her, but couldn't. All of what was out there, the fields battered by balls of ice, the dam, even his memories, seemed to belong to a different time.

He wasn't sure if he wanted to see her ever again.

It wasn't until Rose disappeared around the path's bend that Henry was able to take in the landscape. The hail had ripped through everything. Small trees and brush were flattened. Ice balls stranded in tree branches fell occasionally, breaking the dense silence with soft thuds. Not even a breeze blew—it was as if all weather had ceased, having poured out all at once, leaving the sky empty and exhausted.

The hail balls were the size of peas, and had damaged the paint on Henry's car. The car drove well enough, but struggled on sections of the road home, sections where the balls were the size of cranberries, then acorns. He finally dared to look out at the fields. Flattened, all of them, only the occasional wheat or corn stalk standing upright. *Might be some government money coming our way*, he thought, then cursed the farm. Maybe it was time to give it all up.

Now it was the cave that seemed far away, that seemed to belong to another time. Still, Rose stayed with him, and the smell of her—something like chicory—hung around him. She was right about everything, and he wished he had touched her, just to thank her. Perhaps there was nothing at all to curse—just fields to re-tend, repairs to make, one life to go on and another just beginning.

Up ahead was a person running. A boy. Ives. Henry sped up, pulling alongside him. When Henry got out of the car and approached him, he was unmistakeably clear-eyed. His cheeks were bright red—had the hail pummeled his face?

"Mom fell," he said.

Only the storm knows exactly what happened.
How everything escaped from where it all was supposed to be, Dorrie did not know. When she was finally able to stand up, she noted first the profound stillness. *The eye of the storm*, she thought, but then realized that it was hurricanes that had eyes. Still, this silence could be a hoax.

What wasn't a hoax was The Chief's message. He needed blood. He needed an animal, a live catch.

His destruction was magnificent. The chickens, which had gotten out of their pen, lay dead and twitching all along the exposed side of the hill. Their pen had caved in on one side; no doubt more chickens were crushed beneath it.

Her entire right side was numb, but the power of The Chief's imperative coursed through her, allowing her to make her way down the hill and toward the house.

She had failed, she knew this, but she would redeem herself by carrying out his latest request. Until she heard the bleat of the goat in the distance, she thought she had lost her peripheral vision. Perhaps she had. She needed to turn her whole body to see the goat, which was down on its side, a leg—maybe two—broken, its neck cut and bloodied. Before she could take in all of its injuries or understand how the goat had gotten there, she saw it glow—its whole body shimmering, its desire perfectly clear to her. Its succumbing was beautiful, and she could see why The Chief chose it.

She approached the half-dead animal. Later, she would not remember carrying the goat back up the hill, but now she hoisted it up easily. Then the screams began. Human screams, far in the distance. There was no time to investigate. The Chief needed this animal or there would be more destruction, or maybe he would abandon her.

She approached the well. It was like a magnet pulling her in. The glory and the light, the intense peace—all of it flowed through her. She was happy when she folded up the goat's stick legs, happy as it struggled, hovering, over the well, happy as she released it, happy that it journeyed now to feed everlasting life, happy because of her contribution to her beloved.

The girl's screams were next. They filled her ears. The devil child stood next to her, pointing at her and shaking.

After the storm

The sight barely stopped him: his son, pacing about; his favorite child drenched, her legs bleeding, her eyes bloodshot; his wife delirious and without speech. Other men might have thrown a temper or hit the bottle. But Henry had too much to do.

His wife, mercifully, fell asleep almost as soon as Henry maneuvered her to the couch. He had found her wandering about the smashed chicken coop, tripping over chicken carcasses, mumbling *you whom I should love above all things—in choosing to do wrong and failing to do good—sin no more—you whom I should love.*

Finally, Henry turned to Ives. "What happened?"

"Mom went outside."

"In the storm?"

"Yes, sir."

"Why were you kids out there?"

"Beth heard the goat and ran out. And then I went to get her. And then I saw Mom on the ground."

"Okay. You did the right thing."

Henry looked at his sleeping wife. There would be doctors. There would probably be procedures. *Lots and lots of questions.*

He wanted to see her sleep the way she used to, on her side and

16

curled up next to him with her head tucked just under his armpit. But what he saw was Rose's bare feet, in long grass, water swirling around them and then around her ankles. He saw her knee-deep in flooded prairie, holding on to a canoe filled with knapsacks and burlap bags.

There will be long and severe addictions.

He had not been completely honest with Rose. He read the papers, he heard the reports. People and land: together, they would never be at peace.

It was not enough to say that everyone suffers, that change is inevitable and affects us all. This dam would dislocate the people in an entire area. The dam would bury everyone.

The dam will create orphans.

Why was it that he had fallen so hard for this woman? He realized now that this is what had been happening for months. She was young, yes, and certainly determined. And she hated him. Well, perhaps not hate, but certainly she distrusted him. She knew what drove him more than he did, and for this, maybe, he held her in his mind longer than he should.

Now, though, he needed to get Bethany to stop crying. He bathed her and cleaned and bandaged all her cuts. He dried her body and kissed her cheek.

There, now, peace-dove, you will sleep safely.

Later, to Ives, he said, "Your mother is not well. She sometimes has a problem seeing things as they are. Do you understand?"

The boy nodded.

"She doesn't always know what she's doing. She's not a bad person, but something is wrong and we're going to try to find out what that is."

The boy nodded.

"Your sister is going to need some help, too."

The boy nodded.

"You're a good boy."

At bedtime, Bethany clung to Ives and wouldn't let go. Henry left them together in Ives's bed. Ives had his arm around her and his face buried in her neck, as if to stay warm.

Orphans.

He had something to say to Rose but wasn't sure what it was. He felt that he was meant to be the one to see her and to go to her. He thought he understood now when she said she sat to grieve. It was the grief of future losses, the anticipation of loss; it was the past, present, and future all in the same moment.

He went to his porch and sat. No constellation would appear to him tonight, but he watched anyway, and without expectation.

The next morning he looked for her, but she would never come again, he knew this, but he went to her spot anyway.

In her place were two things: the locket she found in the cave, this time with a picture of her in it, and a small cage with two brown-and-white rabbits in it. The note said that she needed to find a home for them, and would he adopt them.

Bethany's little-girl heart would love them forever. His own would break every time he saw them.

The bunnies huddled together in the cage.

Orphans.

They stayed that way all the way home, all the way up the long, bumpy driveway. His wife stood in the garden. The children ran and screamed.

His fourth summer project would be to build a rabbit pen as sturdy as the walls of his own home would have to be.

These Woods

Hibernation

In these woods, trees sway in the wind like tentacles. They are new growth, they know how to begin from nothing. In time their roots reach far down into the deep clay layers of the earth, unfurling roothairs groping for the raw dirt, holding on tightly for life.

Nadja stands amid the highbrush cranberry growing at the base of a young oak, its highest branch thrusting crookedly into the dawn. The wet leaves below her feet are inches thick, cushioning her step. In this season of transition, she feels her shape shift: she is bulkier in her heavy clothes, and her sluggish body craves breads and grains, the starch her cells will need throughout the winter.

Sister Sky, Nadja's older half-sister, is here too. She is bulky all the time. She pushes through North Dakota windchills like a snowplow clearing drifts. In the middle of a rock-weathering January, her hands are warm and pulsing. She eats fresh root vegetables as long as they are available, and red meat for breakfast. Sometimes she fixes a batch of fried bread and eats it with garlic, which she says is a charm. Nadja, who knows that the caseworker would not approve of charms, adds that it is also an antioxidant.

Arrivals

How long had Nadja been in these woods? She and her husband purchased the drafty yellow farmhouse four autumns ago, in 1967. They hadn't discussed having children, but when Nadja found an abandoned baby girl in the Bismarck bus station, they believed they had received a sign.

The baby was carried off by security personnel—Nadja couldn't get the image out of her mind—and one night she breathed the name "Zola" into the bedroom air and wanted it to be the baby's name. But when, a week after her training had ended, Nadja called the department inquiring about the child, she discovered that the baby's heart, like that of her young husband, was a pulsing flesh grenade quickly counting down to zero. In time, both failed.

The mourning chipped away at Nadja's bones, carved out in the sticky marrow a deep nesting place. She had to remember to move her body forward, preferably into physical labor of some kind, and so directed all her energy into unnecessary home-improvement projects, beginning with the interior of the creaky farmhouse. She drove to the hardware store for cans of paint, rollers, angled nylon brushes, sandpaper, Spackle. After a breakfast of banana and oatmeal, she would sand and wipe the walls, carefully paint the trim, roll on slabs of color—teal, magenta, gold. While the walls dried she went outside to weed or mulch or prune the rose bushes that hung over the stone wall.

But even the freshly painted walls held the energy of grief; they spoke in the night of their emptiness, and when Nadja pushed against them, she decided to believe in ghosts.

One day the department called Nadja with a possible placement: a young girl waiting, it seemed, especially for her. This stringy-haired girl with post-traumatic stress disorder arrived as planned, but Nadja barely had time to get to know her when another arrival came knocking.

Nadja had not seen Sky in nine years. Her hair was still long and straight and raven-colored, her bangs still choppy—she must still use the kitchen knife to cut them, Nadja thought—her expression like an ink blob, her knotty fingers proof of her adolescent training as a potter. "Father said you did not sound so good on the phone," Sky said, and then pushed past Nadja to the stove to set a pot to boil.

Sky found a job at the grocery store in the older part of town, but her blood was that of a healer. The night she arrived at the farmhouse, she sat in front of the fire, her face glowing like melted amber. "I will make an *inipi* out of the shed. It faces east, it is good enough. You will live again."

Nadja said, "You still practice."

"I have no choice in the matter," Sky said.

In time Nadja would see that those who believed in Sky came from miles, in rusted trucks with no windshield wipers or hubcaps, because they knew she'd give them what they needed, that she could sense their energies and their magnetic pulls and resistances, and give them advice they could use.

Nadja had grown up with pharmaceuticals and indoor plumbing and a white mother, a mother born in a hospital, not on frozen ground on the side of an unpaved highway after walking halfway across the state. She was not going to argue with Sky. She remembered how Sky, when just a girl, healed the dying and convulsing snakebite boy on that windless summer day in 1950, and held her tongue.

Inquiries

In these woods, saplings spring up strong and fast. They reach upward and downward, opposites stretching. Nadja breathes deeply in her garden. She can hear Sky banging around in the kitchen, setting out tea and fruit and oatmeal flavored with cinnamon and cream. In a few minutes Sky will emerge in her embroidered denim skirt and the quilt coat with the fuzzy trim along the edges, go to the end of the wrap-around porch, the side facing east, and pay homage to the light of wisdom. She will stand so still she could be a stamen reaching out from a sweet-liquid desert bloom.

Nadja bends to gather chamomile, thyme, rosemary, sage. The light in this northern backcountry is lilac-colored. Lilac comes before pink, pink before yellow. The herbs, which Nadja puts in her basket, will dry over the fireplace and then be put into clay jars. Nadja needs many plants, because she cooks for the millions. That is how she says it. At the moment she might need to cook only for two, but she will cook for anyone, for strangers and the estranged, for Sky's goddesses and visitors, for the delirious and the rabid.

Nadja's children come from all over. The women in the support group, which Nadja attends every other week, nod when she says that these kids are raindrops, they are pollen. The women smile when she says she calls her latest girl Honey-Wheat because all she ate for two days was clover honey on slices of toasted wheat bread. Honey-Wheat's birth name is Julia, but Nadja likes to let the child believe that her new name is a special gift.

When Nadja goes inside, Sky is at the cutting board, silent, preparing the ingredients for chili, and Honey-Wheat is squirming up into her chair, which is pulled too close to the table. She is six years old and on four medications, which Sky glares at when Nadja sets them, in a multicolored pile, in front of the girl, so she can swallow them with some water crackers and juice.

Honey-Wheat is asking about where babies come from, and Nadja jumps in to say, motioning skyward, "My little girl, babies come from above—that is why the clouds have many colors in them." She gets this out quickly because the truth will open the floodgate and then there will be questions she can never answer.

The boy

About a year later, these woods do an amazing thing. It is a glazed, humid week, tornado warnings in all the counties. The sky is yellow-gray and the air so still your ears echo.

On the edge of the tree line appears a boy of about five. He is wild looking, with deep-set eyes, and he crouches in the brush. He wears cutoffs and a T-shirt with a tear in the sleeve. Nadja is putting down a fresh layer of mulch in the garden, and turns for the wheelbarrow when she spots him. She watches for movement, but he is as still as a boulder.

The boy is curious, not afraid. She goes inside and returns to the garden with sunflower seeds and peaches.

"I wonder," Nadja says to the boy, "if you've ever tried a peach." She bites into it and lets the juice run down her chin. She holds the fruit out to him. "And I'll bet you don't know what sunflower seeds taste like."

The boy doesn't answer.

"*¿Tienes hambre?*" she says, but there is no sign of comprehension.

She thinks of calling the police but waits. The boy will come for food eventually.

The next day the boy is there again, but now he wanders to the porch and sits quietly with Nadja, and on the third day he comes inside. Nadja can't take her eyes off him. He looks as though he had sprung, fully formed, from the dank mud on the bank of a stream or from the depths of rotting compost.

Nadja talks to him about anything: her day, her garden, people who mean nothing to him or even to her. She tells him about Sky, how he will meet her soon. She puts out a plate of French toast and watches him closely. There are things—normal, everyday things—that the boy clearly has never seen. The blender, for instance, might to him have been an alien spaceship. Is he interested in spaceships? She lets the silence grow.

She talks to him about a bath: has he had one lately? Maybe he would like one. Maybe he would like to be clean, wear soft pajamas.

She leaves him with his half-eaten toast to run a bath, and when the toast is gone the boy lets her rub him down with a cloth. He has cuts—old and nearly healed—and several bruises that are yellow in the middle. She checks for malnutrition and lice, then dries him and wraps him in a towel. When she runs a comb through his hair he looks down and picks at the chipped spot on the sink.

"You are a sweet fruit," Nadja says, "and you are discovered."

Gathering

Sky has firm ideas about the *inipi*, and stays up all night diagramming the interior, which will consist of a dirt floor with a pit in the middle for the *owihaukeshni*, the fire that burns with no end, and a cedar chest containing several blankets. The sliding door will be replaced with a heavy tarp, which will ease the passing of the hot stones from the outside fire pit to the pit of the *inipi*.

Later, they all follow Sky down to the pond, where they gather willow saplings, rocks, and sticks. The boy takes off his shirt and leaves it by a downed tree. Honey-Wheat sings, rolls on the ground, brings Nadja caterpillars. The boy crouches as he walks, and his diligence pays off; he finds six good-sized rocks and carries them awkwardly over to Sky, who has started piles. Honey-Wheat, after half an hour, drops one twiggy stick. Nadja finds heartier sticks and a whole region of saplings curving around the side of the pond.

Sky joins her. "These are perfect saplings," she says. She pulls out a pair of cutters and kneels by the shoots. "Spirit to spirit, I take you." She cuts a few. "The trees are generous, they help us willingly. Spirit to spirit, I take you, but in your place more will arise." She cuts the last few of the strongest saplings and gathers them in her arms, and drops them near the rocks and sticks.

They walk back to the piles, where the boy and Honey-Wheat

play. Sky looks at the boy. "These are perfect rocks," she says. He adds another to the pile.

Sky looks at Honey-Wheat. "And this is a perfect stick." Honey-Wheat giggles.

The sage will have to wait because Honey-Wheat bolts for the pond. The boy follows. Sky, kneeling by her gatherings, waves them on.

Nadja catches up to the kids. She says that they will lie on a warm slab of rock, and they will listen to the beautiful songs of the meadowlark. She turns to the boy and says, "We will clean your clothes and give you a special necklace to wear." She says to Honey-Wheat, "Come, show him yours," and Honey-Wheat pulls out from the top of her muddy pink T-shirt a silver chain with a turquoise medallion hanging from it.

Nadja says they will all go down and see what the frogs are up to. She says, "What do you think they do down there all day?"

Honey-Wheat is excited because she is allowed to be naked. She smiles, showing teeth stained with cherry Kool-Aid. She yanks at the sleeves of her T-shirt until her arms are free, and then pulls the shirt partly over her head. She lets it hang down past her neck like a nun's habit.

Nadja steps down the muddy slope and onto the rock, to demonstrate. She smells the stale heat of baked earth.

The boy sits beside Nadja. Honey-Wheat joins them and sits, hugging her knees. She scratches a pebble into the rock, brushes at the chalky outline.

Nadja says to the boy, "Do you know this place?" The boy looks at her. "It is a nice pond, don't you think?"

A giant cumulus cloud opens enough for a wash of sun to spread over them. The rock heats quickly, makes their legs prickle with goosebumps. "See?" Nadja says to the boy. "You pulled the sun's rays right out of the sky."

"Sunny sky," Honey-Wheat says to her knees, giggling.

Naming

Nadja calls the department and in fact one caseworker there knows of this boy. "This one is called Russell, and he runs away," the woman says. "He's been placed all over the area." She says that Nadja should hold tight. Someone will come by, she says, to take a history, but the days pass and no one shows up. Calls are not returned.

Nadja searches deep for explanations but there is nothing for a situation like this. She consults her training manual and talks with the support group, but there is nothing regarding a child who is spit out by the woods and does not speak. That the boy doesn't speak does not, on its own, concern Nadja. These kids, they have already tumbled down from strange mountains; they do not necessarily believe in the benefits of speech.

The boy receives his special name a week later: he helps Nadja with the yard cleanup, uprooting with his bare hands stunted bulbs and weeds with stems as thick as Nadja's thumb. And so he becomes Claw.

In the spring Claw digs additional rows for the garden and clears the area around the shed. He pulls wormwood and foxtail for hours, even thistle. Nadja goes to him with lemonade and apples and peanut butter bread. He eats while squatting beside a mass of bent white rudbeckia, the ground dug away and the roots half exposed.

Honey-Wheat wanders over next to Claw. Her dandelion crown sits crooked on her head and her face is smeared with mud and the orange frost of lily stamens. Her ponytail hangs limp at the base of her neck.

Claw counts out half his apple slices and places them, one at a time, in Honey-Wheat's hand. She bites into one and smacks noisily.

Chewing and, imperceptibly, surviving.

Deliverables
Nadja wants Claw to see life in the town, kids playing on the sidewalk, merchandise bought and sold, pigeons and hot tar.

"We will take a trip to town," she says. "To the store to get some yummy things." Claw looks at the floor, chewing on the nail of his index finger.

In the front seat of the truck, Honey-Wheat yammers on about where to get the best oranges; how Mr. Guslander, the store owner, sometimes gives you a lollipop and you don't have to pay for it; that there's a church with ladies sitting in front of it and sometimes the high bell is ringing but sometimes it isn't.

Up ahead is the racket they've heard for a mile: large machines, and then dust rising from the site of a retail complex. The metal contraptions emerge from the cloud, folding and unfolding their grasshopper-like appendages, and Claw is pasted to the window. He turns to Nadja, his eyes ask seven questions. Nadja says they are making a very big building so the workers have to get up in machines with high seats and lots of controls. Claw looks out. His fingers pick at the peel of an orange and finally get a grip, pulling it away. Tiny oil droplets spray into the air.

Nadja has never seen a child so silent. But she will lose him if she coaxes, if her mind is full of ideas of things she feels he must do. She will lay a finger on him lightly, give him a sentence or two, and wait.

When she pulls into the store parking lot, she says, "I will be just a few minutes." Honey-Wheat has questions about what, exactly, is going to be purchased, and climbs over Claw and out of the truck. She goes to shut the door but stops. Claw is moving to get out, and then he does, dropping himself onto the pavement. Even Honey-Wheat is frozen with surprise. Nadja winks at her, motions "shhh."

They go into the store and roam the aisles. Honey-Wheat tosses boxes of cookies into the cart, and Nadja stops to remove them. Claw looks up and down the stacked shelves, but the fruit section stops him in his tracks. He wants a lime, so Nadja bags one and gives it to him to carry.

At the counter Mr. Guslander says, "Is this another one of yours," and Nadja says, "Yes, this is Claw." But Guslander hears "Claude" and says, "Well, Claude, how about a lollipop?" Honey-Wheat grins and jumps around. Guslander places two lollipops on the counter and Claw inspects both before curling his fingers around the red one.

On the way home they have to stop. A train is working its way along the freight line. Nadja stops at the flashing lights. The train rumbles ahead and blows its horn. Honey-Wheat squeals with delight.

The boxcars pass, shades of red and rust and gray flash by. She looks at the children, watches their eyes follow the cars, then flick back to their original position, only to follow again, as if quickly reading lines of text.

Nadja's eyes burn. One boxcar is open and empty; she thinks she sees a drunk man slouched in there, or a child in the corner covered with a burlap sack, breathing the dust of husks and wood chips. When the caboose passes, Nadja looks left at the snaky line of cars disappearing. The sun hits a piece of broken glass lying on the track, and as she pulls forward, it beams out a pupil-piercing glare.

Claw stacks his lime peels against the seat's back, one on top of the other, but Honey-Wheat bounces up and down on the seat and they fall over. He bites into the lime and makes a face. Irritated, he eyes the fruit, giving it a silent interrogation.

Dreams

Nadja stirs from sleep with a vision of Claw running. In a few seconds the vision is gone and Nadja feels consciousness set in, feels the morning light against her closed eyelids.

But when she passes Claw's room she notices that he is not in bed. He is not in the bathroom. And when she goes downstairs she sees that the front door is unlatched.

Her heart races as she opens the door. In her near panic her eyes fly to the light-blue smear passing behind the spindly trees. She makes her way to the woods, where she finds Claw in the brush, crawling around on top of a large mound of dirt. It is as high as Nadja's thigh and is oblong, coffin-shaped. How long has he been digging around in this dirt? And he is not so much piling and patting the dirt as he is sculpting: The mound has an entrance, and the back of it is wedged against the base of a tree. It is big enough to hold a small boy, and as she thinks this, she sees Claw disappear inside of it.

Philosophy

One Saturday night Sister Sky tells a story: There is a man who decides that schedules and clocks and calendars are overrated. The man wanders around the world, through the ancient cities of Israel and India, through fields with rounded stones marking out the vague, overgrown circles of ritual. Commerce has broken him and he needs to find something to make him whole. He is obsessive in his search. He checks along the sides of bluffs, wades through streams, and hunches over earthen pits, studying soggy wood. He is convinced that he will find an answer. He is so certain that he abandons even his books, relinquishes every single one of his material objects. He walks for days in a circle nearly three miles in diameter, looking, inspecting, searching. The man dies of starvation.

Nadja says, "What is that story?" They are all in the kitchen, where she and Honey-Wheat play Uno. It is Honey-Wheat's turn to deal but the cards get away from her and fall, coating the old linoleum. She goes to collect them, but Nadja says, never mind, it's time for bed.

Sky turns to Nadja. "You must not have been listening."

Honey-Wheat takes Claw's hand and pulls him toward the stairs.

"Did Dad tell that story?" Nadja says.

"You do not think these stories are important."

"That's not true."

"These kids are weighed down with bad energy," Sky says. "Their pores are clogged with lead and they have mercury in their blood."

Nadja does not disdain the ancient ways. Karma or kismet or Nirvana or reincarnation are all compelling ways of framing relationships with forces we cannot see. But there are daily battles to be fought here on the ground; here, there is a rising sun to contend with, there are disorders to manage and administrators and officials to deflect.

Nadja says, "The children just need a stable environment."

"And that's what they're gettting."

Nadja picks up toys, throws them into a large wooden bin.

Sky says, "You are still ignorant, then."

"It's just that I think the story is too abstract. They are not ready."

"The story will stay with them. Your problem is that you want to understand everything right away."

Nadja glares at Sky. "You have seen the scars on Honey-Wheat's back. But your answer to all this is philosophy."

"Nadja, your roots, they are smooth and shallow."

Pronouncements

There are times, for instance when all of them are sitting down for dinner, eating silently because of some punishment doled out to the children, knives and forks clinking on emptying plates, that Nadja feels something important disappear: the sheer white curtains billow in an updraft, and she imagines that her purpose has blown under them and out and away. She thinks, who are these children? What are these woods and this house and this roaming half-sister? Where is

28

the origin of the ivory sheen that spreads over this land at midnight?

The other foster mothers, they have strange memories that creep up on them in the middle of a session—memories of failed parents, betrayal, sometimes neglect. The stories differ only in the tiniest details. Nadja herself recalls a depressed father, a critical mother. Perhaps Sky is right about how stories come back to you and deliver messages. Nadja remembers one story in particular, a tale involving a melon that houses a protective spirit, and when the melon is split open the spirit is released.

Sometimes she gropes around for this melon spirit. What is it and how does it work? Will it protect her from the sand slipping beneath her feet and will it keep the wind from whisking up her sunwashed little beauties and carrying them off? Will it tell her that out of grief comes love even though you will feel as if you are drowning?

Nadja knows that the social worker does not think highly of her. She has spoken up about being left out of discussions concerning the children's futures. She has grown frustrated talking with other mothers, hearing about children being thrust back into a dangerous life for the sake of the nuclear family. She is tired of calling for late checks.

On these days and on the days when the social worker drops in unexpectedly to snoop around and formulate opinions, Nadja feels she has sold her body.

One night she announces a new rule. Everyone must knock before entering rooms. No barging in. "Wherever you go," she says, "if there is a closed door and you want to enter, you must knock first. We enter lives with no warning, swing right on in and out of each other's spaces. Knocking on a door is a sign of humanity. A sign of respect."

Sky and the children watch her. Honey-Wheat's brow is crinkled, Claw looks at Sky, Sky looks at Nadja and says, "Now look who is talking about spaces."

It is fall, again, in these woods, the short days descend upon them all. Nadja takes Claw for his first day of school, but he cannot manage it. In the classroom he is as tight as a metal clamp until Nadja touches his arm. After a week he can finally make it through a couple of hours, even do the projects with tissue paper and pipe cleaners.

But he is smitten with cave life, and when he comes home he goes outside and invariably withdraws into his small dirt house pushed up against the base of the tree.

Honey-Wheat's papers are not coming through. The good news is that her mother successfully completed rehab, and this is enough to convince the department to reintroduce the girl into her family. Nadja gets the call well after lunch.

Nadja goes out to the field, where Honey-Wheat sits playing. Honey-Wheat looks up at her and into the low sun. She leans an elbow on her knee, squints her eyes, and says, "Howdy there," pushing the lid of her baseball cap back with her thumb.

Nadja's thighs give out but she steadies herself. "Howdy, pardner," Nadja says, sitting down with the girl in the dirt. The corners of Nadja's eyes tighten. "I reckon I got some news for ya."

Shapes

If the stories Nadja hears at the support group could swirl together and touch down from above, they would do so in the form of lightning, a rare kind, one that strikes in the same place over and over again.

Nadja and the other women watch for signs and clues, and as the months go by they note the tiny steps forward: tantrums of twelve minutes, not fourteen; a child no longer afraid of the bed or of night. Kids are young and elastic, they stretch and bounce back, relearn and unlearn, come and go. They go back to a grandmother's house, a mother's house, they go to group homes or to the apartment of a jobless sister who drinks too much, they walk into hailstorms of promises and fresh starts, to places that cannot support their weight, to ideologues and Jesus freaks, to those who want them for dangerous reasons. They visit prisons, are on speaking terms with adult dementia. They leave town on a midnight bus to New York City. They leave life altogether with a razor blade's slit.

The first snow of the season sifts down in granules and in the noonday sun melts into Rorschach patterns: butterfly wings, profiles of grotesque human faces, crescent moons. The day Honey-Wheat is taken away in a navy-blue sedan, Nadja stops cooking and, at night, waits vainly for sleep.

In these woods the mourning is constant and changing; it aches deeply into limbs. It is a monsoon that flows into every organ and washes away longings, addictions, wishes, intentions.

Sky simmers a chicken, soaks the bones and skin for stock. More marrow, more flooding.

Nadja tells Sky of her latest dream: there are bloody tracks in the snow and she is a girl, she is young, she knows that the tracks will lead her to something awful but then sees the fawn, spotted and still in the center of a field, she is close to it, she can see its breath in the chilly air, and knows that this fawn is not the one that left the tracks and that no matter what, she must find the other fawn, the dead fawn, the bloody carcass.

Sky says the dream's message is simple. "You have encountered fear but you have determination. You gain strength, even now." She says, eat the soup.

But Nadja cannot bring the spoon to her mouth.

"Do not worry, sister," Sky says. "I will dance for you, for your health, for all the miracles waiting just under our feet."

Purification

What they do instead is take Claw into the *inipi*. Nadja tells him they are going into a very hot place, a steaming place, and there will be songs and prayers, and he will sweat a lot, and the sweating will make him feel better and wash all the bad thoughts he has away from him.

He blinks at her.

"And it will smell good, too, not like a sweaty smell. More like a garden smell."

The sacred sticks are placed in the pit, the rocks at the four quarters. The outside fire that warms the seven special rocks that will heat the *inipi* has been burning for hours.

When it is time, the sage is lit, and Nadja and Claw strip down to shorts and a t-shirt. They enter the *inipi*, walking clockwise around the pit. They sit cross-legged on sage beds, Claw opposite the door, in *catku*, the place of honor, and Nadja next to him.

"That's sage that you smell," Nadja says. "We burn it to please *Wakantanka*, which is the Great Spirit. The smell also keeps away bad ghosts, so that we are protected."

Sky uses a pitchfork to bring in the stones. Nadja didn't think the stones would generate so much heat, but the drops form on her forehead and between her breasts, and roll down her back. She hopes that at least the experience will make Claw speak.

After Sky drops the seventh stone, she releases the tarp. The hut goes dark. Nadja takes Claw's hand. "See, we are in a dark warm place to feel relaxed."

Claw uncrosses his legs.

"No, sweetie, stay still, we don't want to offend the spirits."

Sky begins singing a slow chant. Claw stiffens.

Nadja says, "Just listen to the sound. It will make you a little sleepy." But it is too dark to see him, to read his face. He fidgets and squirms, and Nadja feels her hand tighten around Claw's.

Sky stops chanting. "And so, *Wakantanka*, we pray to you. Let the thunders work for you, and the four winds, and all the animals and things that watch over the earth."

Sky reaches toward the tarp and pushes it open briefly. The cool air and light rush inside. In that moment Nadja sees the panic register on Claw's face, and the second she releases his hand, he jumps up and bolts, punching the tarp out of the way before Sky can grab him. The tarp sways, then stops moving. It is dark.

"We can't force him," Nadja says.

"The spirits have been offended. I cut too many corners as it is," Sky says.

"The spirits will understand. He is a boy."

Nadja rises, goes to the window, and opens the shade. Outside, Claw builds up the dirt, bulldozes it with both hands, then pats it down with hard slaps.

These children are like pieces of frayed rope; they come with only a thread of a beginning, with no knots to anchor them, with nothing to stop the continual undoing.

Meditation

Nadja lies on her back in her garden and looks at the tops of the trees through her fingers, which she has extended in front of her face. The sunlight eases around them, turning them a translucent orange. It is November, and winter is already chainsawing through the atmosphere. She has her snowsuit on because she wants to lie comfortably, let the downy thermal layer absorb her heat and distribute it. As the sun reddens her cheeks she sinks deep into her body, feels her chest rise and fall with the gusts swooping in from the north.

The bare branches of the tops of the highest trees sway into her line of vision; a few giant dead leaves of the maples refuse to let go of the mother stem.

She cannot compare her idea of kinship to an oak, maple, or pine tree, nor to a protective forest canopy. It is, rather, like the young underbrush that starts from square-foot one, getting by on what it is offered.

A child can be flung ruthlessly back to a starting point to begin again, Sisyphus-like; but if that child is healthy and fed, then there is a foundation. Nadja has to believe that it is thicker than it seems.

Lost

Claw does not play well with others. The children instinctively avoid him. He has developed a problem with balance; he leans to the left, or when kneeling, for example, he falls over. The speech therapist mentions encephalitis but the caseworker finds nothing in the file. The caseworker says she's seen this happen after a child's head is hit particularly hard, but there is no documentation here, either.

In the special classes, Claw acts out by not participating. Nadja thinks that this is his way of protesting and goes to the teachers to talk. She is embarrassed when she cannot answer questions about his earlier years. One teacher is visibly burned out, stretched too thin, and cannot stop complaining about the lack of resources. She breathes exhaustion into Nadja's face when asked what else can be done.

Cabin fever

It's the middle of winter now, the wind so frigid it welds your nostrils shut, waters your eyes, scrapes the pores off your face, blows dark depressions into your brain.

Sky adds two bags of sand to the truck bed, then rides off to Fargo to visit friends. To combat cabin fever Nadja gets an additional stack of books from the Salvation Army, a clay set, a book of instructions for fun indoor projects. Claw drifts to the clay. Nadja shows him how to flatten it on the newspaper cartoons to get the image to stick. She does this between trips to the attic, where she is storing boxes of Honey-Wheat's things. Honey-Wheat took little with her when she left; the mother did not want to be reminded of her daughter's days with Nadja. Honey-Wheat has five boxes, which Nadja adds to the one box for Zola, bunks them together in this slant-roofed attic, this hollow place, this unlikely heaven.

Periphery

Claw's demons begin visiting him in the depths of February. At two in the morning Nadja is awakened by a shriek. She springs to her feet and runs to Claw's room, flicks the light on, sees the child running back and forth. "Claw, honey," she says. "Claw, what's wrong?" He slows for a moment but there is primal fear behind his eyes.

Sky now stands in the doorway. The hallway light has been turned on. Claw goes to his toy chest, breathing heavily; he glares at it and then scrambles to the closet to hide from it.

Nadja knows he cannot respond to her, that something has taken him away. "Is he sleepwalking?" she asks Sky.

"Night terrors, I think," says Sky. "The snakebite boy used to have those, don't you remember? He'll come out of it."

And he does. In five minutes he crawls out of the closet and registers Nadja, the bright room, his surprising position in it.

"Claw," Nadja says, "you were having a bad dream." The shriek is still in her ears, though, and her heart still beats adrenaline into her cold hands. Claw collapses to the floor, stunned. Nadja goes to pick him up, set him on the bed. She says, "try to be still. Take deep breaths. I'll wait with you."

Three weeks go by and still the terrors visit. Nadja fastens a gate across the top of the stairs in case she doesn't wake in time.

She consults the group and learns that the terrors will not hurt Claw, but their origin concerns her. The loss of Honey-Wheat might be responsible for them, but she cannot know for sure. One night, after a quiet streak, Nadja wakes. It is about time for Claw to scream but he doesn't. She goes downstairs for tea, being careful to secure the gate behind her. When the water begins to rumble inside the kettle, she crosses in front of the window. She stops. At the edge of the woods is a fawn, already sensing Nadja's presence through the glass. It slips away. There are no leaves on the trees to hide it, but the infinite layers of trunks swallow the animal's sleek body.

The kettle's whistle jostles Nadja into motion. Tomorrow she will ask Sky to read Claw's energy. Yes, that might yield some information.

But why her eyes shift to the secured latch on the back door, she doesn't know.

Poof

Was there really any doubt that early one morning Nadja would find that the door was not latched? That she would go to the dirt mound and not find a boy anywhere in it, not find a hint of his presence? See for miles nothing but steam rising from the wet fields bordering these woods, nothing but evaporation?

Transformation

The police search yields nothing. Sky explains terrors to the young officer, says the boy couldn't have gotten far. They will keep looking, the officer says, but when Sky comes in she says, "Claw's run away. I think he's run away yet again, because terrors don't work like this."

Nadja watches Sky pace, then pause, then leave again.

Nadja's layers have been peeled away. She is nauseated in separate, aching waves.

Later, Sky calls the agency and in time someone comes to close the case. "The boy's got to go back to somewhere," the caseworker says. "He turned up for you, and he'll turn up for somebody else." Nadja wants to punch the caseworker in the face but below the sting of the comment are visions of her own girlhood, of a scrubby plot of land, of an eternity of rusted metal and afterthoughts, of resilience and its trick of turning scarcity into abundance.

In time, Claw's dirt mound flattens with the weather. Nadja watches new flora push through it, like a patch of rough skin sprouting hair.

In these woods is a past and future boy, an everyboy, rained on and tackled and pulled down into the mass of roots and rot, smiling, content, as he is coated with the cool, wet earth.

Bethany Writes Letters

3/10/70

The doctor said I'm supposed to write to someone I'm angry with and who has hurt me, and that's you all right, isn't it, Angie? You think you know me, you think your perspective is the only one. It probably wouldn't even occur to you that when something happens, it happens all different ways, and there are so many angles that when you really think about it, nothing ever happens, there are no events, there can only be this assembling of bits into something. And I guess that's what I learned during my vacation to loony land.

The thing about crazy people is that they're no different from anybody else except they are smarter and stronger because their brains are no longer their own. It's like fighting all the time (like we do! ha ha) in this out-of-control way, even if they just sit in a chair and stare at the wall.

I wrote something on the wall in the institution: *We have no friend but resolution and the briefest end.* I don't remember writing it, and guess what? It's Shakespeare. It's *Romeo and Juliet.* I told the doctors the line and they asked people and told me that it's Shakespeare and had I ever read Shakespeare, and of course I laughed at that. So I started to read the play because what else was I going to do. In the play, they thought they had nothing to live for, so deciding to take their lives was sort of compassionate. You'd think I would've offed myself right there but I thought the line was pretty, and then there was the question of who the hell told it to me.

Does this piss you off? Perhaps it embarrasses you. One thing is, I don't care about that anymore. I have been addicted to something or other since I can remember, and that doesn't make me a bad person.

I don't know if you know this, but my first addiction was fucking your boyfriends. Larry wasn't the only one, but that time was different, and there's stuff you need to know.

Do you remember that summer we rode Lancelot along the path that led to that huge culvert, and rode through it? We couldn't believe that Lancelot went. If he had gotten crazy he would have crushed us, and I would've taken you down with me, which is probably why you hate me, now that I think about it. And there were all those spiders. Do you remember that we once rode with our shirts off? Someone must have dared us, and you didn't want to take off your shirt but then you did. How many of the town's boys had their binoculars focused on you, and yet I grew up to be the one with a reputation.

The point is, you failed me. I remember hanging on to your waist, tighter when Lancelot climbed up the ravine. I hung on to you. Later, too, after we were soft and scrubbed down and settled in the sheets, and my stomach hurt from laughing so hard.

It was all for you, and you gave me nothing. You slept that night but I didn't. I traced the hairline scratches on the side of your face from the pine needles that whipped at you during the trail ride. Nature's flagellation—maybe it was the first of that sort of thing for you, always the martyr. But the part that breaks my heart is that you smelled of pine for a week and I felt so safe, like you would never leave me. But this was both the beginning and the end for us, wasn't it? I think of all that happened between us before that as little trinkets that I put in a small wooden box (like that one mom had) that has a lock but no key. Those boxes never have keys—no one ever has them or knows where they are. Is that irony?—it's one of the last things you said to me: "ironic, isn't it?" It was about how you were getting married but I never would. I didn't understand what you were talking about, but I do now. I know what ironic means. It means you think I got what I deserved.

3/13/70

You do not have the right to say anything about what anybody might or might not deserve. Because you do not know the full story.

Let me explain to you what a blackout is. You're walking along, everything is fine, and then nothing. Just being unaware is not the problem, and maybe it's even healthy. It's when you come to. It's days later when people say something to you expecting you to answer or know what they are talking about, except you don't. It feels like something has been taken from you. It also feels like everyone is in on a joke you'll never get. And then there's this: when will it happen again? Or maybe it's happening right now. You can get your brain in a real twist thinking about all that. And all this is under the radar, and the days keep spinning on, and the next thing you know, your mother's got a knife to your throat and you don't know if you're dreaming or not.

Possibly you think I'm making this all up.

The irony is that you got the name Angela. You will deny this, but it is true. People who are favored think the world is full of lies.

3/20/70

Did you ever notice that mom never threatened Ives? Not with her eyes or her palm or a rolling pin or a pen or a cleaver. Ives was the angel, Angela, not you, and he saved my life, and yours in a way, and we owe him totally.

Let me tell you what being invisible is. Invisible is the dead eyes of a mother before the blow lands. It's hiding in the pantry and holding in the piss and shit rather then face the kitchen and the hallway in order to get to the bathroom.

3/25/70

Here is what I thought: how sinful would it be to kill her? There is no anger like that of a child. It's pure and it's correct. A child sees injustice before knowing the word.

Her own books instructed me. Plants. Herbs. Mushrooms growing at the base of some tree. Poison and salvation. I know you are familiar with the concept of salvation. Go get a mushroom and crush it up and slip a piece of it into her goddamn lemonade and watch this world change for the better.

Of course, I'd have the weight of that on my conscience, and I wasn't willing to carry that.

Fucking your boyfriends was revenge. Not purely: I enjoyed the sex, but how wonderful it was to know how stupid you were and how ridiculing me hurt you every time. It was all so easy to lure them— my body is prettier than yours, we both know it.

When they stuck me in that place, I wrote down something else: *sweet are the causes of adversity.* I didn't even know what adversity was—I had to get the warden to let me into that library so I could look it up. Adversity is the hard shit you get hit with. And then I remembered "adverse effects," which my doctors were always saying, because you definitely get hit with those, too, when taking all the pills. But I'll tell you that without the pills, I wouldn't of had the hallucinations, and without the hallucinations, I wouldn't of been scared out of my wits but I also wouldn't of known that there's a whole other world out there that doesn't even really exist. Or maybe it exists just as much as this one.

4/25/70

The problem with you is that you have one definition of what strong is. I will probably hate mom until I die, but with mom, she had a real problem. She struggled with something that she couldn't control. But you were just a bitch, and you still are and maybe always will be. You don't have to be a bitch. You have to keep deciding to be mean, over and over again. I don't know, brother and sisters hate each other, and I suppose it was always this way, but God knows that I once loved you.

5/1/70

Here's why I fucked your boyfriends: to get to this low place. I think God sent me there using my clitoris. It's no different from alcohol, and I sure do know why they call alcohol "spirits." Drink a whole bottle of Jack Daniels, and anything can get into you. I fell that hard for you, Angie. It wasn't about the guys. It was somehow wanting to get really fucked up, it was like wanting to be destroyed. Do you remember how mom would take off all her clothes in the family room and start masturbating? And that weird whispering she'd do? I swear I could hear the crackling in the walls.

All that was adversity, which makes it sound not so bad. No one says "horrific, life-threatening side effects." They say "adverse effects." It's like all the blame gets taken out of the words and they just sound a little pretty, and no one questions them.

5/12/70

I planned to kill mother with *Atropa belladonna*, also known as deadly nightshade or the devil's herb. The downfall of emperors and kings! I was 7, and I read about it in one of her herbalist books. Do you think mom was a witch? That would explain a lot.

I had visions of her staggering over. I saw her dilated pupils. The pulse at her wrist was only a flutter. All I had to do was think of that poor goat down the well and I was putting on my boots to track down the plant.

Ten to twenty berries or just one single leaf.

I am talking here of a woman who nearly killed me.

What I want to know is this—how does it all just go on? Everybody's getting beaten up or yelled at or wrongly accused or wrongly killed and yet the one who says something about it is the one with the problem. So I couldn't of gained anything by telling you that not a single one of your boyfriends was true to you. I'd watch you in front of our dresser mirror, combing out your hair, putting on all that Max Factor lip gloss, thinking about all the stories you must be telling yourself about how the night was going to go.

You might know where I'm going with this.

I am the devil's child and anti-Christian and hateful and spiteful. Boys aren't very nice, either, are they? Your husband, Larry, was a stupid boy once. Probably he still is. Larry is the worst kind: he believes he deserves everything he desires. There's a big difference between being irresponsible and stupid and being arrogant and stupid. The ones in the first group are at least a little bit honest.

5/13/70

Have you ever been punched? More specifically, have you ever been punched in the crotch? After four fingers have gone in to the hilt, is it really that much different to have his whole hand in you? I thought Larry would turn me inside out.

He had been watching me for weeks. You'd think with all that flat land, he'd have nowhere to hide, but men like that just instinctually know how to work it. They also know exactly how to bend an arm behind the back in such a way as to prevent any movement.

He said two things:

1) You like that, don't you, you little bitch

2) I've seen you looking at me.

I still can't believe how fast he got his dick into me, how fast he had me on my stomach and then on my back, how exactly what was happening could not form in my mind, how even the brutality disappeared. I suppose this is an advanced form of protection we evolved to have. And look, he fucked me and bruised me and then do you know what he said? He's zipping up his pants and fastening his belt, and he says, Jesus, that was the best. And he grins. He grins at me.

He almost fooled me: for a few hours, I started to believe that the conquest had been mine. It's an interpretation I could have went with for the rest of my life. At times I adopted it as a sort of persona. It definitely allowed me to understand how stupid you were.

The pregnancy pushed the whole event away, and by the time Russ was born, I was long gone.

Like any mother, I've made mistakes, but the reason I'm telling you this has nothing to do with honesty or revenge or healing or confession or the nature of the soul or which moral is the highest. It has to do with the practical matters of daily life. I'm asking you to stop calling Child Protective Services. In biblical terms, you know not what you do. Your husband's son, whether you like it or not, needs me more than anyone else. He has no one else.

Surely this is not a lot to ask. I don't want money or even an apology. I stumbled out of the barn that day a different person. I no longer needed to prove anything to you, and I no longer needed to fight, and I no longer hated myself, and suddenly I was so sad about all the bad things people do to each other, and right there on the gravel, with cobwebs in my hair and the smell of Larry's sweat coming up through my shirt, I decided that I didn't need to find a man to be complete. Larry raping me was the sweet in the adversity.

When you ask him about this he will surely deny it, but consider that I know he has a large birthmark on his right hip. He is not circumcised. His dick bulges a little in the middle. Remember this when you ask him what he knows about crazy Bethany. Mention a paternity test and watch him panic. Really watch him, dear sister.

Let us make a pact: I will leave you alone if you leave me alone. I have no hope or intention of reconciliation. I just want to live my life with my dear boy, as far away from both of you as possible.

And Christ, don't drag Ives into all this.

Part II: Air

Funerals

The goat

Ives's sister Bethany had a favorite pet: a billy goat named Cecil. Cecil's life was filled with bucolic sunsets washed over flat lands, grasses eaten straight from the prairie, and visits from a little girl who fed him apples and told him stories about princesses and leprechauns. Bethany once found a four-leaf clover and, upon being told that it brought good luck, fed it to the goat in order to preserve him forever.

Cecil's death was gruesome. No one knew how the poor goat broke his leg, or whether that was even true. They did know how he arrived at his premature burial at the bottom of a deep well, and they hoped that he died on impact.

The middle sibling, Angela, slept in the room closest to their parents, and although there was no halo over her head, their mother believed that the child was her salvation. Ives watched his mother very closely. Over time, he noticed that she grew uncomfortable around him. He taught himself to be a light sleeper, and started hanging Christmas bells on the bedroom door at night.

After Cecil's death, Bethany cried every day for a month. At night she'd wake up, whimpering. Ives knew this because he began sleeping in her bed. At first he did it only when she asked, but then it became a habit. In the early morning, he'd hear their mother going down the steps. After a few minutes, he'd wake Bethany. She always had dreams to tell him, and he let her, and sometimes he shared his own, though he didn't seem to dream much.

Bethany's dreams were wild and chaotic and impossibly detailed, and there were times when it took her a whole morning to break from the spell. One day, she said, *Isn't it funny that I used to sleep with*

Angela and now I sleep with you? She said, *I feel safe with you, but my dreams scare me.* She said, *I have dreams about Mother dying.*

On particularly hot nights, they slept naked, and in this way Ives learned about girls. They touched each other innocently, giggling, and sometimes Ives draped an arm over her because sleeping next to her like that kept him close to her breathing, which soothed him. That and the scent of her body, which was of laundry dried on the line.

When Bethany's bad dreams came, neither of them slept. She'd claw at his skin and he'd have to wake her. She'd be panting or sweating or crying, or her muscles would be spasming or she'd be shaking. Once, he decided not to sleep and instead watched her. He watched her body relax, her head turn to the side, her mouth fall open. Soon her face would twitch—first her cheek, then her lips. Her eyes rolled about under the closed lids. More twitching, this time of the arms and hands. Ives touched her forehead. The twitching stopped. He laid a hand on her stomach. Her eyes stopped rolling. He knew nothing of sleep until now.

It was not really sleep at all: he had the sense that his sister was traveling somewhere far away from him, farther and farther with each spasm. He would become anxious and nearly wake her. Would it be possible, in theory, for someone to keep going? To go and go and go so far that waking up would be impossible?

The thought was too much for him, but it didn't matter because Bethany clutched a corner of the sheet, let it go, tightened it again, and then started to breathe the breaths of one being hunted. One arm stretched out and clawed Ives's chest.

She would wake soon.

She would cling to him.

He would hold her until he couldn't any longer. Then, she would have to fend for herself.

Their secret insomnia kept their behavior erratic but their bond even. They went from the swing in the yard to the barn loft to the rows of hot dirt in the garden. There, among the last of the squash plants, they warmed their backs and collected the orange and yellow flowers. As they fell into a pile, the petals and stamens broke away. Bethany would hold a petal high and release it, watch it drift away in the breeze. Then Ives threw up a whole handful of petals, and up they went, an enchanted confetti. Bethany giggled, then laughed, then laughed some more. Then Ives laughed. The laughs were the giddy laughs of tired bodies, laughs that choked and consumed them, laughs that left them, ultimately, silent and reverent.

Finally, Bethany said, *Cecil used to eat the flowers.*

Ives sat up and gathered the flowers. He pulled Bethany up and had her grasp two edges of her shirt to form a basket. In went the flowers. Bethany added her own pile.

C'mon, Ives said.

On the way to the well, they collected other flora—late-blooming daisies, dried Echinacea petals, curled-up rudbeckia and helenium heads, and pale violet morning glory trumpets wedged into the fallen stones of crumbling walls. When Bethany's shirt was full, Ives used his own. Soon, they expanded their scavenging to include seeds, pebbles, ladybug carcasses, switch grass, bits of corncob. Their greatest find, half-buried in the runoff covering the bulging roots of a tree, was a silver locket. Ives thinks that in it he will put his two favorite quartz rocks. He puts the necklace in his pocket, hoping Bethany will forget it.

Ives, Bethany said. *Where are we going?*

To the well.

Bethany's eyes began to water. She shook her head.

To say goodbye, Ives said. *Cecil would like that.*

Bethany froze, but Ives kept walking. Soon, he heard her steps behind him. For the rest of the walk, Ives promised her light and warmth and goat heaven and the songs of angels—angels you can't hear but who are always singing for animals that die.

Are they singing now? Bethany asked.

Yes. Right now.

No, they're not.

Yes, they are. I hear them.

Really?

Yes.

They walked. Ives bent to pick up a smooth stone.

Really? Bethany asked.

Yes.

Ives reached the well first. He kneeled down and piled his gatherings in front of him. As he spread them out, Bethany approached. He looked at her. She was flushed and sunburned. Her toenails, visible in her sandals, were caked with dirt. Bits of debris clung to the soft hairs on her legs. She sat down, spilling the collection in front of her. She scattered it sloppily around her knees.

No, Ives said. *Like this.* He grabbed a handful and tossed it up. Bethany watched everything fall, then threw a handful of her own.

Ashes to ashes, Ives said.

Bethany threw another handful in the air. *Dust to dust*, she said.

Now we have to say the eulogy, Ives said.

What's that? Bethany asked.

It's when you talk about the dead person. So we have to say nice things about Cecil.

I will.

Okay.

Bethany sat squinting out at the fields. *Cecil was a nice goat,* she said. *Once, Cecil ate the candles on your birthday cake.*

Cecil was a good friend, Ives said.

Cecil believed in leprechauns, Bethany said.

Cecil's favorite food was carrots.

No, it was everything.

They giggled. Bethany rolled around in the grass. A squash flower petal hung from her bangs.

Why did she kill him? Bethany asked.

I don't know, Ives said.

I think he's happy.

Me too.

Are the angels really singing?

Yes.

That night there were no bad dreams, no twitching, no disruptions. Ives fell asleep to the scent of grass and clay on Bethany's skin. The bells on the door were silent. And, in the morning, the angel songs had stopped.

The wife (#1)

Not all hard drinkers are selfish. Hapless, yes; this is inevitable. But not necessarily selfish. Lily gave and gave until she couldn't anymore, and then she'd have to drink to replenish herself. That she chose vodka and not water or tea or pineapple juice seemed of no concern at the time because she drank in the security of the home

Ives bought for them after working a few years as a surveyor. Here, they discussed floor plans and gardens and pregnancy. None of these began properly because soon Lily found vodka in new places.

One of these places was a small watering hole in town. The bartender's name was Gene, and he came to Lily's funeral because the guilt was eating him up. He felt responsible. He felt so responsible that he quit bartending and instead opened a diner that closed at eight in the evening and served not a drop of alcohol, ever.

Gene knew things about Lily that Ives did not, despite Ives being a devoted husband for five years. It wasn't that Gene and Lily were lovers; it was that Lily felt she could be more herself with a stranger. Gene told Ives not to feel hurt. He told him that Lily spoke of him with high regard and loved him deeply. Gene said her problem was a lack of focus, to which Ives thought, *still, somebody should have told me.*

Ives, of course, had no idea about Gene, about this man whose life was now inextricably tied to his own.

Physically, Lily was graceful. Ives found her while hiking in central North Dakota. She was resting along a stream when he sat down by her. They finished the trail together, left each other, wrote to each other, and then drove to each other (she took the bus), and never looked back.

Even on the trail, she carried a hint of glamour. She wasn't thin, but her long nose and limbs gave her an ethereal quality. She could have gone to Hollywood and made something of herself. Ives always knew this; perhaps his feelings of guilt began there instead of after that fateful night, the peak of the drama, the beginning of a very long end.

That a woman could in fact disappear into thin air was preposterous. No one would believe it: an empty casket. (Closed so as not to belabor the point.) A woman eaten by snow falling two inches per hour. Everyone in this area knew not to underestimate flakes an inch thick, then tiny and needle-like and blowing so skillfully that they buried entire structures overnight. And now, a woman underneath the layers, dead, because two men thought she had a ride home with the other.

The police officers did not believe in happenstance or coincidence. They said heart attack. They said addiction. They said suicidal depression. They said inebriation and then a lovers' quarrel and then exposure and then suffocation. They said a heart that couldn't find any blood to pump. Out here, an hour is all it would take, if that.

So, Lily, twice lost. First for two years before death, then upon death. Gene, for his part, figured that Lily's husband was one of those men who wanted to put food on the table and worked too hard doing it, which made Lily seek the barstool. Ives thought that Lily needed her time with a friend or two, knowing that she didn't have much family. This fatal miscommunication was the kind of thing that made Ives brood on a whole system of details: that a storm like this should hit just as his wife let the heavy doors of the bar fall shut behind her. How late had it been? How much did she have to drink? These were not the actions of a newly married young woman planted in the dirt of the plains.

The conjecture led Ives in circles, and for a while this is what he wanted because at least it kept the loss at bay. During the eulogy, his head swam and his eyes watered. He had no idea how he could go on.

After the funeral, Gene took Ives out for dinner. This was at Ives's request, but Gene was happy to comply. When the meals came, Gene said, *She didn't talk all that much.* He said she was friendly and sometimes made a joke and sometimes told him things that seemed personal but that weren't notable, not for a veteran bartender who'd seen all kinds.

Gene was a good man, this Ives could see. He had a thick moustache and bushy eyebrows and a wife of seven years and also a daughter.

What did she typically order? Ives asked. *I should know, but I don't.*

Gin.

Ives ordered gin. And when he finished it, he ordered another. Gene tried to slow him down but all Ives saw was an entity with a direct link to his wife during her last minutes alive, and for this he felt that he should not move, and not let Gene move.

They stayed until the restaurant closed. All conversation was a blur. Somehow, Gene had gotten Ives's car keys and maneuvered Ives into the passenger seat. Ives faded in and out on the way home, lucid enough only once, when he noticed Gene's hands moving over the steering wheel. Even his hands were covered with bushy tufts of hair.

Gene pulled into Ives's driveway and helped Ives out of the car. The porch light was on. Ives took one step forward, toward the light he suddenly hated, the light that would, for the next two years, remind him of absence and guilt and disappearance.

The wife (#2)

Growing up, Ives never gave his mother the evil eye, but he did often look at her with suspicion and sometimes anger, and perhaps that registered in the energy field as a type of malicious targeting; and perhaps, stemming from that etheric tide, his mother or someone close to her had initiated a more formal curse.

It was one of the few ways to explain the death of his second wife, Ava, which occurred while she was healthy, and alone. On the way to the grocery store, she stopped at a traffic light. There had been a heavy storm the night before—plenty of lightning—and many tree branches had come down. Ava stopped at the intersection a few seconds too early or a few seconds too late, depending on how you looked at it. A very large tree branch, located about twenty-five feet up the trunk, broke off, gathered speed, and landed on Ava's windshield. That the windshield broke was enough of an uncanny event, but for that branch to isolate, then wedge, a thick piece of glass into Ava's heart was not merely uncanny, it implied premeditation.

Coincidences have meaning; Ives was willing to grant this despite his Christian upbringing. But after the death of his second wife, just four years after the first and in this particular way, Ives was forced to consider evil eyes, hexes, and curses to be a key part of his life.

Thus, vows: never to marry again. To leave his life as a surveyor and buy some land was another. To attend church seemed to go without saying. To live a good, pure life and to infuse every action with kindness and generosity would be his daily task and motivation.

He started his plan as early as the funeral, which was large. Ava had lots of family, most of which Ives hadn't met—he and Ava eloped and did not have a traditional wedding. They had really only just begun their lives together. As Ives sat listening to the eulogy—delivered by Ava's brother and filled with details about his wife's life that he hadn't known—he decided, distinctly and without hesitation, that he would not allow grief to occupy even a month of his future. Upon deciding this, all questions evaporated in the funeral home's dry air. His new life would be one assembled, bit by bit, from the soil. All seedlings would be dedicated to his two wives and to all women who left the earth before having a chance to live.

By the time the eulogy was over, Ives had tilled and sowed his acres, in his mind, five times over.

He looked at Ava in the casket only briefly: he would see her again and again and again. He couldn't remember the last time he felt so free.

When Bethany approached him, he was almost startled.

Ives, she said, *you don't deserve this.*

Who does? Ives said.

Some people, maybe. So they can learn.

Perhaps I will learn.

You're my dear brother, you already know everything.

I've decided to start a farm.

What? Where?

I don't know.

Bethany dug through her purse for a cigarette. *Let's go outside.*

Outside, the dry fall leaves scurried over the concrete lot. Bethany held the cigarette out to Ives.

Thanks. How's Dad?

Seems okay. Has it been only a year since Mom's been locked up?

Something like that.

Long time coming.

They smoked the cigarette down to nothing. Bethany lit another.

Ives said, *Any word about Russ?*

I'm going to fight for him.

I know.

The fire was an accident. You believe me, right?

Of course.

I know I'm no angel. But things happen sometimes.

Yeah, look at me. I keep killing my wives.

One by one, cars left the funeral home. Ives hadn't been able to save or spare his sister from anything. Nor could he get her child back for her, nor could he convince Angela to stop judging her so harshly. He had his own problems now.

He looked at her, blonde hair still long and uncombed, same summer freckles, same bad luck, same resolve.

Okay, she said, *I have to get back to Maddy, or Angie will call someone and cite me for abandonment.* She said, *I'll bring you some food in a couple days and make sure you're eating.*

After a few minutes, Ives went inside, where his father and Angela were bringing the remaining flower arrangements to the doors. He could count on Angela to be proper, and on his father to go along for the ride. Ives understood. His father had only recently been relieved of caring for a mentally ill woman. Perhaps he hadn't been able to feel yet the new freedom he had, or accept it, or recognize it.

Seven huge flower arrangements—Oriental lilies, snap dragons, baby's breath, white roses. All on the kitchen table, the fragrance filling the house. Ives would inhale deeply when he got home after driving around the county, following up on ads he found for people selling land, people eager for civilization, convenience stores, and clean fingernails.

In February he found a nice seven-acre plot and by April had a small greenhouse, a used John Deere, an irrigation plan, a budget, and a crop plan.

He bought seven bouquets, which he placed around the farmhouse, to celebrate.

The mother

The most powerful member of an elephant tribe is the herd's matriarch, whose memory extends to the location of watering holes miles away, and not visited for countless seasons. Together, the members of the herd walk and walk and walk. But if there is not enough water at the hole, even the ancient part of this animal's brain will not save the herd.

The point of the story, which is being told as part of the eulogy for Dorrie, is supposed to be about the inevitability of death and about God's ultimate and unquestionable reign over the hows and whens. We are to be reminded of our smallness and be glad of it.

To Ives, though, the premise grates.

Ding, dong! the witch is dead

This is what Bethany said when she heard the news: *so, the witch is dead. About fucking time. People like her, they just keep living and living and living.*

Ives said, *It was lightning.*

What?

Lightning. It struck her down.

That makes twice.

They had discussed it: lightning striking the same woman twice. It found her, this time, not at the top of a treeless hill, but on the grounds of the institution. She was sitting out on the patio, in the chair the nurse wheeled out, her hands bound and her body lightly sedated in accordance with the recommendations of the resident psychiatrists.

Ding, dong.

The death was instantaneous. The patients nearby saw it all, said that her hair turned blue and then her eyes rolled upward, and then she slumped forward in her chair. The crack of the hit had a hollow sound to it, they said; there was more of a static-filled silence than anything else. Another woman's chair had tipped over and spilled her out on the patio's concrete. Two of the men stayed in their chairs but reported difficulty eating, and fell into a severe depression. The storm had not been a lightning storm; in fact, there barely was any thunder or rain or even wind.

Ives's own thought was that lightning was not what killed his mother. And Bethany had just seen a special on television and thought the aliens took her. *Would I wish abduction upon her? I don't know,* she said.

If air can carry electricity, what else can it bring? Ives asked.

Yeah, maybe aliens.

Maybe the devil.

Maybe the chieftain came for her.

The day before the funeral, more news. Angela's husband, Larry, ran off with another woman.

Bethany said, *Didn't we see it coming? Is sister dearest as crazy as Mom or is she just stupid?*

Crazy as Mom. Because of genetics, Ives said.

And then she's stupid on top of it.

The future present

Ives takes Bethany's hand. Now there is talk about the matriarch's dedication to her family. There is mention of Dorrie's move from a small town to farmland that eats people alive, and how she persevered and brought God to a desolate corner of the earth.

Ives feels Bethany's hand tighten. It is eulogy at its best: all the good, all the youth, preserved in the person forever. There is no *and after that*. Ives was there when his father stopped along the side of the road to pick Bethany up. He saw her bloodied feet from the back seat. He saw his father see her feet. His father said nothing. He drove in silence. At home, their mother was not there. She didn't come back for thirty-six hours. When she did, she started to make a pie.

Ives watched and watched. At night, Bethany woke and complained that her feet itched. Don't itch them, Ives said. They have to heal.

After that, something changed. Their father got quieter and spent a lot of time on the phone, usually when their mother was sleeping. Ives was asked to keep watch over their mother at all times. Soon, after a few months or possibly more, their mother disappeared.

Angela thought Bethany's misbehavior drove their mother away. Angela cried but Ives never went to her.

Their mother would come back, of course, in time, until the medication failed or tissue eroded or the solstice came. Bethany would appear with bruises. The present they all knew would begin again.

The graveyard shift
On the way to the funeral, Ives and Bethany stopped at Lily's grave and then Ava's. First, the flower shop, where Ives purchased two mini bouquets of white flowers. Then, at each tomb, Ives and Bethany picked apart the bouquets, petal by petal, until they both had a handful. Then, they tossed the petals into the air.

Ashes to ashes, Ives said.

Dust to dust, Bethany said.

They had packed sandwiches, and now, at Ava's gravestone, unwrapped them and started to eat.

Angie called me last night, Bethany said. *To accuse me.*

What now? Ives said.

She thinks I've been communicating with him.

Your rapist.

Yes.

Have you?

Bethany stopped chewing. *Of course not. There's nothing left to say. I told her, again, that I don't speak to Larry. That he was born and bred to treat women like shit.*

I'm surprised he's lasted this long.

I guess I will never know why she hates me so much.

It's all going to catch up to her somehow, is how I look at it.

They moved to a nearby bench and sat down. The dew hadn't yet evaporated, and the cemetery was still partly covered in a cloud of fog. Bethany wore a black dress trimmed with lace—surely the best-looking dress in her closet. She had developed a knack for shopping at Goodwill.

So, Ives, are the angels singing?

What?

The angels. You told me they sang for my poor dead goat all those years ago.

I don't know. I guess they have to sing for all souls.

Also on the way to the funeral, they stopped at the grocery store and the liquor store, where they replenished their cigarette supply. When Bethany got back in the car, she said, *I feel like celebrating. I never get to celebrate anything.*

Why can't people celebrate a death?

Sure, they can. Why not?

During the last few miles to the funeral, they planned a party. The food, the décor, the lie they'd have to spread to make the party seem like it was for something else. Like Ives's successful year of farming. Like Bethany being a few steps closer to getting her son Russ out of the foster system. Like the fact that they still had a sense of humor. Like that the day was ending, and there'd be a new one, and that one just might be better.

Consider the father

After the passage about the elephants, the eulogy went on to relay several notable anecdotes, one of which concerned Dorrie, as a girl, taking books off her father's shelf and pretending to read them. Dorrie's father was a medical man, and for a few years worked on a nearby Lakota reservation. He kept journals about his experiences and published them, but the girl's interest was in the heavy hardcover treatises on the history of the Midwest's native populations. Once, she tore out a page that had a picture of a chieftain on it and slept with it by her bedside for nearly a year.

The other anecdote concerned Dorrie's mother, who was also a medical person, but because she was a woman, she was relegated to midwifery, which at that time garnered respect, sometimes considerable, depending on where you had received training. This woman trained in Europe, which at that time taught advanced midwifery.

Even as a girl, Dorrie was interested in anatomy. She received scientific explanations about every procedure and about every stage in a pregnancy. The girl's job was to assist, which she did with considerable skill for her age. She was also diligent with keeping track of how many births her mother attended. She kept the record in a journal, carefully dating each entry and noting whether the newborn was a girl or boy and whether there were any complications, and what remedies were used. Later, her mother would fill in more details.

Birth number two hundred forty-three was notable not because of a complicated delivery but because Dorrie's mother fainted. Dorrie was left to deliver the baby on her own. She was reported to have given the terrified mother precise instructions, and by the time Dorrie's mother came to, the baby was born, washed, and swaddled.

Ives, smoking a cigarette outside after the eulogy, had several thoughts, namely whether the two events are somehow connected, if maybe his mother missed her calling and suffered for it by living the impossible life of the wife of a farmer. Dorrie's mother died violently; she was murdered on her way to a call—what would have been birth number three hundred sixty-eight. Could the curse have begun there? He would have to ask his father about the picture Dorrie tore out of the book.

Ives heard voices. Bethany's. Angela's. The voices were raised and came from just inside the funeral home. He had forgotten not to ever leave the two of them alone together. The voices got louder, then stopped. Or seemed to.

As he walked toward the funeral home, he felt a crackle creep up his spine. He saw an image of horrible violence: his sisters, dead, hanging from the thick branch of a tree. The image came again, stronger, and he picked up his pace even as he drove the image away.

He heard a clunk. Something had just happened that involved

weight. A flower pot? A chair?

He pushed open the front doors. Angela stood with her arm against the wall, the other hand covering her nose. The blood ran down her chin and dripped on the floor. A few feet away, Bethany paced, shaking out her hand. Her cheeks were flushed and her mascara was smudged under one eye. Ives knew the day had finally come.

Bethany wiped her own nose, though she wasn't exactly crying. And she was not finished. She moved toward her sister with a smoothness that surprised even Ives. Angela, cowering and attempting to push Bethany away, was easily thrown against the wall. With both hands, Bethany mashed Angela's face into the exposed brick, the track lighting falling harshly on Angela's red face.

Maybe she is the devil, Ives thought, as he raced toward Bethany and pulled her away, locking both arms behind her. She choked down a few breaths. To Angela, she said, *If you go after Maddy, I'll kill you.*

Your soul will rot in hell, Angela said.

Ives yanked Bethany down the front steps and into his truck. *Are you crazy?*

She might try to get Maddy.

No, she won't. I won't let her.

She will never leave me alone.

Yes, she will. I'll talk to her. Ives pulled out a cigarette and lit it for her. *We'll find someone who can help.*

I hate her. I'm so tired of hating her.

I know.

I don't know what I would do without you.

They drove in silence. Soon, Bethany fell asleep, and Ives switched on the radio. He listened to talk radio, now, and tried to find a program. But only features were on—the lives of opera singers or of the coaches of famous athletes.

He thought of his long, never ending future as a protector for this woman next to him, as a single man, as a tender of the soil. He thought of his mother and how she might have been. Could he blame her if some unknown force sought her out and chose her? As if hearing the question, Bethany stirred. *Yes,* Bethany would say. *Like is drawn to like.*

The witch is undead

The question became not whether deciding to forego grief was right but rather, in the absence of grief, what was the proper way to let go? The question became, what happens if the dead person does not let go of you?

Exactly two weeks after the funeral, Ives planted rose bushes along the fence bordering his new front yard. As he lowered each bush into the ground, he thought of his wives. He held them in his mind as he pulled the dirt onto the root balls and packed them down. He said, *there you are, my dears, be beautiful and bless this farm.* He tapped the packed dirt twice with the fingertips of his left hand, freeing each woman into the finest particles of loam.

The last bush—a bright pink Scottish climber—was ready to go in. Ives dug a hole with a spade, then pulled the plant out of its plastic container. He placed the root ball in the ground. He pulled the dirt onto it. He froze: a distinct presence behind him. A cool, clammy feeling on his back.

He turned. Nothing. The slight pressure on his back gave way to an odd burning sensation that seemed to pass a live flame down his whole body.

Ives lay down on the grass, trying to rest and shake the feeling of nausea that had set in.

Fever in the morning.

He hadn't thought of the song "Fever" for years. He sang a couple lines to distract himself.

Fever in the morning, fever all though the night.

When his heart slowed down, Ives sat up. He felt better.

Fever in the morning, fever when you hold me tight.

By evening, the experience had passed entirely. Ives made himself a broccoli and grilled steak dinner, then went upstairs to bed.

He didn't know how long he slept, but he did know that at some point, and all at once, his insides seemed to vibrate, as if he got caught in an earthquake, as if a giant were holding the bed in the air and shaking it. He felt himself peel away from his body, then a floating sensation, then he was moving fast, above and through electrical wires, the tops of trees, the edges of rooftops. He felt he was communicating with all that was living, as if he were an extension of all things.

He was in Bethany's house, in the upstairs hallway, just outside her bedroom. The bright half-moon lit the space. She was struggling to breathe—no, she was choking, gasping, pushing something away. Ives saw a gray shape, almost like mist, with tendrils tipped in black. He saw Bethany fall to her knees. His strongest thought was to destroy the mist, but as he thought this, he felt himself disappearing, falling away into nothing.

When he woke, he found that he couldn't move despite an intense desire to rise. In minutes, perhaps hours, his awareness fell away.

In the morning, while making coffee, Ives called Bethany.

Hi, he said.

Hi, she said.

Are you okay? Ives asked.

What?

I had the worst dream.

So did I. Mom was coming to get me for good.

What's wrong with your voice?

Yeah, I know. I can't talk. My whole neck aches. I'm going to go to the doctor.

I think Mom really was trying to hurt you.

What?

I saw her last night trying to kill you. I was right in the hallway. You were there. You were choking.

That's weird. I just remembered that I dreamed I was choking.

I have a fever, but I don't feel sick. And I had a weird feeling while I was planting yesterday.

I have a bruise on my knee but I don't know how I got it.

Maybe when you fell. She was choking you, and you fell forward on your knees.

Oh, shit.

Yeah.

Later, Ives drove over. Bethany let him in and then dished out macaroni casserole. They ate in silence.

She can't really kill me, can she? Bethany asked.

We'll go to one of those stores and ask.

Like those New Age places?

They cleaned up the dishes and went to the living room.

I'll go to the library and get a couple books. Just to see.

Ives went to the refrigerator for a beer. When he returned, Bethany was lying down on the couch. Ives sat next to her.

We'll figure it out, he said.

Jesus. Angie on this side and her on the other. That's fucked-up stuff.

We'll figure it out.

I want my son back.

You'll get him. He'll come back to you.

Because you can't force the heart.

No.

Because you can't tell someone to hate and then just have it happen.

No.

Do you think Mom killed your wives?

Ives climbed over Bethany and lay down beside her. They turned on their sides. Ives draped an arm around her.

Will you sleep here tonight? Bethany asked.

Of course.

I mean right here, by me?

From this spot in the room, Ives could not see the front door. He wouldn't know if the doorknob was slowly turning, if she was there, waiting for them to dare falling asleep. And no set of bells sold on the market could tell him that.

The Runaway

Lost, found, melted, gone
1971

Russ stands on a wooded path. There is a draft at his feet, or his feet are cold, or his feet are wet. It is too dark to check.

He does not know how he arrived on this path. He wants to go home—to the woman and the house and the cave. How can there be no lights in any direction? There is a road, and he follows it.

His memory will never bring this moment back to him.

There is the sound of a motor, then it is louder, then lights are upon him. They make him want to run but instead he freezes; already he has learned the art of waiting. If he remains still, he cannot be in error. It's a specious truth, but it is, as such, his philosophy, gained from a historic five whole years of life.

The car is a police car, and then the uniformed man says, "Come with me, boy, we'll get you somewhere safe," and the man leads him to the back seat, and Russ climbs in. The seats are cold, but the air blowing on him from the vents soothes him, and he feels his cheeks slowly thawing.

Doors close, then there are miles covered, more lights, a parking lot, even brighter lights, and hallways with bulletin boards that have papers tacked on them.

The men dart around, and the women all sit behind desks. He is led to one. The woman wears an orange dress. She smokes. Black telephones are everywhere. The woman is stiff and polite and seems to know things about him. She gives him water and grape Crush and tells him to drink.

He will forget her, of course, but hate her just the same.

Heaven is hell on earth
1971–1973

Russ wakes each morning to the bloodied man nailed to the wood. This long-haired man is dead, and he hangs above the doorway. This man hangs in the hallway, too, and the kitchen, and the church, and in the church he is big and somehow deader, and all the gruesome music plays.

And the ticking clocks have birds in them, birds that pop out on the hour. There is roast beef and potatoes, always. There is school, of course, other kids who talk and talk but never ask him to play. One game is kickball, which he watches until he believes he understands the rules. One day he gets in line, and then the ball is rolling to him and then it's in the air, way past the infielders, uncatchable. The bell rings. The kids look at him, look away, and after that he is quietly sought after for recess activities, except for four-square, which is for girls.

In the context of these games, he finds his voice. It barks out requests for the ball, where to run, where to stand in defense. The other boys stare at him, the girls whisper.

The bus dumps him off at around three. There are shouts for him to come play this or that at so-and-so's house. He can't go. Jolene won't allow it.

There is catechism class on Wednesday nights with pale kids who walk in straight lines. The floor is green-and-white checkered. The bathroom smells of antiseptic.

At home, Jolene helps him with his homework, smiling. Always smiling.

There comes a time when the smiles end.

The beginning of the end is the cigarettes. Russ pulls one out one day and lights it. He lets it burn until red ash drops on the table. He runs his finger through it, gray now, smears it in close circles. He holds the cigarette the way his mother does, between thumb and index finger. He brings it to his mouth and sucks. He exhales. Nothing. He tries again and again, and finally the hot smoke pricks his lungs. He coughs, lights another, tries again. He exhales the smoke smoothly but quickly, coughing again.

Jolene finds him, of course. She was hanging sheets out on the line and now stands in front of him. She snatches away the cigarette and tosses it in the sink. "Honey," she says, "you can't do that," but Russ misunderstands. Not only can he do it, he can do it properly, and he shows her by taking out another and lighting it. Jolene snatches it away and says, "Go on, get outside."

He goes, and this is when he starts to dig. He digs a hole and piles the dirt in a mound. The problem is that the dead, bleeding man needs to be buried. He gets a chair from the kitchen and some phone books, and collects all the bleeding men, even the ones on the necklaces. He throws them all into the hole and plows the pile of dirt over them. He needs a little extra because of the large bleeding man, so he brings some from the garden.

Later, Jolene says, "Russ, where are all my crucifixes?"

Russ leads her to the pile. Jolene looks from him to the dirt mound, then back to him. "Did you bury them?"

Russ waits.

Jolene says, barely moving her mouth, "Russ, please get them out."

Russ drops to his knees and moves away the dirt. He places the necklaces in a pile at her feet, and then lays out the crosses, one by one.

"You are going to wash these until they are spotless," she says.

Initially, they are rinsed with hose water, then brought inside to the kitchen sink. Wherever he walks, Jolene walks with him, gripping his upper arm tightly. When she lets go, he freezes because he doesn't know what she wants him to do. She fills the sink with hot, soapy water and gets the step-stool for him. In the water, most of the dirt comes off, but the moisture cracks the cheap finish on the large crucifix, the kitchen one, and it has to be thrown away.

Jolene turns to him. "Why did you do that?" She says it quietly, but heat flies off of her.

Russ waits, looks down, waits.

She goes to the utility drawer and finds the scissors. She approaches him from the side, and then there is nothing but a sort of blurriness, and he folds himself inward, and then the scissors cuts and then his turquoise necklace is in her hand. She tosses it in the trash.

"I knew that necklace was trouble. None of that pagan worship here," she says.

There are meetings with teachers now, and at school, after lunch, Russ has to sit in a small room with a woman who dresses in pantsuits and clogs and wears turquoise earrings.

There is no television anymore, and Jolene doesn't sit with him. He is not allowed outside. At night, Jolene reads a book. Russ sees fear in her and allows himself to feed on it because this feels right. The clock ticks, ticks, ticks, until bedtime at nine o'clock.

The garden of earthly delights
1973–1974

Television sets everywhere in the country are turned to news reports about veterans lashing out at wives and cameramen, to crazed OPEC reports, to a maniacal general stampeding his way through Chile, but Miss Jill doesn't have a television. The inside of her house, a small one-story on a narrow, dead end road, does not have doors. Her entryways and doorframes are draped with curtains, some of them gauzy and light, like the orange and pink chiffon ones leading to her bedroom, and others heavy, like the cotton tapestries held back with braided cords, like the ones separating the dining room from the living room and like the ones leading to a large, open space defined primarily by antique furniture, floor grates, and music equipment. The space was a former used-clothing store owned by the guy upstairs, and is now rented to Miss Jill. Now it is populated with vintage baskets and chests displayed on high shelves, with a sitting area and a new bathroom in olive green and pale yellow. This bathroom has a large shower, and where there ought to be a curtain are instead tall glass doors.

Miss Jill is a ballet and yoga instructor. On the walls of the short hallway separating the former store from the rest of the house are pictures of angry-looking men with hair gelled back off their faces. Miss Jill points: *this one is a Russian dancer, this one is a very well-known teacher from Czechoslovakia, this one is a bodhitsattva from Thailand, this one is a choreographer I once met when I was traveling.* Russ asks about "choreographer" and "bodhitsattva" but can't remember the words later when he tries to recall them.

While Miss Jill is out teaching her classes, a babysitter comes. Rocki lives down the street and is also able to twist herself into odd positions. She performs these moves on the vintage carpet, and Russ imitates her. After a while, they lie on their backs and look up at the ceiling, which has glow-in-the-dark stars on it. Miss Jill comes home dressed in leotards and leg-warmers, and she and Rocki talk for a few minutes. They mesmerize him, the way they are always gesturing with their hands and the way their lips are always shiny and the way they kiss each other on the cheeks when saying good-bye.

Men come, too, especially a man called Nikita, who has fright-ening eyebrows and wears tight shorts. Nikita is the brother of one of the men pictured on the wall. While Russ plays or looks at the ceiling stars or does his homework, Nikita and Miss Jill disappear. When they come back, they take him to the park, or hiking, and sometimes they get ice cream. Later, they have dinner in a kitchen where everything is edible, even the plants growing on top of the refrigerator.

For Miss Jill, there is never a right or wrong answer. Sometimes Russ skips his homework, and often he rides his bicycle far beyond the boundaries of the block. This does not upset Miss Jill. With her, he is compelled to honesty, and tells her everything he finds—bro-ken glass, graffiti, and, in the bike-path turnoffs, what look like pale, deflated balloons—and everything he is interested in, including the motorcycle parked outside, her eight-track tapes, and, inexplicably, her suitcase, which is covered in worn, nonsensical stickers.

Every night, they bathe. There is also a regular-size tub in the new bathroom, and that's where Miss Jill draws a bubble bath. Sometimes Nikita joins them, if he is there. He sits at the back of the tub, then Miss Jill, then Russ. Sometimes Miss Jill lights candles.

The first time Russ sees Nikita naked, he stares. Nikita laughs. "Don't worry, little one, you'll catch up. Touch it, if you want." But Russ doesn't. Miss Jill's naked body is even more surprising, with nothing at all down there except hair, and her breasts are larger than his mother's, and the nipples are large and pink. In the bathtub, if he turns his head, he sees their pores and fine hairs. He is allowed to touch everything. When he does, he gets a funny sensation between his legs. Now it's Nikita who points, and Miss Jill smiles, and Russ cannot keep his eyes open.

The Great Houdini
1974–1976

As far as Russ can tell from what he finds in the school library, Ehrich Weisz, also known as Harry Houdini, did not ever truly disappear. Houdini, shackled and submerged into glass tanks of water or thrown off bridges in locked crates, always defeated his challengers, always broke free. For Houdini, the audience waited.

Russ, on the other hand, falls asleep and wakes up somewhere else feeling unsettled, even afraid. People refer to things he said, things he knows he couldn't have said. He is tired, as if having ridden his bike for a long time, and his lungs feel tight. It is a trick unlike any he's ever read about.

It's Carly who takes him to his first magic show. She gets tickets to everything because she is a librarian. They leave the red brick row house well before dinner and walk to the bus stop. They pass by the basketball courts, where the older boys are always hanging around. They're playing a pickup game now, Ty on one team and Ray on the other, as usual. There are a few girls plastered to the chain link fence. They wear sweaters that fall off one shoulder, and blue eyeshadow, or green.

On the bus, Carly listens to her cello music. Sometimes she plays the cello, too, in the living room. But when she listens to the music, she becomes sad. Sometimes she doesn't hear when Russ talks to her, and he fears he is in the middle of one of his surprise disappearing acts. But then she notices him standing in front of her, or in the doorway, or on the steps going upstairs. "Russ," she says, "you're such a quiet boy." She plays a little while longer and then packs the instrument in its case.

They ride the bus all the way downtown and then walk to the amphitheater. Inside, they sit on cushioned seats. There are kids everywhere—he has never seen so many, except at school.

After the show, they walk to the station. The bus ride home seems much longer, and the whole time Russ is overwhelmed with questions: Did Houdini play basketball? Go to the bathroom? Sleep? Take baths?

In a couple days, there are books about Houdini on the dining room table. It's here where Russ finds out that Houdini tried to talk to his mother, even though she was dead, and that he once ran away from his family and that he died because he was punched in the stomach three times. And though Houdini had to learn all his tricks, Russ never had a lesson in his life.

Life, or lives. There are two of them now: Russ as Russ, and Russ who lives when the real Russ sleeps. There is evidence of this: besides what people say, there are toys strewn about, toys Russ doesn't remember removing from the closet. There are crackers on the table. Carly tells him that they are going to go to the doctor soon to try to understand why.

This is not Russ's only power. At school, his disruptions, which include pounding chalk into dust and swallowing calculator batteries, make the teacher move his desk to the back of the room. When assignments are passed one person back for checking, Russ has to walk to the front of the row to give his to the girl Marie. When the assignments are corrected, she walks his back to him, always with nice red circles around the parts he gets wrong. None of these kids know that he can disappear, that he can just drop through the earth at any time.

He fancies he has other powers as well, probably that have to do with the brain, probably whatever part is responsible for mind control. He first tries this out on Marie. He stares at the back of her head all through class and while she walks to him returning his paper. Still, she has made all the red circles, even when he specifically instructed her not to. He practices every day, on the teacher (to not give him homework), on the busdriver (to forget to pick him up), on Carly (to make pizza for dinner). He knows he is getting better because all of these people, except Carly, get nervous around him. Carly asks a lot of questions. How is he feeling? Does he have a headache? Does he have thoughts about hurting people? She says he can tell her anything he wants to.

One day they drive an hour to a city with a special hospital. In the doctor's office, Carly talks a lot. He is tired of her talking.

She doesn't like his magic. They ride in three elevators and stop at two counters, and then Russ gets a shot that makes him sleepy.

Over summer break, Russ heads to the basketball courts. He offers one of the girls there, Stephanie, a cigarette from a pack he lifted from the corner store. She's dressed in cut-offs and clogs and a lime-green tube top. She takes the cigarette and smiles at him.

In a moment, her boyfriend is there, glistening and razor-eyed. "Who the hell are you?" he says, taking the cigarette from Stephanie, hogging it, smoking it down, down, down. His words are pronounced strangely, and when he speaks he uses all of his tongue. Russ doesn't understand him at first, piecing the words together as the seconds tick by.

But Russ knows this game. He has watched it from his window. He picks up the basketball and dribbles, passes the ball, hard, to the boyfriend with the funny speech and dark curls.

On the court, Russ is the smallest, but without his headaches and with his magic, he dishes out wonders. These kids are fast; he pretends not to notice as he quickly adjusts his game. He has eyes only for the hoop. Even the girls have stopped their chatting and pay attention.

On defense, he's a stealer coming out of nowhere, tipping the ball five feet out, then a few dribbles, then the easy layup.

The kids on his team smirk, but the funny-speech kid has had enough. Russ sees him coming, notes that the pleas from his teammates go unheard. *Fair is fair*, Russ thinks, but the kid is already there in front of him, and his first blow lands in the center of Russ's chest, the air in his lungs gone, the pavement at his back. The kid moves to kick, but Russ rolls to the side.

When Russ sits up, the kid is on him. The dead, bloodied man hangs from a chain around the kid's neck, brushes Russ's cheek. It occurs to Russ that possibly none of this is actually happening. His real self could be in the brick walkup with Carly, finishing his homework or eating dinner. Perhaps he has acquired the ability to be aware of his alternative self's actions.

So why not try the impossible? "Hey, asshole," Russ says, getting up. "Why don't you just learn how to play the game?" Russ turns away and walks toward the bleachers. The kid's footsteps grow closer. But Stephanie, who's on the court now, looks past Russ and at the kid.

"What, you're protecting him?" the kid says to Stephanie, but weakens at the sight of her. "Fuck this," he says, walking off. Stephanie goes after him.

The other kids have regrouped and want to play. Russ joins his team.

One team member says to him, "Are you okay?"

Russ nods.

Dream, magic, or for real, Russ decides that the biggest kids have big weaknesses. Still, his shoulders are knotted, his right hand clenched, ready for the fight.

The Mccluskey Residential Treatment Center
1976–1978
These boys are hedons, sinners, and skeptics, but inside each of them is as much raw material as that which can be found in an unexplored mine or riverbed.
           —G. T. McCluskey, activist and educator, 1870–1936

Originally, what was known as the McCluskey Orphanage took everything—strays, bastards, criminals, loners, the sick, and the deranged—which was in line with the desire of its founder, George T. McCluskey, who himself began as a wayward lad in a new country ripe for trans-regional expansion. A railroad worker turned social activist turned, in the late years, alcoholic, McCluskey built the school himself, brick by brick, then drew up its mission statement with the help of his socialite wife, Anne. The statement combined the practical language of a long-time day laborer and the archaic language of a Catholic saint: "This New orphanage, looked upon with beneficence by the Glory of Heaven, shall take upon itself to Protect & Serve, those children who for whatever reason, stand in need."

In the 1950s, a minor scandal involving an administrator forced all state eyes onto the orphanage. Fueled by indignation, it continued operating for another two decades until orphanages in general came under scrutiny. The organization was told to make changes or close for good.

Regulators, health insurance specialists, bureaucrats, nurses, pediatricians, and child psychologists descended on conferences in Denver, Boise, Madison, and Chicago. After the dust settled, the state funding came, first in big chunks, then in bite-sized pieces that barely covered expenses.

The day Russ enrolls is in the middle of a year that has almost eaten through the latest bite-size chunk. Two boys to a room, a common toilet down the hall, a strict daily schedule, no food after dinner, inconvenient visiting hours, and rotating chores numbered among the tedious and undesireable; but healthy meals, a new baseball diamond and game room, extra counselors, updated medical equipment, and a library were among the amenities.

Russ is here because his blackouts have become a burden for the average foster mother, who understands his condition well enough but who doesn't, after all, have nerves of steel.

The classes incorporate instruction, but at varying and mismatched levels. About half the boys are medicated. Russ himself is taking an antidepressant, which makes staying awake difficult and makes concentrating even harder. Sometimes he puts his head down right on top of whatever is in front of him, and falls asleep. Sometimes his arm twitches and he bolts awake in his desk only to fall asleep again. Later, the teacher wakes him up and walks him to his room.

The center also houses a well-established hierarchy with a stronger foundation than the building itself. The boys at the top wear bandanas around their heads and are physically tall and have an early outcrop of facial hair. They are volatile, not mad, and are held together by fear and paranoia. They, like Russ, can sense the lack of control the facility has, the way the boundaries shift every time a boy makes a move.

Russ stands out in the crowd. He is new, small, quiet, and therefore suspicious. After he falls asleep in class the third time, his fate is sealed.

It begins with taunts and pushes when he ventures into the tall boys' proximity, then progresses to rough shoves and insults wherever he might be. He avoids the bathroom and waits for the lunch line to dwindle to nothing before making his way through, sliding his tray along for his helping of meatloaf or lasagna. He sits, and eats quickly.

What he keeps tucked in his belt, a relic from a past bully, is his own business.

They call him stupid, a retard, a faggot. "What's the matter, you need to hold the teacher's hand?" the boys say. "You need a babysitter? You want your mommy?"

One day Russ is called to the office that has all the secretaries. A man appears and tells Russ to come into his office. This man is the head man, a principal, maybe. Russ sits in the leather chair opposite the man. The man says that Russ's mother has been trying to get him released from the center and that soon Russ can go home. Russ studies the man's face, his large shirt collars, the thin wisps of hair on his head. A mother: this triggers nothing in him, not even curiosity. The man says, "How do you feel about that?" The man says, "I've spoken with your mother personally, and she's made great improvements, and she'd like her boy to come home." Russ kicks the desk with his toe. There's a headache coming on. He asks to go to the nurse for his medication.

When he leaves, the secretaries stop typing and watch him.

He hates these women looking at him. He feels the blood rush to his face as the urge to destroy gathers in his arms. Later, in his room, he throws books across the room. He watches the way they land, how the pages curl and bend under the weight of the spine. With one book, he tears the pages out one by one, and crumples them into tight balls.

Then, all at once, the top of his head shoots a bullet of pain into his skull and neck. He drops the book and makes his way, again, to the nurse.

He feels himself stumble as he rounds the corner. The edges of his vision are closing in, and the pressure has moved from the top of his head to his forehead. He feels queasy. In front of him are two boys—two of the tallest boys. But he can't stop walking. One of them says something but he can't understand. In a moment, he is pushed from behind and held tightly against the wall. Its coolness comes as a tiny relief, but now there is a strong hand clasped around the back of his head, which is totally immobile. The other boy spits on him; he feels the hot glob slide down the side of his face.

They are laughing, monolithic. They don't know that they have trapped the wrong boy, on the wrong day. They don't notice Russ squirming—in their calculated attention to his upper body, they forget the lower. They don't notice Russ's free hand slip under his shirt, grab the pocket knife tucked in his belt, and pry open the blade.

Russ waits for the pressure behind his head to lessen. He waits until the tallest one is in the middle of a sentence, laughing, cracking himself up. Russ rolls his head out of the kid's grip and frees himself long enough to swing his extended arm behind him, like a tennis player backhanding a killer shot.

The swing, though uncalculated, hits the mark. Russ's vision is so clouded now, and his head is pounding so much that all he sees are a few drops of blood at his feet. The other boy seems to have disappeared, but then Russ's vision is gone entirely, and his knees give out.

Russ sits near the lobby's windows, watching. In his suitcase are several medicine bottles—a new drug this time, something that might work better—and a slip of paper with his next four psychiatrist appointments written on it.

This new medicine doesn't make him so groggy, but still there is the unrest from a particularly active dream life. Last night was another of the merry-go-round, except that instead of horses, there were cars attached to the poles. All of the cars were black, and all of them had ripped-up interiors. Sometimes the doors of the cars didn't work, and Russ wondered how anybody got in them. But there were people on the carousal platform, and people getting out of the cars. But then the ride started up, and a man in some kind of uniform told him to sit down, but Russ couldn't because he couldn't find a car that worked. And then all of the cars were gone, and there was a strong wind, and Russ grabed an empty pole to steady himself.

In the lobby, he waits for another woman, a woman who has seen him before, a woman who knows him. Finally, she drives up in a little green car with rust spots. He grips his chair.

Home isn't where the heart is
1978–1982

Russ has a younger half-brother, Madison, who snores all night and reads books instead of throwing them. He doesn't carry a knife, and he doesn't play any sports. He does everything that their shared mother, Bethany, tells him to do. He draws in little notebooks and in the upper right corners of thick books, so that when you flip the pages, you have a cartoon. One is of a dump truck driving up and dumping dirt on two people. Another is a pirate forcing a crew member to walk the plank, and when the crew member jumps, he sinks and starts to swim with small fish, then bigger fish, and then one of the fish eats him. This one makes Russ laugh, even though he himself is more interested in the thicket of dense trees that line the edge of the backyard, past the lilac bushes and pines. This is where he goes to smoke, which, miraculously, Bethany does not mind. She doesn't even mind when he smokes one of her cigarettes. She doesn't even ask where he got his, and sometimes she smokes one of them. She is thin, with shoulder-length blonde hair and high cheekbones. One large wave of hair always falls in her face.

She looks out of windows a lot. She says things like *I finally got you back* or *You don't know how hard I tried* or *Those bureaucrats have straw heads*. This woman takes more pills than Russ does—two for every one of his, and she washes them down with anything that pours out from a tall, narrow bottle.

The kid Madison has a mechanical mind, this much is clear. He takes everything apart. One morning the toaster oven is gone—it's spread out on the living room carpet, piece by piece. Bethany says, *Damn it, Maddy, get that thing together and back on the counter.*

As Madison screws in the back plate, Russ says, *Madison is a girl's name.* Madison looks at him, keeps rotating the screwdriver. *Why do you have a girl's name*, Russ says, and Madison gets up and brings the toaster to Bethany. *Thank you, love*, she says, and she brushes her hand over Madison's head. Russ sees that his words have no effect on the kid, that the kid lives for her, that he disappears into corners where he plays quietly, disassembling, assembling.

Russ wants to punch this kid, but Bethany is looking at him there in the corner, she's smoking, she's looking out the window, she's dressed in her brown-and-gold uniform again, the one that smells like a dirty frying pan. It's a sight that fills him with rage because it's supposed to mean something but it connects with nothing.

Russ is in seventh grade, and he's flunking, but this fact doesn't connect to anything, either. He disappears into the woods and, in short, finds everything: railroad tracks, a stream, one half of a rotted picnic table, and, the real gem, an old tree house with dirty magazines, lighters, and syringes in it.

The day Russ decides to follow the tracks is the same day that Madison decides to follow Russ. They walk the tracks for a half hour, Madison trailing behind, past dumpsters and blown-out warehouses and middle-class backyards and apartment complexes with the word "landing" in the title. Russ thinks, this kid isn't going to stop, and walks ten more minutes, just to test him, then finds a path and veers off.

They sit on a downed tree, near where the base was uprooted. Madison says, *We should go home*, and Russ believes the kid to be weird, possibly crazy. A kid like this is never going to make it, Russ thinks, and so announces that they can go home when Russ gets back. *Where are you going?* Madison says. Russ says, *To look around a little.*

Russ comes back fifteen minutes later to find the kid in the same spot, white-faced, shivering. Again, he wants to punch him but not in the same way he's wanted to punch other kids. Plus, this kid wouldn't understand being punched.

Russ has candy from a store. He knows no one will question the cut on the inside of his forearm or the sore right knee, both acquired when his shirt caught on the chain-link fence, causing him to fall.

It's dusk, and soon the tracks will be dark, but the more familiar darkness visits Russ again in the form of the edges of his vision blurring, the old queasiness, the legs that betray him.

When he wakes, Bethany is above him, checking his eyes. Russ realizes he's in his room. Madison is doing a puzzle but stops when Russ sits up.

Bethany holds a thermometer and says, *I don't know what the hell happened out there, but Maddy came running in the back door, said you might be dead.* She shakes the thermometer. *And he hasn't left this room.*

The thermometer gets thrust in his mouth. She says, *Russ, what's all this about? You're going to have to help your mother a little bit.*

The love of a good woman
1982–1983

Russ could have stayed. He could have helped a little bit. But the railroad tracks call to him in the night. They speak to him of freedom, of motion, of a recklessness that thrills him to his core. That the thrill is part and parcel of anger does not occur to him, of course, and since the anger feels a lot like strength, Russ walks rejuvenated, even brazen. He is lucky; he does not understand fear, and this is why, on the day when he decides to follow the tracks, he 1) brings nothing at all along with him, and 2) doesn't stop walking or turn around.

After three days and four petty thefts yielding Hostess pies,

Twinkies, an assortment of pretzels, orange juice, and cigarettes, Russ abandons the tracks and instead camps in alleyways and dumpsters.

He is too hungry for snack food. After five days, he no longer tastes it. Meat is what he wants, in all forms. Just outside the back door of the fish-fry joint is one place to go. He lifts a little coke from the pocket of a passed-out junkie and gives it to the cook, who in turn gives him battered cod and discarded French fries. Cole slaw, too, and sometimes beans from a can.

The system falls apart when, one day, the cook gets fired. Russ is back to striking stray matches on stone to bring up smelly fires in garbage barrels. He's rolling newspaper into a torch in order to start another fire when he buckles at the knee and his head spins so fast he doesn't even feel the ground hit him.

When he wakes, the first thing he feels is warmth under his back; no not warmth, exactly, but softness, a cushion. He opens his eyes and sees that he's in a room—the wallpaper is brown and curling off the walls, and there is no normal furniture—but a room is a room, and he tries to trace his life backward to piece together what might have happened. He stops, though, when he sees the girl: what good has piecing anything together ever done him? It's what's in front of him now that matters, and although he doesn't realize he's turned a bad streak, he understands that he will exploit this girl for everything she has.

Which is not much, but coke in all its permutations can turn time into the best friend you ever had, so Russ steals it, borrows it, buys it when he can, even begs for it when the smallest hours creep up on him and are more than he can bear. The girl's name is Marci, and together they live on a sea of mattresses. When she's naked, which is often, they talk about many things they'll never remember; when they fuck, which is also often, he slaps her when she asks for it and sometimes when she doesn't; he hates her stale-sweat smell and her stinky feet, but after a while, he can't smell anything, not even the broken bathroom toilet that everyone uses with limited success.

By "everyone" he means all the men who find Marci, and there are quite a few. That they emerge and disappear from his consciousness does not bother him, nor that they all sleep with her and leave wadded bills on the floor, nor that they trip over him and swear at him.

Marci feeds Russ tomato soup and crackers. She heats the soup in a frying pan on a hot plate. He knows three things about her: she grew up in a different country, her mother was a stripper, and she is able to dream the future, but only after eating eggs. When she wakes up screaming, she's had another dream omen. *This one involved you,* she says one day, but he doesn't ask. He thinks maybe she's lying about the dreams and her ability, but what difference would it make? Her story would be like all the other ones he can think up, all of them plausible, all of them true.

What he wants is to control time. One night he and Marci take some cash and go to a club, which they get into because Marci knows the bouncer. She's dressed in stilettos and fishnet tights, and she buys men drink after drink, passing or taking with each one a small plastic bag or pill, pushing her knee into the crotch of some heavily mustached man. When they are gone, Russ drinks two more shots, then climbs the back stairs looking for them, which he easily does: not only Marci and the mustached man, but others, too, in soiled corners and stained-velvet chairs. Three wallets, Marci's purse, and four days' worth of powder enter his poorly stitched pockets, and he's gone before the red light blankets them all.

He hides in plain sight, disguised as himself, pacing on sidewalks and the steps in front of public buildings. He allows himself a good meal, so good that he glimpses his future: there can be more food like this for him, couldn't there?

There is a girl in his past: she huddled with him around a fire. She had freckles and a red ponytail and pink lips, and black boots with loose heels flapping when she walked. She emerged from the same path they all did, the one that took them in and out of the woods and to and from barrel fires.

She hadn't been a true runaway, and this fact broke his heart. She made up stories, this he knew. She was his companion, though she didn't know it, and when she left, he buried his face in his jacket.

The buildings he passes now all have gray faces and awnings and neon glows. He goes into one and buys a pizza with money from Marci's purse. He watches teenagers just like him smiling and flirting with each other. That life is miles and miles away, but the girl he likes the look of best could be any girl, even Marci, if things hadn't gone so wrong. He wants to hate her, but cannot.

So he returns to her that very night. She's passed out; her mascara is smeared, and she's drooling onto her pillow, her bruised veins darker than plums, her skin streaked red and green. His one regret is not asking her about the dream omen, but it is too late for all that, so instead he drops her purse, intact and unsullied, on her ice-blue face.

Outside, a rainstorm impedes his view, but there is indeed a car following him, and, omen or not, he ignores it until he can't anymore, until a man in a trench coat steps out and yells his name. Russ freezes. It is another sedan coming to pick him up. The man says, *Russ, we've been looking for you.*

What can he do? There are dead ends in every direction, an open street slicked with oily water. He knows that the man is there to take him somewhere, possibly jail, but the man says, *Your mother wants you to come home.*

He gets in: it is like saying goodbye to himself. But even ghosts have to make appearances.

Last ditch
1983–1984

That summer, after rehab, Bethany gets Russ a job at the farm of an uncle he doesn't remember. It is purely a labor-for-food arrangement, and also, Russ is to live at the farm. Madison is there, too; they have their own bedrooms on the second floor.

It becomes obvious that wherever Russ goes, so does Madison, and yet they can't be said to be working together. Now it's Russ who follows Madison, and sometimes Madison tells him what to do. *I worked here last summer*, Madison says, *I've done all this before*, and it's true, but Russ still can't shake the feeling that he's being watched.

Watches as in scrutinized. As in monitored. As in, one day after inventory, Madison takes the clipboard and checks the numbers. They stand by a row of wooden pallets. Russ says, *What, you think I can't count?* And Madison says, *I was asked to double-check. It's what we always do.*

But there is more: there are Madison's trips out to the barn long after Russ has showered, to the barn Russ was asked to lock up. There are Madison's hands flashing around keys Russ has never seen, there is the cash register till put into the safe each night, there are small tasks for him to do the moment a customer comes into the store, there are breakfasts made and eaten before Russ even comes downstairs, there are notes left for him about where to report to next, and there are reminders about things he's been reminded to do so much that he hears voices in his sleep.

He knows there are moments where he loses himself—when he can't remember where he is or what might have happened the last few hours. There are moments where he loses himself in other ways— when he can't remember the last town he lived in, when his mother's name escapes him, when he cannot fathom a self beyond these tree-lined borders. It is especially these moments when the rage creeps up on him, when he feels a panic slipping in, when the only thing to do that makes sense is to strike out: a statement, a cry, and plea.

The day comes when Madison's face is on the other side of that plea, and all because of a parked tractor, which is now in a deep gulley filled with low-lying water and cattails. Madison tells Russ that he parked it too close to the edge, and in all seriousness, Russ doesn't know what this means because he has no recollection of parking it anywhere, nor of being told to do so. But the tractor is undoubtedly in the ditch, and Russ is guilty, guilty, guilty.

It's easy to hit Madison, of course; Russ has wanted to for many years, but even he is surprised at how hard the throw comes, how the cracking nose bruises and bleeds. He is even more surprised at the repercussion, which comes not in the form of physical violence but is delivered in a look, a look of pity, and at his own instant understanding of how far he is from anything that makes up a conventional life.

Madison says, *Uncle Ives is taking you home tomorrow,* and there are nothing but apologies welling up from Russ's insides; and here's a kid with a bloody, broken nose and a good heart and an instinct for preserving it.

Russ is gone the next day. He sees a "driver's wanted" sign in the window of a brick building in an industrial park, and decides to let whoever works inside that building determine his next move.

Confessions

Breath

I watch the dead, but not in the way you might think: that is, as spirits, as cold-cloud entities hovering in the corners of rooms said to be haunted, or as they appear in horror films—gray-blue zombies hobbling rancidly down abandoned urban streets or in moonlit cornfields. Rather, I watch the *ni* of my old and sick ones break down and lose its vitality. I watch until the *ni* cannot keep wrong thoughts away, until they swirl down from the mind to the soul, already hollowed, as if awaiting them. In time I watch the *ni*, the strong ghost, move on and up and away; sometimes this happens before my eyes—my sweetie in a bed or on a couch or even a wicker chair on some porch. When it's over, I take the time to watch the body not breathe.

The first last breath I saw was that of a man, drawn in deeply, with gusto, and released through the top of his head. This breath was the color of a ripe cherry and I held it in my hand for exactly three seconds.

Secrets

I, too, move on—to the next one and the next one. I happen to have had many men, which is different from having had many women, though tissue is tissue, thin blood is thin blood. This is my career: the dead I am often around to watch during the first minute of their deaths are alive with me before that, for any number of months, sleepwalking or getting lost in walk-in pantries or softly praying or mumbling bitterroot under breaths of day-old syrup or potato.

I get my latest sweetheart, Henry, from his kitchen. He has forgotten where he left his tea, but it is on the front porch, shaded by a giant awning. I can see the tea there, half-drunk, getting cold. I guide him by the elbow, his hand dangling and weakened from the cancer, across the living room. I have just put a CD in the stereo and say with a raised voice, "Listen, Henry, it's Ella."

Henry stops, looking around for the sound. His eyes brighten. "A real siren," he says.

I will dwell later on that word, *siren*. It has *vixen* in it somewhere, the fox, the sharp wit and the lies, the short gait, the hop. The Greek enchantress and the warning. It has Henry's age all wrapped up in it, in its allusion to another era. He has also said *jaunty* and *screwball* and *dapper* and *gumption*, even *cut of his jib*, which I like and try out—just for fun—on my caretaker friend, Jo, and the girls in my book group.

I sit Henry down on the porch, in his cushioned wicker chair. It's spring, petals of the earliest daffodils curling inward, already drought-ridden. Sometimes I send him out with a watering can. He says he likes to hear the crackling sound of the dirt taking in the water, which I don't think is possible without the hearing aid he refuses to get, but here we are looking over the daffodils on his huge front porch, a porch bigger than my first remembered home. His lungs are eaten away, cancer-pocked at the tissue-laden, gas-exchanging surface, and now his spine suffers the spread and warp. What's left of his hair is yellowed and silky. His voice is hoarse because there is little space for breath.

We live-ins—sequestered, toeing borderlines, squished by family members who hire us but never listen to us (I am the fly on the wall and they swat at me if I rub my magic wings)—have a certain definition of fun, a certain idea about humor, and this is necessary, in my view, to do the job well. Henry is my sixth employer in six years, and even though we are taught about the importance of detachment, I don't like to say *employer*. The problem is that although I am the employee, I get possessive with my charges, my sweeties. Seven weeks ago Henry's daughter Angela made him go to church. I disagreed with that—Christianity, like other diseases, having long since swept through my land—but what can I say? And so I drive him to Saint Michael's and walk him in and wait in the car for Mass to end.

Angela also made Henry give away his rabbit to a high school kid down the road. I do not understand why Henry allows her to dictate the terms of his final months. *Made him.* You can talk as high as the clouds about the positive effect animals have on sick people, talk yourself ridiculous about the money you can save on doctor bills and therapy bills, but none of this can change the outlook of a self-described martyr, a daughter with an ax to grind on the subject of pets.

Henry has not been the same since his rabbit was taken away. A week ago, in fact, while getting his walking exercise around the house, he removed all pictures of her from the walls and bookshelves, and stacked them in a corner. We have been together something like a year, and still, Henry won't tell me certain things, like even the name of this rabbit. Like the reason for his aversion to lemonade. Like the reason for his map collection, extensive enough to fill the upstairs closet, which is as big as an old-fashioned pantry, and spill out into one of the unused bedrooms. Like why it is he thinks he is being punished with lung cancer given that he's never smoked.

Must I know these things? When the last breath leaves him, I want to have a vision to focus on—I want to see all his elements flow away from him in a foamy, gaseous release. It's the rippling away I throw my own rock into, so I can't say my watching is selfless; I always take my ill with me, I always choose theft. I want the secrets he would tell grandchildren in that way they wouldn't recognize: confession disguised as a morality tale or as a casual observation or even as the early babblings that mark the onset of senility.

Men

My first was eighty-seven, Clayton Thompson, a weasel-eyed spitfire who ate pickled eggs out of a jar, chewed tobacco, and drank whiskey. If not whiskey, then scotch. Despite his decaying liver, there was no doctor who could set him straight, or dared to. He said, "If drinking is my life sentence, bring it on." He was a loose cannon, a rhubarb-necked desperado with hands the size of grizzly paws. I brought him fruit that rotted away in bowls.

He mostly wanted to eat out, so I took him wherever he wanted. I called to ask the family, but he said, "To hell with them all, I don't need no goddamned permission." We ate at upscale Italian places, fish-fry joints, sandwich shops, and cafés with menus on blackboards. His coordination was lost to the early stages of Parkinson's, but really it was his mouth you had to look out for: he cursed red and purple, let the fury streak his face and knot up behind his ears. He ranted about gas mileage and OPEC and the decreasing whatever and the increasing everything. His advice to me? "Fuck a lot of women."

But his tirades required no reply and thus no participation. He could be calmed by a nod or grunt in agreement or approval, because if you approved, you were his friend, and if you were his friend, then he had nothing to convince you of, and if he had nothing to convince you of, then there was no show.

He died of a heart attack seven months after I moved in, and I call him my sweetie because his blue streaks left in me a love of silence.

The next three were all terminally ill, bedridden, toilet-prone. All fluids left them, their tiny bathrooms a chrome-barred prison. I cleaned these men and their bathrooms until I was raw, until I understood the concept of creative warfare: battles that took place in cube-like rooms and in impossible hallways and in laundry rooms with tired machines and in dresser drawers that wouldn't stay full and in my men shamed into silence by their failing bodies. Their children came, their siblings and their friends, but my men, in their patterned pajamas, hid from them by blending into the wallpaper, into stripes and dots and miniature flower bouquets.

But they tricked me, every one. Herb Winkle, my youngest sweetie, asked me to page through a photo album filled with wartime photos—eighteen-year-olds with thin moustaches, cigarette packs rolled in shirt sleeves, parachutes ballooning down onto scrubby hills, bars lit in neon, topless women encircling yet more chrome bars. He pointed to a bald, tattooed man and said, "This man saved my life with a hairpin that"—he pointed to a naked woman hanging upside down on one of the bars—"he happened to find in his pocket a week later. Do you believe it? I was chained to a street grille in a piss-stained alley in Seoul. Because I took some asshole's girl. Would've had to cut my arm off."

Benny Lindser's family never visited except for a daughter, once. He was in the final stages of Alzheimer's, so mostly I moved him: from the bed to the wheelchair to the toilet to the wheelchair to bed. His jaw hung slack. I talked a lot of nonsense, a lot of cheery drivel. When I ran out of drivel and patience I put the radio on—talk shows to fill the room with chatter. Benny had been a geology professor and cave spelunker. He had four ex-wives. He had a scar along his spine.

He had a fear of rodents. The daughter had the answers: an inability to connect emotionally to women; the collapse of an abandoned underground coal mine in Haynes; a friend who died after contracting hantavirus. One morning I brought his oatmeal over to him, tied his bib, and went to raise the window shades. After the third shade, I felt the static slice up my body. I let the ghost rise before making phone calls, before writing 8:53 a.m. on a scrap of paper and tacking it to the kitchen bulletin board.

The only woman I took care of, Hazel Sonnenberg, sat for hours on the edge of the couch sorting her *National Enquirer* magazines. She drank one and a half glasses of red wine every day, and ate her eggs with ketchup. Hazel asked *me* the questions—how old was I, did I have children, where did I live? I said, "I live on beams and rafters, like a bat." The real answers confounded her. I tried to explain, but she shook my replies away. With Hazel, I did not provide twenty-four-hour care, so at night I stayed with Jo or my friend Nadja to save money. Days, Hazel and I sorted magazines. Or read coupon booklets, remarking on all that was on sale. We just clipped and sorted. One day she folded up a large tampon coupon (from the "not using" pile) into a butterfly. The *Pla* of Playtex spanned one wing. Then she folded Grey Poupon mustard into a crane. Johnsonville brats into frog. Cool Whip into a fish. We hung them on a mobile.

Hazel started getting tired a lot. She'd say, "I have no pep." Tests were run. She had four weeks left. In one week, almost all of her *ni* dissipated—I could practically see the fog whispering out through her eyes and ears. I heard that, in the hospital right before her death, she lashed out at one of the nurses and had to be restrained and given Thorazine.

The wife of Nate Claibourne, my fifth sweetie, died from breast cancer, and two years after that Nate was being fatally poisoned by his own blood. Nate told me that his wife had been a stage actress and that they first made love backstage at the Blue Moon Theater in Chicago, in a huge wooden bin filled with costumes. Her career ended a month later, and she would be pregnant for nearly nine consecutive years. He said, three weeks before he died, his brown eyes watery and faded, "I took her from the stage—I thought it was the right thing—but she was no good at being herself."

I thought, *Now is your chance to speak, watch your treasures gleam, say your peace keepsakes in this room, your haven, my presence your witches brew.*

Games

Months go by. Henry and I fall into playing long, nonsensical card games. The cards we use have a purple fleur-de-lis pattern on the back. They are worn and soft from his hands, from years of his skin's oil and warmth. Angela hates these games. "Next, you'll have him gambling," she says. She worries about his soul, which she says is blackened from sins she'll never utter. But I am not paid to keep Henry holy. I am here to keep him clean and fed and medicated.

There is no name for the game we play, and this is because the rules keep changing, and this is because Henry's mind is not consistent. I pretend to strategize and then put down an ace of spades, which might be an important card in this particular game, which began as something resembling gin, but now Henry layers cards upon each other, as in solitaire.

I am tempted to reach for the book my group is reading this month, *The Last Salamander*, because Henry could take twenty minutes to make his move. Susan, the group's leader and a part-time librarian, chose this title. We meet at people's houses. Angela does not like that I get this time off, but it's in the contract. She rolls her eyes when she shows up to relieve me. Jo says, "Remember, you're the one doing her a favor." I say, "If I don't take this time off, when will I get any?"

I bake things for the meetings. Before Angela arrives, I get Henry situated on the porch with Ella or Louis playing. I make sure he has several issues of *Scientific American* nearby, and then cut, slice, or arrange whatever I've made and bring a plate of it to him.

Henry holds the index finger of his right hand up in the air, as if an idea has struck him. He says, "A very good move," and I smile. Sometimes I get to pick a card from the "pot" and sometimes I don't. This is okay, that the game changes colors; these games with no reason are not always entertaining, but they are lifelike, and this is what I try to remember: good plays at the end of a lifelike life.

Confessions

Let me tell you about the future dead and their confessions. They will all begin with an argument over whether a certain shirt should be washed. He will wear it, I will want to wash it, and he will not want to take it off. I will let the matter rest for a few minutes while I go to get tea or pills or cough drops, and when I come back, he will offer me a clue, he will blurt out an almost random thought about someone I don't know, the person who would most appreciate it being gone or lost or long dead. So I try. I say *you* a lot. I nod my head, say, "I know she would understand how you feel. If only you would have known." I say, "You were right to tell her when you did." I say, "You did what you could." But I have no way to measure the accuracy of what I say. I soothe in the way only a bystander to near death can: by walking my old and sick across their last street, like a child in a fifties documentary, doling out my belief and trust, professing my faith in their good intentions, derailed by time or not.

A woman

There is a distant phenomenon brewing for us, a treat from the heavens, and this phenomenon corresponds to Henry's life span.

Henry's middle name is Halley, and one of his last wishes is to view his namesake, Halley's comet, which he was not able to do seventy-six years ago, which was when it last appeared. I know that Henry has watched comets before, that for a period in his life he sat vigilant under the night sky keeping tabs on certain celestial endeavors—Comet West, in 1976, and Comet Kohoutek, in 1973. So lately, on his good days, he reads about a space ball several miles in diameter, tiny by sidereal standards, packed with solar debris and ice, an ancient projectile whose orbit has been altered by planetary activity and now brings us an orb with a fiery, gaseous tail.

His plan is to sit in the field beyond the yard, where the darkness is unobscured by fluorescent effluvia such as traffic signals and street lights, and wait. And how can I resist? He is very specific about what he needs: a view of the horizon, since the comet will be low in the sky; his wide-field telescope, which he thinks is in the attic; his Adirondack chair, which might be in the shed; and his wide-brimmed straw hat, which is probably lost.

I find him in bedroom closets or lost in the middle of hallways. I find him upstairs, pulling down the attic panel with its attached step ladder. I ask him what he needs so that I can get it for him. "I want," he says, feeling the air with his fingertips, "my telescope." His hand flies to his temple, and he squints, thinking. "My Meade telescope."

In the attic, I stumble around boxes and pails and iron bed frames. Bug carcasses and mouse scat litter the floor. Drafting boards and collapsed tripods, white with dust, lean against the walls. I sneeze repeatedly.

"Henry, you have mice," I say.

"What?" Henry says.

"Mice."

I wipe my nose on my sleeve, then bend to open boxes. I grab the flashlight sitting on the ledge and shine the beam on their contents: rolls of steel and cloth tape, piles of *Scientific American* and *National Geographic* and *Reader's Digest*, calibrated cylinders with metal loops on one end, large compasses with metal bracketlike appendages sticking out of them, cameras of all sizes, one box filled with cases stamped Keuffel and Esser Co. in gold lettering, several editions of the *Illustrated Price Guide to Antique Surveying Instruments and Books*.

Between the boxes I find more equipment, all of it covered in old sheets.

"Henry," I say. "Can you give me a hint?"

"I think it's in a blue case," he says. "No, a wooden one."

I come over to the attic door and look down at Henry. He sits, wheezing, on a rung of the step ladder.

"You have mice up here."

His head bobbles a little. Then the creases in his neck appear, which means he's going to speak.

"Well, they don't eat much," he says.

"I'll tell Angela, she can deal with it."

I go back and start pulling at the sheets. Eventually I find the telescope. It is indeed in a wooden carrying case, which is bulky but manageable. I climb down and close the attic panel. Henry has disappeared to the spare room, where he digs around in the closet, looking for his wide-brimmed hat. So I kneel down and rummage through the boxes and tins and rolled maps and drafting supplies.

I'm pulling at a box at the bottom of a stack and in the process knock over another. A few drafting pencils and what looks like a silver chain fall out. A locket. It's a fine one, oval, engraved, heavy, barely rusted except along its tiny hinge. I open it quickly, and in fact there is a picture in it. I gather it in my hand, quickly, and put away the pencils and boxes.

There is no sign of the hat, so I take Henry downstairs to the porch. It's dark; a storm is blowing in. I push him in closer to the glass-topped wicker table, where he begins wiping down the telescope case with a damp cloth.

The telescope project will busy him for days, because he will have to rest his hands and his back often. I go inside to make chamomile tea. Angela buys the stuff in bags, but I get it fresh from Nadja, who grows it and mixes it with just enough lavender. I put the kettle on, feeling the locket, smooth and magnetic, in my pocket. I lean back on the counter and fish it out. The picture is of a Native woman, unsmiling, long black hair flowing down her shoulders.

I dump a tablespoon of herbs into the infuser. This face does not match that of any on Henry's walls. A locket: an exchange, encapsulated hope, pure youth. I decide that if Henry ever confesses anything, the confession would be of her, this anonymous woman, this portion of all that his *ni* comprises.

Provocations

Henry ignores his children's fights. Angela seems to provoke them— she gets on the phone and yells at the brother, her husband, somebody—and then hangs up and huffs and sulks. I do not like the cut of this woman's jib, this woman who sees only the bruises on people. The bruise on me is that I exist, and that I help her father. That I will allow him a peach if he wants a peach, that I will give him coffee if he wants coffee, that I will let him stack photos wherever he wants, that I don't believe there is a "wrong" way to organize the cabinets.

I was hired initially because Henry began to have accidents. He'd fall, he'd forget to eat, he'd take too many pills. The son said he had slowed considerably, that he had aged more in two years than he had in the last fifteen. He got in a minor car accident that was his fault.

A month after I arrived, I found bloody tissues in the bathroom garbage can. His regular coughing had turned into near spasms that ended with a deathly choking sound. The bronchoscopy revealed a large mass growing quickly into the lumen and obstructing the airway. The cancer had already spread to his spine.

I hear a car pull up and look out the window. Angela is in the driveway taking some groceries out of the trunk of her car. I go to the front door and hold it for her.

"Hi, Nina," she says. "Thanks."

Her mood is not so bad today. Instead of putting the bags on the counter and unloading them, she leaves them and walks out to the porch, where Henry sits. I hear a faint "Hi, Dad."

I don't hear a reply.

I take advantage of the opportunity to put away the food myself, and be spared the commentary she typically has for how I have chosen to arrange the refrigerator. I see she bought oranges, which I've told her Henry cannot eat.

They talk out there for ten minutes. When she comes back in, I'm making coffee. I have a vase of wildflowers on the table. She looks at them coolly.

"Our one-year anniversary," I say.

"It's been that long?"

This is how the relationship begins: a couch and a loveseat, the family—a son or daughter, usually—and me. The employer on a rocking chair or in a bed nearby, a representative from the placement service flipping through papers. Pictures in faded frames tracing faces up stairways and down hallways. The what to do, the what not to do, the lists and schedules of medications, the signatures, the handshakes, the contractual alliance. The smell of Old Spice and Brylcreem. The shifting glances from members of my latest family.

Angela pulls Henry's diet chart from the clip magnet on the refrigerator.

"I'm not giving him tomatoes or citrus—the acid is too much for him," I say.

Angela is a real estate agent. Besides yelling at people on the phone, her other interests seem to be buying jewelry and getting manicures. She wears her permed hair in a banana clip and smells of honey, and she's always brushing herself off.

She puts the chart back. "I'm sure you know what's best. I'll be by on Friday."

Friday is Henry's next chemotherapy appointment. I see her out, then make Henry a grilled cheese sandwich. He's got the telescope out on old towels and tries to maneuver the red strawlike attachment on a can of WD-40 into the joints. I watch him struggle with the nozzle, then put the can down, his hand shaking, and consult the manual.

Angela has provoked me. There are times when my *ni* sits too low in my body, in the depths of my gut, a heavy, stagnant rot. I feel it now, giving me a stomachache. I cannot go to Henry. I cannot pour him more juice. I cannot take the weakness from his hands. I cannot lead him across the street.

I am hired to know what's best.

I sit down to watch one of those evening dramas, and as the night's story segment unfolds, I put myself into it: how I would announce my intentions, how I would stride into rooms furnished like hotel lobbies, how I would come by the gun; these people are crazy, these people who are everyone and no one. They make me cry, and yet this universe does not contain them or any part of their scripted lives and hospitalizations and deaths and funerals. I hear their plastic speech and try not to believe a single word they say.

The swimming hole

The man whose death breath was cherry colored was not one of mine. When I was twelve, I was dropped off on a dirt road near my favorite swimming hole. I was going to meet my friends Genevieve and Ida, and off I went through the brush and thorns to a pond surrounded by cattails and reedgrass.

Genevieve stood at the pond's edge in her hand-me-down polka-dotted suit. I skipped down the slope of matted muhly leading to the water. Jo and Nadja and Penelope were there also, already in the water, having contests to see who could do the most somersaults. They emerged laughing and holding their noses. Across the pond a young couple sunbathed, and near them a family sat having a picnic.

I'm sure we all felt as rich as I did, as rich as anybody outside the reservation borders, because we had a swimming hole to hide in and nothing to lose.

I walked. The sun warmed my face. Ahead to my left, off near the trees, the even grass line buckled. I saw the old man's foot first, then the top of his head, covered in a green fishing hat. His eyes were half closed, but he wasn't sleeping. Nor was he awake. I slowed and then stopped. Jo and Nadja splashed in the water, Genevieve screamed, a squirrel chirped. Then his breath: a sharp inhale, there and gone before I even turned to look at him. I saw now that he lay between two logs—his feet propped up on one, his head on the other. Behind his head, a crimson air mass, ill formed, illuminated. I thought a swarm of flying ants had risen from a nest behind the man's head, and I considered running to him to fan them away, or to wake him up before they bit him. But there was no sound, no buzz, no hum.

I went to the man, who looked heavier than he probably was, and waved my hand over the crown of his head. My hand tingled with heat, the way the blood pricks the skin when a numbed limb revives, and that's why I thought at first of life—that he was dreaming—instead of death. I panicked and ran to my friends.

We played at the edge of the pond for twenty minutes. I scooped up a tadpole in a handful of water. Jo buried her knees in muck. The people who had been picnicking rose, looked around, shaded their foreheads. They made their way to the slope leading to the water. I heard the woman's cry first. Then the children, bewildered, ran in small circles. The young couple came running, and they all crowded around the heavy man, and that's when I knew for sure that he was dead.

Threads

It's dusk. Henry and I walk out to the spot he's chosen. I carry the telescope and tripod, Henry two lawn chairs. We have done this for a week—carry out the telescope, set it up, wait for Henry to position it, settle into our chairs. And each night, when we come in, we hide the evidence. The story we tell is that Henry is refurbishing the telescope in order to sell it.

Still, Angela finds out. The other daughter and the son have called to warn me. They say they have talked to her but she has the final, contractual word.

Now Henry and I sit in the field brazenly, and Angela and the appearance of the comet compete for first sight. Henry peers through the giant Meade contraption and tells me that Newton believed that comets produced the best part of our air. I tell him that I have always only known them to be bad omens.

When I was young, the northern lights meant something too, magenta swirls that held my teenage self in adolescent vertigo, moonshine—both types—washing through us, bottle rockets exploding a few yards away, in the light of a small bonfire. On the hood of a pickup truck held together with duct tape, it was easy to cast fantasies into that black tank of a sky but harder to pin them down. We grew up, watched part of our land flood, got out, grew up more, got our hearts broken, grew up for good.

A coughing fit overtakes Henry—the ground shakes with it. I wait for the wet splat of his insides to hit the ground.

With a caretaker, you purchase a human being to administer some rules. You purchase a pair of eyes to anticipate and a pair of hands to prod and guide. You purchase a person to know another person in a way no one else will. You purchase a person's judgment, a person's trust.

Henry's finger is in the air. "People once thought Atlas held up the sky. You know, Atlas."

I nod.

"On his shoulders." Henry bends his arms over and behind his head as if carrying a weight. "They thought Hyperion rose from the water to light the earth, and then sank under it again at night." Henry pauses to wheeze, winded from the effort of speech. "But how did Hyperion keep burning after being under all that water? No one knew, but instead of changing their ideas, they just kept believing. This is how my daughter's mind works."

It was the most I had ever heard from him at one time. "She's going to yell at me."

Henry looks at me quickly, as if I've shocked him. "And what of it?" he says.

No air gets to his lungs, but it doesn't matter.

"She hates me because she hates my sins," he says. "And now she's responsible for me."

I think, *You should tell her what you know.*

"It's about her mother, but she doesn't know the whole story. She doesn't know what the woman's mind was capable of."

And then there are confessions that sound all true, all sane, undisguised.

I think, *You were right to not tell her.*

The picture of that woman. A wife's mind lost to jealousy? An old story. Still, would that be enough to turn a daughter so vindictive? I look through the eyepiece at a color I've never seen before—purple and gray, deep and dark but somehow also washed out. Light everywhere, globs of brilliance, pinprick stars, even magnified, a depth that pulls at the edges of your eyes and holds you spellbound. I sit back in my chair, dizzy and disoriented, urging myself to cast yet another fantastic vision, because I am on the pickup truck's hood again, a girl, safe before the catastrophe, mesmerized by the power of wishing.

I watch the dead.

I shift my chair closer to Henry and do what feels like the boldest thing I have ever done. I reach for his hand—my own fingers trembling more than his—and hold it in mine. It is cool and fleshy. I turn to him, but he has nodded off, chin to chest, and can't feel any part of me.

Endings

Dying fathers and mothers, dying families, dying trusts, final words, confessions, last honors, last shreds, last parents.

Henry and I play cards. I have made him a dill pickle sandwich with potato chips on the side. Sometimes he wants the potato chips on the sandwich but then forgets that he wants that and becomes confused and sometimes irritated.

I play my card, a six of hearts, and Henry grins. I have lost something, some points perhaps, I'm not sure.

Henry plays three cards, two tens and a five, lays them out one at a time, triumphant, and declares that he has won. He says, "Twenty-five is the highest score." This is news to me, but then, if you get to make the rules, you always win. Still, he's my favorite white man.

Angela didn't think it was right for me to allow Henry to watch for his comet. To be "dragging him out there" every night. Without even bringing the cordless. How she got the information about the phone, I don't know. Perhaps I'd been watched more closely than I knew.

I think, *Swat me if you can!*

She can, of course, and does.

She didn't fire me in person. She called the service, which is the correct protocol. She registered her complaint, and it was done. Jo says, "Good riddance to the bitch, that ingrate," and I'm inclined to agree, except that she's tied to Henry, and I to him.

Henry never sees his heavenly namesake, but the comet-omen

finds him. Two days after I get the call from the service, Henry doesn't wake up. I'm almost glad—I am selfish that way, with the end of my sweeties—but I can't deny it, his *ni* is intact. Finally he stirs and croaks out to me that he has pain in his chest. I barely detect a pulse. He twitches with cold and sweat. The room is humid. I remember the nasty headache he had two days ago. Pneumonia could take him down. He says there is an anchor on his lungs.

Angela drives him to the doctor. It turns out to be a chest cold, but that's bad enough. She and her son, Jeff, will take over when I'm gone.

The last tasks for me are all of my usual ones: clean, bake, make casseroles that can be frozen. Water all the plants. Wash Henry's clothes. Revise Henry's charts and hope they will be followed.

Ask the right questions.

Henry and I make our way, slowly, to the porch. I am angry with this comet and my slip into superstition. How did he catch this cold, is what I want to know. I say, "Henry, how did you get sick?"

"Don't know. Never smoked."

"No, I mean how did you get this cold."

"Germs!" he says. "That daughter of mine brought them. She'll kill me yet."

I can't tell if he really believes this. "You mean she brought you germs, on purpose?" I lower him onto the wicker couch.

"I won't say it."

He is tiny on the cushion, pale against the white sky. "Won't say what?"

I sit beside him and take his hand. But that is the last I hear from Henry.

The day comes when Angela and Jeff arrive. They drag suitcases and bags from the car. I go to sit beside Henry. "Goodbye, Henry," I say. "You're a good man." I don't want Angela here for him, carrying him, tying him up on her cross.

When the confessions come, shot off with a last breath, churned up and launched at you, or layed out like a bed of nails for you to walk on in the dark, they can kill you—these altered memories, these *screwball* outtakes. Whatever version you get is the only one that matters.

I leave by the front door. I shake hands with Angela, who thanks me quickly. Her son looks at me once.

I check my bag. The locket shines up at me from the corner of it.

I make up some kind of ending for my favorite sweetie and never know how close I get: *I know you loved her. I know you hear her, even now. You will open your palm to her, a shooting star, the night air your heavenly indigo peace.*

Part III: Fire

Smoke Signals

Dreams

Take the one of the burning pyre in the middle of an apple orchard. The body on fire is that of a male child but I don't know whose child. A few rotten apples hang from gnarled branches. The sun sets in a pink sky.

Take the details: the mourners around the pyre, mourners dressed not in black but in green. Take the women, who don't wear veils, whose fingernails are orange. Take the men's umbrellas shielding their broods from the puffs of ash released from the blaze.

I hear what they say. They say he was too young. But we all know that youth is no antidote to death. We all know this, but we remark anyway on the intricacies of consequence, on history that won't go away.

I watch the consumption, quickened by the evening breeze. I have seen this violence before.

Soon the pyre becomes a coffin and the apple trees mere stumps. Everyone is older but the child's body is still there, inside the wooden case, untouchable, suffocated.

In time, I believe these dreams. I believe them when they come to me in the high school hallways, when I run laps around the cornfields, when I stand in the Communion line at church.

Eventually, I come to believe that the child's body is the body of my younger brother Ryan, a new kid in a new grade school in my family's new town, but I cannot prove this.

The dream comes and goes. In time, I almost forget about it.

Sights

Ryan pounds three hundred nails into his bedroom wall. Somehow my mother and I don't hear this happening, and I realize that my brother has an active life beyond my awareness. The larger nail heads form the shape of the Centaurus constellation, which I know because Ryan has left the book open on his dresser. The other nails, representing lesser stars, begin at the floorboard and end at the ceiling. The likeness to the book image is striking, but my mother and I can only stare mutely when we discover the project.

I hear my mother comment on Ryan's creativity but note that the nail mural, specifically, goes unremarked on, goes unseen by any visitors.

Watch closely, I am told.

This is what I do.

The summer begins: my friend Leah and I practice jump shots in the driveway, listening to Casey Casum's top-40 countdown on my new boom box with detachable speakers. Ryan sits cross-legged on the lawn, thumbing through his *Apocalypse Survival Equipment and Supplies* catalog. He turns his hand around his chin, encircling it. Later, he kneels in the grass, his face pointed down at the conibear trap he ordered special months ago. Already Ryan's eighth-grade mind has advanced in science and math beyond me and the rest of the senior class, even the minor geniuses preparing for elite East Coast schools. Tools lie strewn around him, and he reaches for them without looking. He makes an adjustment to the trap's joint.

The basketball gets away from us and rolls to him, just two feet away, but I have to get it because he won't toss it back. I ask him what he's doing and he looks at me sullenly, and I regret even faking my interest. He watches Leah, shooting basket after basket in the driveway, for too long.

"Watch this, Danni," Ryan says. He picks up a test tube filled with a pinkish liquid. He corks it and shakes it, then uncorks it. A heavy white smoke drifts across the yard, hangs in the air like a thick ribbon. He stares at the tube in silence.

"Pretty cool, huh?" he says, grinning.

It is not a question for me to answer.

"Pretty sweet," he says.

He drops the tube on the grass, the liquid foaming at his feet. He spins away from it, half walking, half dancing, toward the house.

Appointments

Again and again, I wait for Ryan in the car. I work at a nearby country club, but my shifts are at night, which means I am charged with taking Ryan to his afternoon counseling appointments. I drive him to this building and wait.

I want to watch closely but I cannot.

Finally, Ryan appears and runs to the car.

"Danni," Ryan says. "Can we go to the park?"

The park I drive him to is the one we went to as kids. The seesaws still poke up out of their dirt ruts like splintered bones. Ryan runs to one and straddles it, pushing himself off the ground uselessly. I am the counterbalance he waits for, and I mount the rough wooden plank, watch him float upward.

"Do you want to go on the slide next?" he says.

He is only a boy, really, and in my mind I take his hand.

"Okay," I say. "Then we have to go."

"You always say that," he says, biting his nail.

"Because we always have to," I say.

Ryan climbs off the seesaw and bolts to a nearby tree. He sits at the base of it. As always, I go to him.

"Danni," Ryan says, smirking, hugging his knees. "I left a note for you underneath my pillow."

"I'll read it later, Ryan."

"I don't want to go to the doctor."

"We'll figure something out."

His head turns slightly to the side, and I know he almost believes my silly lie.

"We'll figure something out," I say.

Church

On Sundays, my mother gets us into the car and takes us to church. We drive the road along the bluffs. I see wisps of dark grey smoke drift above them, then curl into each other and disappear. The puffs come in threes, many times in a row.

I don't know where the smoke comes from or what it means or whether I only imagine it. I forget about it for the rest of the week, and then when Sunday comes I see it again. It never occurs to me to ask about the phantom smoke, in the way that you don't ask about giant culverts or those strange antennas planted on hillsides along highways.

We arrive late and sneak into an open pew in the back. My mother sits nearest the aisle, then me, then Ryan. Today he is dressed in fatigues and black lace-up boots, which draws too many looks.

I play hangman with him on the backs of the bulletins until he pulls out his electronic football game and punches the buttons madly. I sense the people around us trying to focus on the sermon.

I look over at Mom. By the time the priest sings *through Him, with Him, in Him, in the unity of the Holy Spirit, all glory and honor is yours, Almighty Father, forever and ever*, Ryan is falling apart, clawing at his clothes. He mumbles something I don't understand. I try to distract him with a crossword puzzle, but he's losing his limbs, and out they fly as he twists and twitches. I look over at Mom, who's putting away the hymn book and motioning to Ryan. He ignores her, so she goes around to the other side of the pew. I push him toward her. He turns and glares at me, then squeals as Mom, red-faced, yanks him out by the arm.

Outside, Mom shoves Ryan into the car. I sit next to him in the backseat, holding his hand. We are quiet. Mom drives. Away from church, the silence grows, and by the time we get home, Ryan is asleep.

A visit

Leah and I shoot baskets in the driveway. We're comparing tans—she's darker from her job as a lifeguard—when Ryan shows up with his traps, plopping them down between us and the hoop.

Leah rolls her eyes.

"Ryan," I say. "Can you move?"

"Leah doesn't know how to shoot." He looks at her. "Do you?"

"Of course she does," I say. "We played together on the team."

"Danni, look," Ryan says, holding up one of his traps. "I painted them black."

"Can you maybe go do whatever you're doing somewhere else?"

Leah drops the ball and goes inside. Ryan watches her.

"I'm going to screw her someday."

"Yeah, Ryan, okay."

"You watch."

"Okay, Ryan, can you move now? We're trying to practice. Just go over on the grass."

I am almost surprised when he gets up to move. He lays out his traps, lost in them already.

We both stop when a car pulls in. It moves slowly up the driveway. Inside is our priest. He gets out of the car.

"I'm here to see your mother," he says.

"She's inside," I say.

When he's gone, I look at Ryan. He lies on his stomach picking grass.

I don't go to him. I launch the basketball to the hoop, again and again.

After the priest and Leah have left, I go inside. Mom sits at the table, crying. "I told him that Ryan needs God now more than ever, but he won't let us back in the church."

"Can't we go to a different church?" I ask, but I know what the answer is.

Mom had made the priest coffee, despite the heat, so I pour myself a cup.

"When did you start drinking coffee?" Mom says.

"Breaks at the country club," I say.

Outside, Ryan has started a new project.

"Mom," I say. "He's dragging wood around the yard."

"I know," she says, waving her hand. "If it keeps him busy."

In two weeks we will have a makeshift jungle gym, complete with a slide—from a neighbor's old pool—and swings.

"Where does he find all this stuff?" I ask.

Mom pauses. I can see the question sticking in her mind. "The shed. There's all that stuff in there." It's an incomplete answer, but I can't question its believability.

We watch him pound yet more nails. "Danni," Mom says.

I wait.

"I try disciplining him the regular way," she says. "But something isn't working."

Ryan sets up sawhorses and lays the two-by-fours on them. He has a pencil tucked behind his ear. I believe this to be the most endearing thing I have ever seen.

"He needs to be engaged. I understand that," Mom says. She goes to the refrigerator and feels around on top of it. I watch her unwrap a pack of cigarettes.

"When did you start smoking?" I ask.

"Just now." She leans back against the counter and cracks open the windows above the sink. She exhales toward them. "I used to smoke," she says. "I also used to have friends and certain ideas about my future. I thought I'd go to college." She puts the cigarette out. "Now I have to avoid people."

I pull out a chair and sit.

"Your father left for a reason," she says.

"You said you weren't right for each other anymore," I say.

Mom joins me at the table. We watch Ryan measure the wood. We watch him saw it. The sliced-off ends fall to the ground.

Appointments II

In the car, Ryan hugs his backpack. I pull up to the curb in front of the doctor's office and watch as he nervously grabs at the door handle, then slips out.

The note Ryan left for me under his pillow was folded in quarters, and consisted of two notebook pages stapled together. On the first page was a description of a typical day, with commentary after each event. The last few lines listed all the things he believed to be beautiful, including fire, galaxies, dandelions, and blood.

The second page was a crude map of our neighborhood, but only certain houses were drawn in. There were a few trees, and the railroad tracks that ran near our house. Under the tracks, he wrote, "We will all be denied."

I folded the papers back up and put them in my dresser drawer.

He started disappearing into the woods behind our house. I played a game: if he stayed out there for longer than an hour, I'd tell my mother. If he was out there for less than an hour, I would convince myself that I hadn't seen anything.

"Danni," Ryan says when he gets in the car. "Can we get ice cream?"

"No, I have to get some stuff at the store," I say.

"So?"

"So, there isn't enough money for both."

"What about the money from your job?"

"What about it?"

"We could use that."

We order waffle cones and sit at a shaded table at the town square across the street. It is not long before the ice cream covers Ryan's chin and neck. I go to the water fountain to wet a napkin.

"Ryan," I say. "Wipe off your face." I toss him the napkin.

He grabs it and swipes the whole front of him. He misses a lot, but his crossed legs, swinging rapidly beneath him, tell me not to bother.

Soon he drops his cone, the melted ice cream oozing out onto the ground before I can bend to pick it up.

"Ryan," I call, but I am only a ghost mother, and he can't hear me.

He runs to a bench and crawls under it. He folds his body into a bundle. I hear the gunshot noises he makes. A woman and child pass him and look around, unsure of where to step. Ryan expands his game to include an army of enemies, and he rolls out from under the bench and into the legs of a young couple passing by on the way to the parking lot.

I go to him. "Ryan," I say. He draws patterns in the dirt with a twig. "Ryan. The car. Now."

He lies there. "Ryan," I say. "You got your ice cream, and now we have to go."

"You always say that."

When we finally get in the car, he uses his imaginary machine gun to "take out the disbelievers." The car sways when he flies to the floor. After a few seconds, he pops up, angles his body toward me, and shoots me in the head, spit flying at my cheek and ear.

Tremors

As kids, we roll our sleeping bags out on the uneven ground. The tent cocoons us. We are only in our back yard, but in a tent, the land turns exotic. Ryan's sleeping bag is my old one, purple with a paisley design on it, but we exist in a time before color and pattern. We settle in our bags and position the flashlight so we can play our puppet show game, except we don't have puppets, only our hands, and we make them into shapes and watch the shadows project on the tent wall.

Our stories are astounding and always take a violent turn; one recurring character, the Blob Man, moves across the vinyl before getting squished by a boulder. But the boulder only makes him split into smaller blobs, each with new life. It's an old story that's over before it begins, a story with no end.

We eat vanilla sandwich cookies and let the crumbs fall around us.

"Danni," Ryan says. "Watch." He stuffs his mouth with three cookies. He cannot chew, and his cheeks are puffed out and veiney, and I laugh because he is idiotic and mesmerizing. Because I laugh, he laughs, and after he snorts and chokes, we laugh some more. He has to spit half his mouthful into his hand in order to chew what's left.

When he's finished he lies down facing me. Only the flashlight is on, and I aim it away from us. His eyes are dark pools.

"Danni," he says. "My teacher says I'm a genius."

I sit up and arrange my sleeping mat, then turn off the flashlight. "But do you want to be a genius?" I ask, rolling toward him.

But he is already asleep, one hand curled beneath his chin. I touch his forehead with my fingertips. He is dry and smooth.

Then there is just the sound of the crickets. I watch him and wait for my own sleep to come.

You're it

In grade school we all have recess at the same time. The doors are Kelly green, and at ten o'clock the kids pour out then clot together, heading for the swings, four-square, basketball. A random tribe starts a game of tag on the grass.

I'm on the swing, and I can see Ryan, slow and uncoordinated, run straight into the game, taunting the tagger.

I am a fifth-grader and his sister, and I know I could call to him, make something up about thinking he was hurt, or say that I thought I saw him fall, but I can only sit on my swing and watch the boy I have a crush on allow Ryan to tag him, only to spin around, catch up with him in two short strides, and send Ryan sailing through the air.

Ryan rolls to a stop. Then I truly do think he is hurt and am about to go to him when he raises his head and props himself up on his elbows. He is trying to look uncaring, but he is out of the game. The other boys race around him, tackling and wrestling each other.

When he comes to me and sits on a swing, even I ignore him, swinging higher and higher until the sky burns me up.

Announcements

In the middle of summer, I begin packing. I move all the things I will take to college—a bedding set still in the store plastic, cheap lamps, a shoe holder, a telephone, a plant my mother promises me will survive even if I sometimes forget to water it—into one corner. The university assigns me a roommate who lives several towns away.

Ryan watches me from the hallway. "Danni," he says. "Let's go to the park."

"I can't."

"Let's go to the quarry."

"The quarry isn't open right now." I slide a box full of school supplies to the corner pile.

"Danni," he says. "What's it like in high school?"

"You'll switch classrooms every period," I say. "Otherwise, it's not that different."

Ryan lies down on the carpet. "I don't care what it's like."

"Then why'd you ask?"

"I'm probably not going to be there."

"You have to be there," I say. "It's a law."

He looks at me. "I'm not going to be there. Or maybe I will, but not for too long."

He wants me to ask questions, but I don't. I want to go to a new school of my own. I want to go to a new state and see people I've never seen before.

I push another box to the corner. Ryan lies on his back, quiet. I close my eyes and see a leafless tree with a trunk as thick as four men standing back to back, branches stretching outward and uplifted at the ends, like upturned palms. The light is yellow-orange and the sky is splotched with lavender and blue. A hint of motion in this tree, up high: Ryan perched like a gremlin in the crook of three branches, planted there forever in a vast and tragic hinterland. He has binoculars and looks out over the swampy, low ground. He turns to look at me and I look away.

When I open my eyes, Ryan is gone. His elbows have left indentations in the carpet and I run my fingers over the smooth, compact fibers.

Collections

Ryan materializes one day with scratched hands and a cut on his face. When I ask him where he's been, he looks around for a moment, as if he hasn't heard me.

"Hunting," he says.

The day comes when he disappears in the woods behind our house for longer than an hour. This means I need to report him, but I change the rules of my game and decide to track him instead.

The narrow, grassy path I follow leads, ultimately, to the swamp. As I walk along the path, careful to avoid sticks that could snap under my feet and give away my presence, my skin itches with tension. In the distance, I see a movement. My heartbeat quickens as I cut through a patch of young pine and brush.

I crouch near a clearing, a hilly, tufted, low-lying patch of tangled grass and mettle, chalky and phosphoric. Ryan kneels in some tall grass, then springs up, carrying his backpack, and runs to another spot, where he kneels again. Each time, he pulls something out of his pack and sets it on the ground.

Ryan pops up and kneels several more times. I don't have binoculars, but by the cylindrical shape of the objects he sets on the ground, I suspect they are the M-80s I know not from his catalogs but from kids talking black market in study hall. Then, the confirmation: three explosions that throw dirt and debris and tufts of fur into the air. My stomach knots up when I see Ryan bend to collect his bounty. I look back only once as the white flash-powder puffs feather upward from the pines.

That night I wake up. The house is blue and electrified. I hear footsteps on the stairs, in the kitchen. When I sit up, I see light at the end of the hallway.

Downstairs, Ryan makes a sandwich. "Hey, Danni," he says. "Ham on rye." He shakes a slice of ham and makes a face.

I smile. "You like it now?"

"No, but there's nothing else."

"Are you okay?"

He pauses, mustard knife suspended in the air. "Probably not.

108

I'm so hungry all the time."

"Did you get new medications?"

"No, just more of one of them." He sits on the counter stool and slides the plate over.

I go to him. The scratches on his hands are healing already.

"It's like I'm not real sometimes," he says. "Like I'm disappearing."

"Maybe you can switch drugs."

"They all feel the same. I can't sleep, either."

I take a bit of his sandwich and choke it down. I watch him chew and kick the cabinet in front of him. It's a low and frail sound, like a weakened heartbeat.

Abduction

Undisputed facts surface: a young boy, a Cub Scout, missing for three hours, the young boy's identification of Ryan as his "captor," the boy's bloodied wrists, and the fire that the boy started while Ryan went to "obtain provisions," a fire that secured his rescue when a neighbor saw smoke emerge from the spindly treetops of a tiny woods.

Ryan's backpack contains knives, lengths of frayed rope, stakes, nails, and foot-long lath boards. There is gossip, there is speculation, there are neighbors who hover and talk while they wait with their children at the ends of gravel roads.

My mother signs papers for the psychiatrist.

What's left is the residue of story: a boy went missing, then was found—a nonstory of disappearance and discovery.

Incidents

Leah and I shoot baskets in the driveway. We talk of college and college guys, of our imminent freedom, of our futures so close we can feel the heat of them on our faces.

By the time I notice that Ryan is running toward us, it is too late, and suddenly he is in front of Leah, in full Rambo posture, blasting her chest with his freshly filled Super soaker. A rope hangs crossways over his shoulders.

"Oh, you shit!" Leah yells, running into the yard.

Ryan drops the gun and grabs at the rope, which he swings lasso-style. He moves toward Leah.

"Ryan, what the hell are you doing?" I ask.

A smile spreads across his face. He leers at Leah. "How's the slut," he says. "Here, slutty, slutty, slutty."

There is something in his face I can't identify. I get up and walk quickly toward him. "Get the hell out of here," I say.

He ignores me. "Here, slutty, slutty, slutty," he says to Leah. "I have a nice big dick for you. Ha ha."

"Ryan. Get out of here, now."

Grinning, he lets the rope fall and walks away.

"He's going to do something," Leah says. "Did you see his face?"

"No, he's not," I say. "Don't worry," but by the time I say this Ryan appears again, this time with a slingshot.

I turn to Leah. "Just turn away and crouch down if he aims it at you."

Ryan looks at me. "What'd you say?"

Leah says, "Shut up, Ryan, nobody's talking to you."

"Oh, so the slut knows how to talk back."

"Ryan, just get out of here," I say. But it is too late.

"Just get out of here," Ryan says, mimicking me. "Let's get out of here." He turns to Leah. "Hey, slut, I bet you show your tits to anybody, bet you love it. Bet you suck cock every night. Fucking trailer trash."

Leah, stunned, stands perfectly still. Ryan aims the slingshot at her and she turns away just in time—the rock misses her head by only a few inches.

I bolt toward Ryan. I catch up with him after only a few strides and tackle him in the yard, pinning him.

He is nothing but a scrawny boy and I will not set him free.

I push my knee into his spine and hear a genuine shriek of pain. I lean in close to his ear, see the saliva from his wracked jaw ooze onto the grass. "You don't realize that I could beat you right now to a pulp and blame your injuries on one of your stupid ideas, and watch you get carted off to a fucking loony bin." He gasps for air.

I extract the slingshot from Ryan's hand and feel around in the grass for a rock. I release him. He struggles to get up.

I aim the slingshot at his head.

"You won't do it," Ryan rasps. He backs away clumsily, turns sideways, and quickly ducks behind the house.

I sit with grass stains on my jeans, knowing that no lessons have been taught. I look around guiltily, as if caught on tape. There would be no apologies for this, no effective means of erasure.

There are times when the fleeting moments of life gather in one spot and become events, and times when events, grown up and matured, become incidents.

This event would live on in some form; it would cower and wait, gaining strength, growing ever more eager by the day.

Appointments III

After the slingshot incident, my dream changes. This time I stalk Ryan. He's a robber sneaking into our house. I sit on the horizon of his crime, wait to see the whole thing: setup, entrance, transgression, exit. His leg crosses the window's threshold first, getting a grip, say, on the back of a couch, his small body stretching forward and flattening, his back skimming the bottom of the window as he eases his way in. The moonlight projects his shadow-image on the living room wall, a dark grey elongation of an everyday boy, an accidental criminal.

I dream of vomit—my own—with streaks of blood swirled through it, of a body burning on a bed of branches, of a spherical spirit levitating softly over the charred carcass.

I give the note Ryan left for me to my mother.

On the way back from his next appointment, Ryan is quiet—no inquiries about plans for the next ten minutes or hour, no requests for food or entertainment, no invisible machine guns blasting me in the face.

He is pale and confused-looking.

I stop at a red light.

"Danni?" Ryan says.

"Yeah?" I say.

"Do you ever feel like you can't feel anything?"

"Sure, yeah. Sometimes."

"Really?"

"Yeah."

He stares into his lap. "Because the doctors think I'm always going to be like this."

"What, they said that?"

"No, but that's what they think."

The light turns green and I continue down the street, through town, and out. I park at the market stand, pick up what is on my mother's list, and get in the car.

"I don't want to be like this," Ryan says.

Betrayal

At the country club, I get the brunch tables from the storage wing and wheel them on a cart through the carpeted, mauve-and-teal corridors. I lean them against a wall in the banquet room. A couple of us snap the legs of the tables into place and line them up along a wall of windows leading from the dining room to the kitchen. I haul buckets of ice from the freezer in the small room off the bar area to the station in the dining room, and begin setting tables. Outside, two older men start a golf game. As I fold my napkins into little tents, one of the men swings, throwing up a clump of earth.

Mom and Ryan show up around ten-thirty. Ryan's hair is slicked down, and there is trouble on his face. There has been ever since his last appointment.

After they are seated, the regulars glance at them. Mom digs for something in her purse.

I stop by the table to pour coffee. Ryan doesn't look at me.

"Are you going to order the buffet?" I ask.

"Maybe," Mom says. I know she's hesitant to move.

"Ignore them, Mom," I say. "We have a right to go to brunch at a country club."

"Brunch is stupid," Ryan says.

The comment is meant only for me.

"Why's that, Ryan?" Mom asks.

"Because."

"Just because?"

"You wouldn't even get it even if I told you.

"Because I'm stupid? Is that it?" Mom shifts in her chair.

"Well," I say, "if you order the brunch, try the French toast."

I check all the other tables, topping off coffee cups and water glasses. In a few minutes Ryan and my mother head for the buffet tables. Ryan is taller than my mother now, but I can't seem to remember when he grew to such a height. And yet he disappears; with each step, he fades further into the background.

My own steps slow as I make my way to a table that needs clearing. When my mother gets up for seconds, I go to Ryan.

I pour him water.

"I want coffee," he says.

"No, you don't."

"You don't know anything."

"I'm not getting you coffee."

"You think I'm stupid."

"Ryan, you almost really hurt Leah the other day. Do you understand that?"

He looks at the tablecloth, smearing a crumb into it with his thumb.

"You weren't supposed to show anyone the note."

"It wasn't a note, Ryan. It was some kind of map. What are you planning to do?"

Ryan freezes.

"I have no life because of you. I have always had to watch you. And what do you do? Terrify my friends. Draw weird shit. Pound nails into walls."

"The note was for you."

The breakfast crowd thins; I have tables to clear and set.

"Okay, Ryan, fine. I didn't realize you felt that strongly about it. Okay? I didn't know."

He smears jam into patterns on a napkin. "Danni," he says. "Look. Hieroglyphics."

Distance

On campus, I walk to classes and join clubs. People I have never seen before comfort me just by forming random patterns on the quad. The clock at the center of it strikes each hour, marking my days. I have new dreams. There are so many girls on my floor of the residence hall, and they hang around in each other's rooms as if they have come from an obvious, shared origin.

An almost-boyfriend takes me one night to the campus planetarium. Arcs and angles draw themselves on the ceiling, mapping out the Big Dipper, but all I see are the tiny stars, the farthest of the farthest-away stars, and in moments I am standing in front of Ryan's bedroom wall again. I do not have to wait anymore, but I realize it is possible for Ryan to discover my hiding spot.

In my dreams, Ryan shows me the maps he makes and how he digs for treasures no one can fathom. He folds the maps into paper footballs and flicks them, one by one, out the window. When I look out, I see them scattered on the lawn like balls of hail.

When Mom calls me one night, her voice is soft. She wants to know how I'm doing. But next time she calls, there is no voice at all. There is silence, and I have to ask her if something is wrong. Finally she tells me that Ryan disappeared one night and was found two days later walking the railroad tracks. She says, "He wouldn't really hurt anybody, would he?"

"Who found him?" I ask.

"We don't know. Somebody called in."

"He's okay?"

"Yes, he's fine." I hear her light up. I say nothing.

"I'm going to be asked to send him somewhere."

Mostly, I'm relieved about this because I'm preoccupied with the railroad tracks. I know she means the ones that run by our house, and I panic, wondering if these tracks somehow pass near this college town.

After I hang up, I go about my new life: I have papers to write, boys to meet, friends to dance with. I get a job at the school newspaper and tell myself that this is the path to freedom.

Negotiations

The day before Thanksgiving, Mom picks me up at the bus station and tells me that we're giving up Thanksgiving dinner with my grandmother in order to head to the Winnepoag School for Boys, located about fifty miles west of our town. I am eager to see this school, eager especially to see if there are guards and alarm systems. These thoughts exist because I know Ryan still believes in me.

The corridors are barren, but the grounds are well-tended. There's a basketball and tennis court, and even a view of a lake. The classrooms have desks and look mostly like regular classrooms except for the bars on the windows. We pass at least three nurse stations before getting to the check-in desk.

"Most of the kids here are on medications," Mom says.

I think of Ryan's wild brain. "Do you think the classes are advanced enough for him here?"

"I don't know. But at least it's a school. They know how to keep him focused."

After we check in, we sit in a waiting room. I tell Mom that she can go first, that I want to wait a little while before seeing him.

Mom comes back in a half hour and gives me a weak smile. "He wants to see you," she says.

I go to him.

He's in a seating area much like the one I just came from. He sits, still, by a window.

"Happy Thanksgiving," I say. I sit next to him. He's quiet and too calm. His eyes are dull, all the manic life drawn out, no energy for mapmaking or following tracks. There are hairs sprouting on his chin and upper lip, new acne on his neck.

"Can you do any of your projects here?" I ask.

"Sometimes," he says. "But I'm always supervised. It's like you said, I always have to be watched over."

"They're just afraid that something will happen because of your medications."

"Everyone's tyrannical here, and they give us plastic forks so we don't kill each other. Which, I don't understand, because if you wanted to hurt someone you could do it with plastic totally easy."

"It's just a precaution. The important thing is that you feel better so you don't have to be here anymore."

"I don't want to be here."

"But you have to."

"I hate it here. I don't belong here. They tell me how smart I am, then treat me like a kid." He looks at me. "I didn't tell Mom, but sometimes I get so angry."

"I know. But it's only for a little while. Until you feel better." His eyes become focused in that way they do when a thought strikes him, when he's about to ask me for what he needs. I already know I will have to deny him.

"Danni?"

"What?"

"You could write a letter. You could say that I just made a mistake. They'll listen to you."

"I'm not sure about that."

"Tell them that I wasn't really running away. I was just walking."

He's looking at me now, excited, pleading.

"Where were you going, Ryan?"

There's no answer, of course.

"Danni. I was just walking."

"Okay, Ryan."

"Just tell them that."

"Okay."

"You always say that." He pulls his knees to his chest and traces patterns on the dirty table with the back of his fingernail. It's possible that because he has nothing to lose, he'll try anything.

Premonitions

A month after New Year's, I get a call from Ryan. He talks in almost a whisper, and quickly.

He tells me a secret: that he is losing control, that he knows it, and that he doesn't know how to stop himself. I know that this is both a confession and an apology and that it is offered as the only gift he can give.

I envision a boy's funeral. Everywhere are gladiolas and white lilies, the sky can't get any bluer, and the coffin shines like a long polished fingernail.

My point of view in this vision is from several rows back. The priest reads scripture. The midsummer day is already humid, foreheads are shiny, curled tresses have already gone limp. An older relative can't stand up anymore and buckles, and people scramble to find her a chair. Two kids fidget; they are antsy and want to play. One of them slaps the back of the other's head.

The coffin is lowered into the ground. A giant maple leaf follows it down into the hole and goes unnoticed. The sobbing grows louder, into groans and grief, and I stand there, incapacitated, believing that Ryan represents all that is unfair and inscrutable in life, that he might be my savior, that I'll get over him, and that all I ever wanted to do was help.

Checkmate

Jeff Basco and I played chess all summer in the barn that smelled of manure and mold, sawdust and leather. We chewed on bits of sweet-feed and spit the naked oats on the concrete floor. We stared at the chess board, stringing games together back to back. We logged our gambits in our notebooks, in code, like spies. We set out bales of hay to stretch out on while we decided which moves to make. We examined each other's faces for hints. We ate bologna sandwiches with mayonnaise and drank Dr Pepper.

This is what I shared with him. These were the hours I felt him live, when the backlight from the setting sun touched me, too, a flame at my toes, when the warmth moved up my legs and into my body like a spirit.

Jeff could have asked Mr. Kraus, the calculus teacher, to be reassigned, but he drove to my house every day to be with me, an inferior player, a young man of unremarkable intellect, a late-bloomer, quiet in the classroom, a fan of stars and lakeshores, and I believe he did this because he loved me.

I had not seen Jeff in the hallways before school let out, but there his name was on the sheet tacked to the bulletin board, paired with mine for summer chess practice. He was tall and thin and had a facial tic—he tightened the left side of his mouth, released it, then blinked both eyes hard, in an almost single action. On the right side of his neck, extending up to his lower jaw, was a large scar the color of an acorn.

We walked to the barn, where I had the bales spread out. "We can play here," I said. "It'll be quiet."

He dropped his backpack on the ground and pulled out a Thermos. I went to get the chess board, which I kept by the harnesses and saddles, and as I set up the game I watched him pour steaming liquid into the cup.

"I drink two cups of green tea every day," he said, "to improve my intuitive grasp of the game."

Later, he referred to a particular Karpov-Spassky game as a superb specimen that contained traces of magnificence.

He lived with his mother and sick grandfather in a big house near the center of town. He watched over his grandfather in the morning and early afternoon, and his mother took over when she got home from work.

"I don't know what's going to happen when school starts," Jeff said. "It was a rash decision to move here, but then, my mother is not known for her foresight." The side of his face tensed, his eyes blinked hard.

It took me only six moves to realize that Jeff was tournament material. He had an expert's repertoire and a veteran's intuition. I found out that he'd been playing since the seventh grade and by now was beating all the math teachers from the nearby high schools. He said that their games lacked elegance.

The tea came and went; I would listen as he peed in the crabgrass outside. I turned to look, once, saw the edges of the scar hook around the back of his neck. When he returned, I said, "How did it happen?"

"I fell into a fire, apparently," he said. "I have no memory of the incident."

As summer went on, I pieced together, but never could confirm, a fuller explanation: that his aunt had once dragged all their living room furniture to the center of the room and set fire to it, and that Jeff, a boy at the time, had wandered in at that moment from his nap, stumbled over a toy, and fell into the blaze.

Sometimes when I looked at him, I envisioned a child, hair on fire, a black spot on his neck where the flames bit. A kid who didn't wail, a kid numbed and tranquil with shock, a kid who never again lost his way in the night.

Sometimes I wanted to reach out, with burning palms, to touch that scar.

My love that summer was Mandy. I met her at a church retreat. She wore tight jeans and heavy eyeliner and had tiny freckles across her nose. Her voice cracked bewitchingly. She stole miniature bottles of booze from her dad's truck. She smoked marijuana. She had obscure origins and mysterious parents and sisters who were dropouts. She kept a flashlight in her purse.

At the retreat, we wanted to play a pop rendition of *Alleluia* on piano and acoustic guitar but never did. Instead, during the nights when we were supposed to be rehearsing, we sat out on the hill at the far back of the church lot, smoking and groping each other. I identified constellations for her: Ursa Major, Draco, and, using my binoculars, the M13 cluster in Hercules. She was actually interested. I watched her watch the stars. I watched the smeared white stripe in the sky, two sides of space sectioned down the middle.

Then her hand was on my chest, light and fluttery, her tongue in my ear, her cool fingers under my arms. Her touch became his touch, we were kids again, restless in sleeping bags scattered in bedrooms or living rooms. I lay closest to my cousin Phillip; I smelled his skin, felt the heat of his shoulder. He grew so still he moved in other ways I could only sense. He turned and placed his hand on my chest—an accident, a message. I sank into the earth, his elbow pushed into my ribcage.

We grew up on hillsides and scrubby woodlands, we grew up on weekends, unsupervised.

I nudged Mandy. "It's midnight," I said.

"Past curfew," she said.

"I'll walk you back."

But we stayed on that hill, our hair and clothes pulling in the moist night, our faces washed out under the moon. She grabbed a magazine from her bag and used her flashlight to read me horoscopes.

"What sign are you?"

"Taurus."

"I'm Leo." She paused. "We're not a good match."

"I suppose we should stop talking to each other, then."

She turned a page of the magazine. "It says here that you should prepare for conflict with someone close to you, possibly a relative."

"I barely talk to my relatives."

She read more. "This is a good month for me for love."

"But not with me."

"Right."

I tore off a piece of the page, wanting to write her a note. But I couldn't think of what to write, so in the margins, I wrote gibberish, which started in my family as a car game. *Turd spankle writ large gangrenes to the left*, I wrote, and passed the paper to her.

She read it and snorted. "I don't get it, but it's funny." She took my pen and wrote something back. *Don't cookie-flutter my dangles.*

"Hey, that's pretty good," I said.

After the retreat, I pulled out the notes and dreamed about lying with Mandy in a sunny field. I forgot the sleeping bags and the dangerous cousin, and wrote the most sincere gibberish notes I could. Even gibberish poems. When Mandy came over, we'd go up in the loft of the barn, where I'd show them to her.

I gave her all of them, all of what I thought I was supposed to give. Nobody told me that my body spoke more languages than I possibly could.

Mr. Kraus called Jeff and me asking whether we wanted to participate in the chess tournament run out of the home of a local grandmaster. The winner would proceed to the next competition, and the winner of that to the next, all the way to state level. We'd have to practice hard.

A few days after the call, Mandy showed up unannounced. Jeff and I were in the barn, an hour into a game. When she came in, I introduced her to Jeff.

"Hi," he said. His eyes never left the board.

"It's his move," I said to Mandy, making a shh sign.

"Oh," she said, and sat down on a nearby bale of hay.

We played for ten minutes. Mandy said, "So, like, you guys play this every day?"

"Almost," I said.

She looked at the board. "Who's winning?"

Jeff rubbed his eyes.

"What?" she said.

"Nothing," I said. "It's just that you can't really tell sometimes who's winning. It's more about who's developing a better position."

Mandy got up, sat back down. She pushed back the cuticle of each fingernail. She dug around in her purse. She lit a cigarette, offered it to me, then Jeff, who fanned the smoke away with his hand.

"Whatever," she said.

Jeff's right knee began to bob up and down.

I moved my knight, then said, "Mandy, let's go up to the loft."

I led her up the ladder. She fell back on the bales. "What?"

"Shh," I said.

"He's weird," she said.

I lay down next to her, on my back. She threw a leg over me. I felt her breath on my neck. In my ear, she said, "We could fuck right now and he wouldn't even know."

"When he leaves we can do whatever we want."

She sat up. "Forget it. I'll just go."

"I'll call you later."

We climbed down the ladder. I watched her go to her car and pull away.

Jeff's eyes were on the board, his head cocked. "Knight to c1 was an excellent move," he said. "The more I look at it, the more I realize its depth."

Realize its depth.

I watched him for several minutes, let his focus and single-mindedness pull me in, down onto those sleeping bags, into that terrible scorched neck.

He said, "Tarrasch thought that chess consists of only three things: force, space, and time."

Sometimes I didn't even record my moves. I made it seem like I kept them all in my head, arranged in neat columns. Sometimes I just stopped and listened: a cat playing, rustling the straw in an open stall; the dull thud of hooves in the paddock; a mouse shooting along under the warped stall doors.

Sometimes I just watched his slender fingers sliding polished wood.

It was my cousin Phillip who proposed spying on the girls swimming in the quarry. He had been there many times before: he knew dates and times, which girls, how long. He knew when to leave the garage on our bikes and how to navigate the barely distinguishable path through the woods and where to put the bikes in case someone else had the same idea. He had his favorite girl, Samantha, and he knew all of the girls' names even though he didn't go to school with them. He knew how to climb the slope to get the best view, how to crawl forward and up without making any noise. He had a backpack, and there were binoculars inside, which he pulled out and adjusted. He had dirty magazines. He threw one to me and said, "That's what they're going to look like in three years."

I peered through the binoculars while propped up on my elbow, the way Phillip did. There were four girls out on the floating platform and two swimming out to them.

"Samantha's the one in the red suit," Phillip said.

Samantha and the other girls were rubbed down with oil, brown and slick as seals. I heard the two girls in the water call out to each other, but could not make out what they were saying.

"Let me see," Phillip said.

I handed him the binoculars and grabbed a magazine, which I paged through until I felt dizzy.

I looked at Phillip. *We could do anything right now and no one would know.*

"Oh, man, she's on her stomach now. Straps untied," Phillip said.

I stared up at his chin, his open mouth. *Take my hand again, put it on your chest. Remember?*

There was a commotion. I grabbed the binoculars. The girls had tied their suits and were jumping in the water one at a time, from the diving board. They were talking more now, and screaming.

Samantha was not the prettiest. "Who's in black?" I asked.

"Katie."

"Where do they live?"

Phillip took off his shirt. "I'm going to go out there."

"What?"

"Let's go, come on."

You can't. But he was gone—over the edge and down to the sand, to the waterline, where he stood momentarily before jumping in.

He must have talked to the girls, I don't know. I didn't look. I ran back to my bike and pedaled home.

What I meant was, *Don't go.*

Mandy was already at the park by the time Jeff and I got there. She was over by the monkey bars with some other girls, talking and turning the sand around with her foot. I couldn't get Jeff to leave the game for a day—he brought along a magnetic set, and during the car ride had arranged pieces and flashed the board at me, his face twisted up behind it. I was supposed to respond with the best series of plays given the configuration he set up. "Jeff, I'm driving," I said.

The tournament was coming up, which meant that Jeff wanted to practice more than ever. I watched him hunch over the chess board, notebook and pen propped on his knee, squinting against the evening sun angling in through the narrow windows in the loft walls or through cracks in the warped boards, watched him slap at the mosquitoes feeding on our ankles. In addition to his formal play and directed chess study with Mr. Kraus, he pursued secret chess projects—new twists on opening gambits, several personalized defenses.

Jeff and I walked across the wide shaded street to the park and found a spot under a large maple tree, which was located near the sand volleyball court. I spread out the blanket and set the cooler down.

"I'm going to find Mandy," I said.

Jeff propped himself against the tree. "She is a singular distraction," he said.

After a few volleyball games and a couple trips to the snack bar, I sat down next to Jeff, who was writing in his notebook. He put it down and flashed the magnetic board at me.

"The snack bar was out of green tea."

"Very funny."

"Wanna play volleyball?"

He looked at the court. "You want me to jump around hitting a ball over a net?"

"Yes, that's what I want."

"Maybe later."

Around dinnertime, the games broke up. Mandy had to babysit, so I offered to drive her home.

We loaded her things into my car. Jeff sat in the back seat, quiet. Mandy and I played twenty questions. Then I asked her what she wanted to do with her life. She said she wanted to be a florist, or else nothing. Maybe a teacher. But she wanted to work with younger kids, teach them every subject, so that she wouldn't get bored.

Jeff snorted.

When we got to Mandy's house I helped her carry her things to the porch. Then I got into the car and slammed the door.

I looked at him in the rearview mirror. "What's your problem?" I asked.

We could do anything right now.

"Mandy's friends were really hot," I said. "Don't you think?"

"No, they weren't," Jeff said. "Not to me, anyway."

"Come on."

"Did you ever stop to think that maybe Mandy likes you because she's easy?"

"No, she isn't."

"She doesn't even want to do anything with her life."

"No, she just doesn't want to play chess."

"She couldn't even if she tried."

I pulled out and turned onto the main road. We drove through town, past the new apartment buildings, then, farther on, past the abandoned drive-in theater.

"Okay, maybe not. So what? She's smarter than you think."

"You can do better."

I looked at him in the rearview mirror and gripped the steering wheel.

Jeff said, "I won't be able to come over for a few days. My grandpa's really sick."

Streetlights and shadows passed over him. I saw a one-story house on an open, rural road. I saw the bright and burning child, skin flaked and curled, eyelids singed, three stages before the final stage: brown, dimpled, permanent. I saw the living room floor with a hole in it; I saw how it was repaired but how the cinder stayed behind, lodged in the polish, merged into the fresh wall paint. How do you fall into a fire and live? The miracle of flesh: it grows back. From a gash in the neck to a new neck, from absence to substance.

Jeff said, "I have to make sure he's breathing."

I couldn't see Jeff bending over a bed, his ear to his grandfather's chest.

Don't go.

Mandy and I were driving along the bluffs when the sky turned a brownish-gold, then dark gray. We went to Dairy Queen and ordered cones at the drive-through window. We had just gotten the order when the rain came down, so we parked and ate, raising our voices over the pounding of the drops on the car's roof, tasting ice cream off each other's tongues. By the time we pulled in my driveway, the sky had brightened.

We went around to the backyard and sat on the picnic table. Within minutes the top was too hot to touch. The humid air was hard to breathe, and left me winded. Mandy yanked off her shirt and re-tied her bathing suit straps. She passed me a folded piece of paper. "Naughty gibberish," she said. "For later."

I lay back on the seat of the picnic table. The heat traveled along my spine. In the distance I heard a shovel striking dirt, a man's voice calling out, the wind chimes from someone's porch.

We went to the barn and climbed up to the loft. From the window we could see the storm moving east—black clouds tumbling over themselves, blowing endlessly into counties, lakes. From her purse Mandy pulled out miniature bottles of brandy, gin, and vodka. She gave me the vodka and opened the brandy for herself. She threw her head back and guzzled. The contractions of her throat hypnotized me.

She lay down next to me, stretching out on her stomach, hic-cuping softly, her hair falling on my forearm and giving me goose bumps. As she rolled onto her back, her hair dragged over the length of my arm, and a beam of sunlight washed over her. She raised the bottle to her mouth again.

I crawled over to her and kissed her stomach. She twisted and moaned. I reached down to unbutton her cutoffs.

She tugged at the waistline of my pants. "Let me ask you some-thing," she said, and stopped. "I'm totally serious. Do you like guys?"

"What?"

"Guys. Do you like them?"

"No, I like you."

She said, "Would you ever do a girl and a guy at the same time?"

"I don't know."

She ran a finger along my belly. My stomach buckled. "No, you wouldn't," she said.

"Okay, so?"

"I think Jeff likes you. Do you ever notice that he never talks to me? Or to you, actually, when I'm around."

"I think he just really likes to play chess."

She is a singular distraction.

Not to me, anyway.

I turned on my back. For three summers, Phillip's trick was to jump fire on the sly. All the relatives sat around these small bonfires concocted in somebody's backyard on the Fourth of July or Labor Day weekend. It started as a dare, one cousin to another, to jump the firepit. The parents had gone inside—or almost inside, chatting on the steps of the back porch or finishing their beers in the driveway. We were overtired and hyped up on roasted marshmallows, and that's when someone would challenge someone else to eat a charred caterpillar or moon a passing car or jump over the fire.

Phillip was fourteen, athletic, coordinated, but his jump began too far back, and his foot slipped on some dry leaves, and when he landed he fell backward, which seemed to put his whole body into the flames, but as it was, only his left side caught the edge of the fire, and his shorts were smoking to prove it.

He shrugged it all off, but later, in the bathroom brushing our teeth, I smelled singed hair, saw the reddened arm, saw the shine of fresh burn above the waistband of his underwear.

Let me see it. I envisioned pink skin bubbled and blistered, felt the heat of his wound on my own skin.

In our sleeping bags, our feet were warmed on the calves of other legs as our child bodies twitched into sleep. The spaces between them let in cold drafts; as we slept we turned in to each other, closer—our dreams warmed our pillows, which were coated with evidence of deep sleep: loose hairs, tiny feathers, occasional specks of blood.

Our hips touched. I must have turned to him in the night, faced him with closed eyes. In the morning, the covers were disordered, some of them thrown off intentionally, some of them pulled away from another in the chilly stage of half-sleep. Our bodies had cooled, all of the night's suspicions carried off with the smell of pancakes and sausage as we kicked each other awake.

The tournament was on a Saturday. Jeff and I parked along the curb in front of a two-story house with lavender clapboard and light-blue awnings. Mr. Kraus, who had just arrived, parked across the street, then walked over to us. "You boys ready?" he asked.

He led us up the walkway and opened the front door, then led us through the kitchen and a hallway, then down a few steps into a damp, sunken living room, which had large windows all along the side of it, and which looked out onto a small fenced-in lot. On the walls were framed photos of famous matches, and the bookshelves on either side of the fireplace were stocked with matryoshka dolls, Civil War memorabilia, and chess books. On the piano, an old baby grand, were two antique chess sets—a turned wood and bone set, from France, and a Chinese ivory set with a silk-lined box.

Five boards had been set up on fold-out trays or card tables. Two had been placed on the dining room table.

A woman approached us. Mr. Kraus introduced her as Lilian. We all shook hands. She was thin and pale and had her hair pulled back in a low bun. She asked each of us to pick a number out of a hat. A few minutes later, she hushed the group and explained that we would play until eight o'clock, break for dinner, then play again until midnight. Any games that weren't finished by that time would continue the following night.

My number four matched a number four belonging to a woman in her thirties. Jeff sat at the dining room table and was also paired with a woman.

Eleven moves into my game, I captured my opponent's bishop but realized too late that doing so might leave my king side too exposed. Two moves later, her position outweighed my material advantage. When we broke for dinner, Jeff came over to examine the game.

"You got too complacent," he said. "Your weakness."

A couple weeks ago Jeff had loaned me all his strategy books—five-hundred-page behemoths. From them I knew that complacency in an aggressive midgame is a common pitfall.

"What about you?" I asked.

"Position, excellent; development, fantastic. Plus, Mr. Kraus told me she's known for her terrible endgame."

We regrouped. After two hours, my center fell apart and my own endgame virtually collapsed. My opponent didn't have to say checkmate.

I can't say I was disappointed, though Mr. Kraus might want to know how the game went. I'd tell him the truth: I played my best and lost.

I wandered over to the dining room table. Jeff's game seemed too quiet for him, his center not as secure as it could be, but he showed no sign of fatigue or frustration. I watched him shred the board with his eyes, watched his tic carry away his face in nearly consecutive spasms.

By midnight, the end was nowhere in sight.

During the ride home, Jeff was twitchy and excited. His postsession analysis told him that he was in an even better position than he thought.

He said, after a couple minutes, "So, what happened with you?"

"What?"

"You could have beat her."

"Maybe."

"Probably."

"I don't know," I said. "The game started out as one thing, but then became another." I cracked open a soda can. "I don't even feel like finding out why."

"You need a more effective philosophy," he said.

"I just do what seems right at the time. That's how I play."

The road got darker as we moved into the suburbs. Jeff said, "We'll go over some strategies tomorrow. Don't worry, we're in this together."

Mandy and I sat at the edge of the park's gravel parking lot eating sugary snow cones with plastic spoons. I couldn't take my eyes off the ice crystals and syrup melting on her tongue as she talked.

Mandy's father owned three Italian restaurants in the area, and today was the annual picnic for all the employees. The central feature of this park was a hill. It was more of a slope, really, but when I was younger the incline may as well have been that of a mountain. I'd trudge to the top and roll all the way down, the trees and flowers in the distance flickering in front of my eyes like the frames of an old filmstrip. When I finally rolled to a stop, my brain seemed to slide out of my ears.

Two sets of creaking bleachers bordered the softball field, where two teams now warmed up. Mandy and I sat along the first base line, picking crab grass and holding it between the outsides of our thumbs, blowing on it, trying to get it to whistle.

I had thought ahead enough to bring a blanket, so when Mandy nudged me and said, "Let's go to the hill," all we had to do was snag a few beers from the giant cooler located along the side wall of what were probably the skankiest bathrooms in all of the Midwest. She grabbed a few cans, wrapping them in my blanket. "Boss's daughter," she said. "Privileged status."

We walked to the side of the hill facing the pond. Eventually a bunch of younger kids came around, yelling to each other and gawking at us, so we ran down the hill to the opposite side of the pond. We looked at tadpoles and clumps of frog eggs, gelatinous clots anchored to a mass of underwater weeds. We were on the very edge of the water, and as she scanned the milkweed and cattails I stared at her feet squished in the muck, foamy aquatic curls circling her ankles. A long snarl of her hair trailed down, skimming the water's surface. I turned away from her slightly, to hide my erection.

Mandy said, "My friend thinks Jeff is cute. Should I call her? You could call Jeff."

"Nah," I said. "I mean, yeah, but let's do it some other time."

Two kids were drifting toward us. "Is it true that he has a messed-up family?" she asked.

"I don't know."

"It's totally okay with me if you like guys. My brother is gay."

"Seriously, I haven't really given this much thought. I don't think it's an issue."

"Maybe you're bi."

I rubbed my face. "Can we just change the subject? Please?"

She looked at me. "Whatever."

Two kids started splashing us. Mandy chased them for a few yards, then tripped and fell in the water. I ran to her and extended my arm to help her up, but she yanked on it, pulling me in. By the time I turned over and wiped my face she had straddled my body. Her eye makeup had smeared, and strands of hair were wrapped around her head and tangled in her earrings. We swam underneath a huge willow branch arching over the pond, and made out. As she sucked my neck I could smell her, salty and sulfuric.

I wanted to wrestle her to the ground, rip her top off, thread her hair through my fingers.

I came, quietly, in my pants.

It got dark, finally. We walked back to the field. The softball games were over. Mandy's dad loaded up vans with coolers and softball equipment, jangling his keys as he walked back and forth. The parking lot lights buzzed as winged night insects fluttered beneath them.

Jeff won the match and would proceed to the next level. I congratulated him when he came over to practice. "Though I can't understand how I'm helping you out," I said.

"You are essential to my progress," he said. "Which is more than I can say for my home situation."

Jeff sat in his car, the engine still running, the window halfway down. "My mom has to work longer hours all of a sudden." He squinted up at me. "I haven't had the proper atmosphere for serious practice."

"Maybe I can come over to practice with you," I said.

"My mom would never allow it," he said. "She's quite religious, but the 'sanctity of death' apparently means no one else gets to live. So to speak."

It was the most I had ever heard from him on the subject.

After he left I went out to the paddock and drained the raised water trough, which was permanently stationed against the barn wall and partially shaded by a giant clematis vine tangling its way up old chicken wire, and wiped it down, being careful to not give away too much of my presence to the family of swallows camped around the corner, under the roof's edge. I stuck the hose in the trough and turned on the spigot: in moments the scent of hot aluminum, rust, and riverbank.

No Jeff the next day. Or the next, or the next.

My mom was the one who told me that Jeff's grandfather had died, when the funeral was, and that Jeff would be gone by the end of summer.

"What do you feel like?" I asked. Mandy and I lay facing each other on the picnic table, resting our cheeks on the splintered wood.

"Play-Doh," she said. "What do you feel like?"

"A bag of sand."

"Sand fornicates ugly against wicked ramblings," she said.

"But can you wiggle medley after dark?"

"Only after snow cones die idiosyncratic."

"Die idiosyncratic," I repeated. "You have become an excellent speaker of gibberish."

I heard a car door. In moments, Jeff appeared around the side of the house. He looked down at me.

"I learned a really sweet variation and want to try it out," he said.

I sat up. "Are you okay?"

He blinked hard and followed it with a succession of lighter blinks. "Are we playing or what?"

"Um, I don't know. I suppose." I looked at Mandy and shrugged. "Just for a little while."

The barn was pleasantly cool. Mandy headed up to the loft with her headphones. We opened with the Spanish game, and now, five moves later, Jeff had just fixed a k-side pawn to strengthen his wing and, I suspected, to develop the bishop. I didn't detect a variation yet. "Are you going to be able to go to the next tournament game?" I asked.

"The future is uncertain."

"Where are you moving?"

"Probably back in with my dad, which won't work, and then I don't know."

A few minutes later, Mandy came down the ladder. "I have to use your bathroom," she said. She leaned in for a kiss and bumped the board with her knee. The pieces jumped and shifted, a few fell. "Oh, sorry," she said, and picked them up.

Jeff glared at her.

"Look," Mandy said to Jeff. "I'm sorry I ruined your stupid game. But you were only going to play for a little while anyway." She turned to me. "Eric, why don't we just get out of here."

"Well," Jeff said, checking his watch, "it has been forty-five minutes, an eternity, I know."

Mandy whirled around to face him. "Hey, asshole, why don't you just admit you want Eric."

Jeff laughed. "That's classic," he said.

"Hey, guys, let's do an experiment," Mandy said. "Let's watch while I give Jeff a big, sloppy kiss. What do you think, Jeff?"

Jeff froze. Mandy moved toward him but he jumped out of the chair before she could even touch him.

"Fag-got! Fag-got!" Mandy shouted, pumping her fist in the air.

Jeff, red-faced and shaking, kicked the chess board off the bales, and tore off.

Mandy laughed. "God, he so loves you."

"Fuck off," I said. "Everything was fine before you messed it up."

"Messed up what?"

"Go to hell. At least he's not in love with himself."

"What?"

"Why can't you just leave people alone?"

"Oh, I *so* will. Starting now."

At the funeral, I stood around nodding and smiling weakly. In the receiving line I said to Jeff, "Sorry about your grandfather," and moved on to the next person. I actually wanted to hear him drone on about Tarrasch, about how the queen acquired her mobility, about historic chess moments and trendy strategies. Mostly, though, I wanted to tell him that I didn't care about what Mandy said.

The next day, I drove to his house, ostensibly to return his chess set. I knocked on the door, but there was no answer. I left the box on the porch.

On moving day, late, I biked over but hung way back. The moving vans were gone, and the car, the only vehicle left, was packed to the brim. I got off my bike and watched Jeff and his mother lock up the house. They got in the car and backed out.

I wanted to wave as the car moved closer, but I froze. It pulled forward and turned out of sight.

The afternoon was quiet: nothing but the scratch of leaves blowing across the cement, a dog's bark, the hum of residential air conditioners. I pedaled away, grateful for the rush of wind in my ears.

I didn't see Mandy after that day in the barn. School started, and at times I almost forgot about her. During the last warm days of fall, I lazed around, mostly. I didn't open a single chess board. Instead, I took my favorite books up to the loft and read until dusk. Once, in the pale blue of the emerging moonlight, I peered over the ledge and saw a shadow out of the corner of my eye, heard the faintest of rustlings; but when I looked closer I saw nothing, and I knew that the sound was only that of a field mouse, maybe a toad, and that it had nothing at all to do with me.

Trespassers

Establishing borders

In the wooded area that surrounded our house, the rusty-toothed barbed wire was the only sign that someone thought of the land as taken, might in fact refer to it as a *parcel*. The wire was almost completely hidden, locked in a twisted, leafy hold. I don't know who strung the wire, who decided, *here must be a boundary*, but it lead out of the thicket and into the area we converted to a pasture, a five-acre sprawl where we kept a few Holsteins and the old palomino with one brown eye and one blue eye.

We had white geese, and cats too; they ran where they pleased. I'd pass them in the woods, where they pretended not to know me. I'd kneel down and call to them but they wouldn't stop. Their tails hung low and they held plump mice in their jaws. Above, spiny tree branches fanned across portions of sky, overlapping intricately. I'd look up and let the sun come seeking me in boxy tubes of light. Among these rays I played out fantastic battles between Good and Evil. The Evil marauders descended in black capes from the treetops but my forces dodged them and killed them mercilessly. We had the home-team advantage—we had grown up here—and knew the traps and pitfalls.

I could distinguish a single tree from all the others, or a rock, a rotting stump, a stream, a vague, leaf-covered trail. I had my bearings. Moss grows on the north side of a tree. The sun sets in the west. Red skies at night, sailors' delight. The stream begins there, and ends here.

Our house had walls but no borders. Privacy was not a recognized right. None of us, except my sister, Junie, waited until reaching the bathroom to start stripping down for a bath. Sometimes we made small efforts to conceal ourselves, but when my father crossed through the living room one day dressed only in "what God gave him," Junie screamed and ran to her room.

So I thought perhaps it wasn't so strange when, early one fall morning, we woke to find my father, naked except for rubber galoshes, outside chopping wood. His penis jiggled with each blow of the axe. The white puffs of his breath came quickly. He bent to pick up the logs and hoisted them onto a pile. My brother, Alex, and I laughed but my mother watched him closely, her jaw set.

Twisters

My science and nature books taught me that the Greenland shark sucks in its prey from three feet. They taught me that fire can be orange, blue, or white and that white was the hottest. They taught me about warm and cold fronts and how, when they clash, the warm one slices upward and begins to spin, forming a powerful funnel that can rip houses and trees from the ground and toss cars for miles. They taught me that this funnel can perform miracles, like ramming a single piece of straw through the trunk of a tree, like leaving an entire mansion in shambles except for a coffee table with a vase on it, completely untouched. This wind was not the wind I knew. This wind was a phenomenon.

For a while I thought that if I left gifts for the wind, we would be safe from it. I set out dishes of acorns and berries to appease the gods and goddesses. I was proud of myself, secretly protecting my family this way.

But in the middle of one summer's ancient heat, I stopped negotiating with unseen forces. Every week, somewhere, a small but belligerent tornado pruned back human expansion. The community newspapers reported on children found hiding in empty barn stalls, paralyzed with fear. Now and then a pet or spouse wandered off and never came back. The palomino tossed her head, snorted, pawed the ground. Everyone glanced nervously at the sky, at some approaching bulk of drifting stillness, and thought *how fast is it moving* and *how much longer*.

In the beginning there is fire

Our summer bonfire is no ordinary fire. Its flames lick up twenty feet, and not even the mosquitoes, heat-seekers by nature, drift into its glowing orb. This fire spits embers six feet out. This fire does not comfort or soothe. It kills.

But we—Alex, Junie, and I—scream and run head-on toward the massive orange smear. The fire takes everything we give it. We toss in brown glass bottles, cardboard from twelve-packs, the plastic dolls Junie and I outgrew. With demented grins we watch the smooth faces hiss and pop and melt into themselves, watch limbs curl and twist. We light thick branches and race around at the edge of the woods, keeping away (we imagine) the trespassers my father broods over. After those branches burn we grab new ones, thicker and longer, and thrust them into the fire until the flames take to them, and then run away, the cool night air hitting our skin, and we stop, gasping and gagging in the golden perimeter of our fledgling torches.

Our parents sit with brothers and sisters and neighbors and finally look around, scolding us, telling us to *stop playing with fire*. So we slouch in lawn chairs, huffing at the injustice. Uncle Riley comes over, sits in a chair, and cracks open a beer. He is a housepainter with no kids of his own, so he sings us songs and tells us improbable stories while we stick marshmallows on the ends of the longest sticks we can find and brave the fire, leaning forward into the hot wind with our chins tucked to our chests.

By midnight we all sit quiet, transfixed by the dying fire's sizzle. Uncle Riley says, Bertrand, how long you been now at that factory, and my father says, fifteen goddamned years. And then my father says, union's coming in, and we sit, staring, again. Junie's head falls lower on my shoulder, and I finally knock it away.

Neighbors start to leave, but my father and Uncle Riley stay with the fire. The rest of us go to the house, carrying one cooler each. My body loses its ability to walk straight, and I am aware, suddenly, of my sticky hands, the smell of pine and grass, and of hair stiff and stringy with grit. My mother makes us empty our pant cuffs and brush off, strip by the door, and tells Junie and me get in the tub.

The water turns a dark gray before the tub is even filled, so my mother empties it and starts again, this time aiming a sprayer at us, one by one, rubbing us down head to toe. She says it would be better

135

to just hose us off and be done with it.

I pull the drain, watching the water flow out of the tub, a small funnel forming on the edge of the chrome, whirling around until I suffocate it with my foot.

Vagabonds

My father is a quiet, skinny man. At one point everything he says is a variation on two themes: First, my mother is the strongest person he knows. She can start fires with her eyes. She has an aura that sharpens senses. She is a protégé of St. Francis—just watch the geese and the cats and the old mare follow her—she, with magic in her fingers and dreams in her voice. Second, land begins and ends with theft. And because of its criminal origins, you have to fight to keep it and to keep it safe. Here's this land, he says, his arm sweeping over the flat yellow landscape. All this land and no way to monitor it. Vagabonds could be living out there, *right under your nose*, and you'd never know it. He is obsessed with what he calls "siphoning," the slow thieving he thinks goes on and on, little by little, practically everywhere. One time we stopped for fuel on the way to an amusement park, and he was gypped a quarter, which he promptly went to retrieve from the clerk. Imagine, he said, if that guy cheats every person who passes through here. Think how much he siphons off of people in just one day.

My mother, though not a religious person, believes you will be judged upon death by how you treat any living thing on earth. She is temperamental but has high hopes. She wears tube tops and hoop earrings, and her legs are long and tanned. She has a frizzed-out hairdo, and she ties long scarves in it.

On some nights she brings brownies and casseroles to neighbors. She is a powerhouse of beneficence. Once, she bought a birdfeeder for a neighbor because she thought he might be lonely. She looked out the front window, saying, I wish Mr. Thompson's son would visit more often. These wishes are not invoked between other idle thoughts but are themselves the subject of contemplation. She wishes with conviction, the way others might pray.

A younger sister of hers died at the age of ten of a reckless, protracted illness. The death of the young, my mother says, inspires humility.

She operates within a two-mile radius. The next town, for her, might as well be China. She has faith in the immediate vicinity and she bosses people around with a hard, gentle manner.

My father soon begins to rail on about her humanitarian interventions. He thinks *those people* are taking advantage of her. But wait. This is St. Francis. This is a woman with spells in her eyes and steel in her bones, a woman who runs from here to there and back again, a woman who can hold the foundation of a family together with just the sound of her voice.

These contradictions float freely over and past the weeks and months, then hover, heavy and silent.

The devil

My father spray-paints a florescent-orange line at the end of our driveway. He says if we cross it and go into the road, he'll skin us. He says you never know who could come racing down our quiet road at eighty miles an hour, swerving in some state of drunkenness. Alex and Junie and I sit at the dinner table, choking down our peas as he speaks. Alex rolls his eyes at me. I smother a giggle because my father is looking at us with that serious and cracked-up face. My father says, you'd hit the windshield and fly through the air. He makes an upward-slant motion with his arm, and then lets it smack down on the table's thick top.

My father begins to see evil falling upon him. He sees the devil in the woodpile, the devil overhead, in airplanes and nonexistent hot-air balloons, in Baptist churches and in the town clerk's office.

The day our house smells like a swimming pool is the day my mother tells us that he has taken the bleach and added it to his bath water and soaked in it in order to purify himself. He has these notions, she says, her hand gesturing helplessly.

I want to believe that a chemical agent, such as bleach, can in fact cleanse the soul if added to water in the correct quantity. But I know the power of superstition. I think of my gifts to the wind and the tornadoes that rip throughout region nonetheless. I think of Uncle Riley's unlikely stories and of how true they seem, regardless. When I think of purification I don't think of water or blood or penance. I see a disembodied glow traveling at the speed of a human walk, I see a naked, bearded man in galoshes whose skin is red and raw.

Sundays

The summer of my tenth year is record-setting hot, driest since 1902, parches everything in sight. A month straight of asphyxiation. Grass like needles, air the color of fog, everything warped and still, heat lightning flashing up the sides of the sky, animals panting, elderly people dropping dead during their walk to church. Farmers set back entire ledger-lengths; the numbers, wedged in narrow columns, are spooky and static. Fields nothing but puckered, brown sheets.

I open the garage door and see, first, a used Harley-Davidson, then my father in black leather chaps. He sees me and grins like a hyena, his front teeth the color of smoke-stained walls.

This machine he now owns deafens his family and neighborhood every Sunday afternoon, but attached to it is a horde of new friends: women with turquoise-studded cigarette cases, red-white-and-blue bandanas, and permed hair crushed from helmets; men with beer bellies, shaved heads, and unearned swaggers. A pile of metal and chrome in the driveway, gooey brown chew dotting the pavement. And my father on the perimeter, quiet, enthusiastic. My father, beaming, helmeted, a bulbous-headed cartoon bug.

The women smile at me. One day one of them turns toward my father, says which one is this?

"Miryam," my father says. "My tomboy."

I say hello and give a quick wave.

They tease each other, talk of people I don't know. They put out their cigarettes, swig the dregs of their beers, raise helmets, tighten straps, start engines, roar out of the driveway like a swarm of black beetles. I watch the crusty structures carry them away, millions of tiny engine explosions propelling them into new towns with identical streets, streets lined with pool halls and family restaurants and convenience stores.

My mother does not approve of the Harley crowd; she joins the Unitarians. My father calls them heathens, but every Sunday afternoon, while my father "sees the world," my mother goes to the service and doesn't come home until dinner, when she throws pizzas into the oven and lets us fend for ourselves.

Scenic tour

From the back of a motorcycle, in the open air, things you never

138

notice barge in on your vision: the rusty piping in a ditch, the particular type of dust thrown up at a given intersection, the smell of your own skin. Weeds growing through split concrete, flora crawling over itself, working everything under it into its dewy clutches.

My father and I pull into the lot of the town store and find a spot near the main doors. The cycle's engine stops but my blood still fizzes purple. Beyond the store is a field of yellow yarrow and white coneflower; a close look would reveal dried crowns, but from this distance the color is crisp, the image convincing.

The store smells of cardboard and freezer burn and cellar. Canned goods strain the shelves with their weight. Huge jars filled with candy are lined up on the short side of the L-shaped counter, behind which stands a sliver of a woman with her hair in a ponytail. The sleeves of her denim shirt are rolled up, and she moves slowly, as if in pain, and if you look closely you can see that she never looks directly at anyone but rather slightly off to one side, as if something of interest were happening just over people's shoulders.

"Hello there, Roxie," my father says to her. I grab a can of pop and turn to see him standing by the counter, his helmet dangling from his right hand. His left hand is in his pocket, and he sways from side to side, overpolite, like an embarrassed schoolboy.

I bring up the pop and a box of Twinkies. My father brushes everything toward the register, and the woman starts ringing up the items. "This here is Roxie," he tells me. I smile at her but she seems to be looking in the direction of the restrooms. I almost turn to look when my father says, "This lady been through hell and back. Thrown fifty yards from a motorcycle and lived." My father raises his eyebrows at me, his way of emphasizing a lesson of some kind. Roxie keeps scanning the items, a quarter of what is perhaps a smile stillborn on her face.

Outside, we eat standing. My father has corn chips and Pall-Malls.

"Miryam, I want you to get baptized. You wasn't, you know. But that was wrong."

I am already on my third Twinkie. I didn't know people my age could get baptized, so I listen.

"I want you to enter God's kingdom someday."

"Okay," I say, my mouth full.

"It was wrong. It was something we did wrong," he says.

"Okay."

Then he really comes after me: Do I know what evolution is? Do I have a boyfriend? Do I pray at night, say the "Hail Mary"? Do I have "longings," and of what type are they?

I see shadow boxers behind his eyes.

That night, in the basement, Junie and I play video games. We hear my mother get home, but nothing prepares us for the sight we get when we emerge from our electronic dungeon: my mother and father holding hands, staring at the television, which blares the top news story, a report of a small fire that has started on the edge of the state, licking around in the underbrush of a small woods, but that is now a hungry flaming giant on the move.

Memories

But what is a fire in the shallow part of some young woods in another state? What are flames that multiply and divide and multiply again? An abstraction, an event *out there.*

This fire crosses the state line, gulping oxygen and eating land by the mile. This fire's heat grows so intense that fifteen acres at a time self-combust. Meteorologists predict plenty of wind; the grossly underequipped towns bank on faulty foresight. But by the next morning the wind—which materializes at a steady thirty-eight miles per hour with gusts up to fifty-five—sucks the flames forward and upward on a greedy, historic binge. This fire has nothing to lose so it jumps streams, crackles through marshes, feeds itself violently and fills the sky with its filmy exhale. This fire knows no borders, and, town by sparsely populated and sleeping town, it overtakes what can't outrun it.

Every channel airs continuous coverage of the fire. Old men speak of past fires, of entire families destroyed. Teary-eyed women talk of charred cars and skin, of standing in ponds to escape lurching flames, of ash pelting their cheeks like needle-hail, of trees holding lumps of fire—small, glowing omens—in their stripped branches. Tragedies relived, wounds opened, footage flashing, and wherever you look, wherever you go, there is talk of *largest ever,* of *nothing like it,* of *spreading even faster.*

Clues

I imagine sometimes that the roads that slither past our part of town can take us to the end of the earth. I know that the end of the earth is an impossibility, there is no *end of earth,* but I am eager to imagine it. And if not the end of earth, then the end of America: some sandy path descending from Provincetown into Cape Cod Bay, a crumbling bridge tipping me into the Gulf of Mexico, a rickety California pier dropping into a Pacific Ocean inlet.

These images of roads that flow across the earth have an origin. We all pretend not to notice when my father drives off somewhere for hours on end. My mother concedes that his lies are becoming more sophisticated. She calls Uncle Riley, warns him, then goes to the file cabinet and pulls out the last three phone bills. She runs her finger down the pages.

"What?" I say.

"Clues," she says.

That night, over a supper of pork chops and green beans, my mother doesn't answer questions, doesn't comment on anybody's day, on needy neighbors. She says "pass the milk," not looking at anyone, and I know that what I'm seeing is not benevolence but obligation.

Revelation

Three days pass and still the fire burns. Its origin reveals the workings of an arsonist. Who would do such a thing, we want to know. My father says, some bastard vagabond, that's who. *Criminal scum.*

The fire crews call in extra strike teams and brush units from two cities, but still, the fire lopes along through the night, a snaking magma wall belting out flaming debris.

We can hear the planes dropping retardant and the choppy sucking sound of helicopters flipping out water bombs. At one point three of the helicopters hover over our house, low, and we run outside to see them heading east. My father is looking up, his eyes glazed over, his lips moving with a message or prayer, but the helicopters are too loud, and I can't hear him, and I think I'm glad of it.

Evacuation

When our town is called to evacuate, my father prays the rosary and takes a bleach bath while my mother packs blankets, thermoses of water, first-aid kits, and cans of fruit and vegetables. She tells us to load the suitcases and ourselves in the car, and we leave her to get my father out of the tub. When he comes out he has his Bible tucked under his arm, and after he opens the car door he says, "You kids belted in?" We nod, stiffened by the smell of bleach and tobacco. My mother locks the house. She gets in the car and says, "Thank our stars the animals have been moved."

We're barely on the county road when the first signs of a traffic backup appear. My mother turns on the radio, which is reporting alternate routes out of the area. A couple cars ahead U-turn and head in the opposite direction. My mother begins to follow when my father says, "Out of our way." My mother says even so, with this jam we'll be better off forging our own path, but my father's hands are shaking and he's looking up toward the sky and saying "and the smoke of their torment ascendeth up" over and over.

Junie hits me on the shoulder and says, "punch-bug yellow," and then we stop again. We are behind Mr. Thompson and his son. My mother puts the car in park and gets out. She runs to Mr. Thompson's car and taps on the window. My father looks up from his Bible. I can see in his profile the weight he's put on, how his stomach bulges over his belt. Alex keeps Junie busy with car games but she knows too much and says, "Is the fire going to get our house?"

My mother gets back in the car and waits as Mr. Thompson turns his car around. Then she puts our car in gear and follows.

"No, Gloria," my father says, "you want to get us killed? Let me out and I'll get back in that line my own damn self."

My mother hits the brakes. The seat belt digs into my shoulder and hips. The screech from the tires echoes in my ears but over the ringing I hear her say, "You will sit in that seat and shut your mouth. I am going to get this family out of this town, so help me God. You want to get out, you go ahead and get out."

We hold our breaths. Nobody says anything for half an hour, a half hour of cars, heat waves, oldies songs, sticky skin, highway dust, and disbelief. Junie starts to cry. She looks up at me, then Alex. Her tears fall on my thigh and they tickle vaguely as they crawl over my skin.

Accidents

I'm at the edge of our own green, lucky woods, helping my mother drag large fallen branches into a pile. A blackbird caws.

We all looked out of windows that last day of burning. We were in a Best Western sixty-five miles west of our home and the fire. My mother looked east. I looked north. My father looked south, eyes narrowed.

Shifting winds and a drizzle brought the fire under control. The blaze was traced back to a lone, disturbed man from a nearby town whose pregnant girlfriend left him. He drove, wandered around in a drunken daze, passed out, dropped a cigarette, and died quickly of smoke inhalation.

I'm angry with this idiot man and his rotten luck. I think, maybe he's an asshole and if he hadn't been such an asshole his girlfriend wouldn't have left him. Or maybe she loved someone else. It could have been our woods he wandered into, stupidly and blindly. There are too many possibilities.

Since the evacuation my father had gotten worse: when he wasn't locking himself in the shed he was in the living room, glued to the television. We all avoided him instinctually. When he stopped going to work my mother took him to the clinic, and then to weekly appointments at offices in other towns.

"At first I put it in his terms," she says, approaching me with a stack of maple branches and twigs. "I told him, 'A man who doesn't feed his family hasn't done his duty, and goes to hell.'" Her jeans are rolled up, white scratches visible on her ankles. A tiny drop of sweat peeks out of her hairline. "I think this worked for a little while but it doesn't matter now."

That night my father disappears for too long and we get a call from the police station. He ran into a state trooper's car, which was parked alongside a low section of the county road. The trooper found him creeping around, stunned.

At the hospital, my father announces the good news. He is changing his name in order to start fresh. "From now on, my name is Jeremiah Wilson Gauge, but I'll go by Wilson."

The doctor gives him an injection, and on the way out of the hospital he says, "Junie, honey, how's my girl?" Junie scowls at him.

My mother says, "We're going home. Do you understand?"

He tells us he understands alright: he was brought here against his will, he doesn't need to come here and mix with all *these people* buzzing around, trying to tell him things that aren't true.

Drugs

My father's body wastes away, sinks into itself as the shrinkage loosens his skin. My mother lays out a small pile of pills for him to take in the mornings, a small white pill at night. In the morning, while we eat Corn Flakes and Pop Tarts, he stands at the kitchen counter setting the pills out in front of him. He takes them with water, sometimes grapefruit juice, knocking each one back expertly, in one gulp. Sometimes he sets the glass down and stares into it. He is a molecule frozen in space. If he were to turn and look at me, I'd see that his face is like clay that someone has molded incorrectly; there are hollows and shadows and protruding bones where none existed before.

Uncle Riley comes to visit one day, then again the next week. After a while he and my mother take my father to the hospital for a shot, which he is to receive every month. Two weeks after each shot, my mother gathers us together and says now we have to be on the lookout. We must *keep our eyes peeled* for unusual behavior. Listen for nonsensical speech or sudden small obsessions. We must not push him. Be patient, watch carefully, and report to her.

She says the most dangerous time is the three-week point. He will push limits; he might not take his drugs, he might flush them, he might disappear when he knows Uncle Riley is coming. He could begin to believe that those who are helping him are conspirators in a plot to keep him drugged and down and helpless.

Rain

Summer pedals on. Uncle Riley comes to pick up my father or sometimes just to have long chats with my mother outside in the garden or in the woods, by the blackberry bushes and wild thistle. Three days before the August shot day, my father holes himself up in the shed. Mom and Uncle Riley spend nearly two hours trying to get him out.

There is the garden to weed, the alfalfa to cut, the fences to mend, the apple trees to spray, the mare to lunge, the tractors to fix, the vet appointments to arrange, the retaining wall to reinforce. Each day brings a new task and several offspring tasks, which each then birth two- and three-headed tasks. The land is too much for my mother alone.

A week after shot day, sheets of rain are delivered express to our county. Flash floods drown low-lying intersections, ponds appear spontaneously in fields, ditches, and dirt roads, horses cramp together on hills, bewildered. The gardens drown, mud everywhere, the corners of the basement damp, then holding tentative puddles in the uneven spots. Outside, underground critters race to the surface just to catch a breath, the sky dirty-bone gray and not blinking.

The rain keeps my father housebound, wandering about, a trespasser in his own home. He points and criticizes, babbles and argues, occupies the moral high ground in the bog of barbarianism that he fancies has seeped into our lives. He tries burrowing into the garage, but my mother, her benevolence shot to pieces, says no way, no telling the trouble you'll get into in there.

Two days later mudslides submerge parts of Highway 20. Alex calls from a friend's house and says that they were driving along the bluffs when the traffic was wiped off the road like crumbs. If they hadn't stopped a few minutes earlier at a station for fuel and some ice, he says, it would've been him down there with mud up to his chest.

In the space of the living room I lie listening to the call. I count to sixty, then to sixty again. In this time I can follow a rusted wire fence from woods to pasture, an updraft can begin to swirl, and the wind can blow half the leaves off a tree on just the right day in fall.

Keys

By September there are fewer chores to do. My mother starts working thirty hours a week at the new megastore two towns over. She picks nights, when she can, so she can watch my father during the day. This doesn't always work out, so she and Uncle Riley have more talks, design a system, and now when I get home from school I see my uncle in front of the television or on the phone with someone who wants a living room painted Tawny Taupe or Brownberry. On days that Uncle Riley is too busy we are told that we are in charge, and that means we have to have a discussion about keys.

All of our keys are locked up in a secret place, and the key to that place is hidden. This key's hiding place is top secret; we are not to tell anyone, not neighbors, not friends who might happen to come over after school, unless there is an emergency, and even then we are to call my mother first if possible. She leaves her work number by the phone and we are shown the metal box that holds the keys to every compartment in our lives. This box is underneath the sink, and the handles of the cabinet doors are fastened together with a chain, which is padlocked. Now, she says, what is the secret word? We look at her. Beethoven, she says.

She leads us to the old upright piano she played when she was a girl. She opens the bench, which still contains piles of music, and fingers down to the Beethoven collection. Inside the front cover is a small silver key. What's the secret word? she says. Beethoven, we say.

How to hide

When fall comes the pine trees drop their brittle needles, which blow and circle together at the edge of our yard. With two or three sweeps of my arm, I have a mound the length of my body. I return with a quilt and lay covered on the cushy needle-mattress. If I fall asleep, I will wake covered with the needles, and in the space above my bent knees will be two or three pinecones. When I roll on my back I will have to wedge out two more, one under my neck and one under my shoulder.

From here I can watch the sun slide across the sky, I can watch a bird crack a berry open with its beak, dig out the insides, and let the skin fall. I can watch how a spider's legs negotiate the tips of grass blades, how each leg feels ahead for a sticking point. I can smell how much water is in the air, the nearest fire and the type of wood burning in it.

I can imagine becoming part of a tree, that if I lie still long enough I will sprout roots, and they will plunge into the dirt and join with the mature roots, tangle themselves among the worms and pebbles and bark.

From here I can watch my father walk crookedly to the garden, watch him pace back and forth in front of it.

I once yanked a weed from the ground and pinched off a segment of root. My book said that the hairs on this root suck up water like tiny straws. The water travels the length of the root hair, the root, the stem. I learn that its pressure keeps all plants green and upright. I think, with water and light, maybe I could grow my own forest.

Clues II

My mother is vigilant with the phone bills, and one day her persistence pays off. She checks out a suspicious phone number that shows up six times. The phone company says the number connects with a place called the Spiritual Consortium, in Utah. My mother calls the number several times and gets nothing but endless ringing. The telephone directory contains an entry for the consortium but indicates that the number is no longer in service.

A man acutely aware of swindles has been bamboozled.

From the phone bills, my mother goes to the credit card statements, which show two payments of five thousand dollars each. She calls the bank but can stop payment only on the most recent check. Now he's giving our money to the fundamentalists, she says, running her hand along the side of her face, going to the kitchen window to look out, rub her eyes, look out again.

My mother is so quiet that I know two things for sure: one, that the amount of money must be large, and two, that I shouldn't ask.

I slip away and leave by the back door. Once in the woods, I veer off to the right, to the east, the direction of fire.

I have not played Good versus Evil for a long time but I have no desire to look up toward the tops of trees and imagine faceless hooded creatures. I keep my sight grounded. I get to the three birches, the group where one grows sideways and out, and note that only the flat, low leaves of the wild Lady's Slipper are visible. I remember my father telling me not to touch it, not to accidentally step on it, because it is a rare plant, and destroying rare plants is illegal, and doing so will cause the police to come and pick me up and fine me for upsetting nature's balance. I looked at the orchid differently after that, waiting until April to go to the spot and look at the stiff stem, the hard green knot of flesh at the top beginning to elongate, then brighten, then crack open. I crawled close to it, wondering whether, if I picked it, how anyone in the world would know, and wouldn't balance mean that, if picked, another would spring up somewhere in its place?

When I get to the stream I smell something dead. White foam gathers in a rock-pool and I stoop to break it apart. I have some hazy idea to check for footprints, that perhaps my father sneaks off to the creek bed as well, that maybe this place is where he decides how he is going to divide up his money.

I drop to my stomach and slither along the ground, eyeing it masterfully, pushing into it to check how spongy it is, to determine whether rain might have already washed away evidence. A funny arc near a rock big enough to sit on reminds me of the heel of a man's boot.

I think that it's best not to return to my mother with this information but rather to hold it close and see what comes of it.

Robbery

A huge carpenter ant, left over from summer, crawls along the kitchen counter. I brush it away, hear the faint tap of it hitting the floor. I don't crush it because I'm busy stirring batter for pancakes, knowing that if I do so, someone will have to make them for me.

It's Saturday, and the house is quiet except for the small television showing cartoons; Junie sits in front of it now, wrapped in an afghan. We've been sneaking cookies but I tell her we have to stop, we're having pancakes, and later we're going to rake leaves into giant piles and jump in them. She lets out a hideous giggle.

Saturday mornings are timeless; they thrive solely on anticipation. Alex sleeps in, greedily, my mother and father too, and I can sense the freedom—I can walk anywhere I want, open any cabinet or drawer I like, imagine alternate uses for objects I didn't know we had, play with the cookie cutters and dream of Christmas, lie on one end of the living room and roll to the other end, until I hit the piano stool, until Beethoven stops me.

I hear my mother's footsteps and soon she's in the kitchen, not dressed but in her bathrobe, a series of small wrinkles disrupting her usual Saturday-morning face, making her look uneven, and I know a question is coming, and the question is, where is your father.

I say I don't know and can we have pancakes, but she is running to the bathroom, the garage, then finally she goes to Beethoven, picks him up, watches the silver key fall, doesn't bother to put it back. Then she rushes toward me, toward the sink, and says goddamn that shit. Her hand holds a length of chain. The other half, smoothly severed, falls to the floor.

Uncle Riley hasn't heard from my father, but in an hour we hear from Aunt Sissy in North Dakota, who says that she spoke with my father, that he asked her if there were any airports by her, that he was going to buy a plane, fix it up well enough, and see more of this beautiful country before God struck him down for good.

Dust to dust

I read that smoke is a mass of volatile compounds that slither out from the pores of ruddy wood chunks, its gray tendrils curling. When I hear damp wood burn, I hear a soprano hiss, a baritone sizzle, and in the background an occasional pop, a staccato bass line. The smoke seeps out, blackening even a black sky, spreads through the night air like ink on linen.

The phone call comes from Mr. Davis, who owns the town store. Then another follows, this time from the local police chief. He says, come down here right away.

Alex isn't home, so my mother has no choice but to take me and Junie along. We approach the dark smear in the sky. Then, at the last turn, flashing lights spin everywhere as we near the gravel lot. For a brief moment I think that the police know something about the orchid in the woods, and are going to accuse me of doing something to it. Then I see my father sitting on a bench, handcuffed, looked over by a police officer.

The fire, which had begun on the opposite end of the building, had ripped easily through the century-old wood. The store resembles a giant rotting molar. Everywhere, black char drips like saliva and flows down into piles of ash. The flashing lights of the police cars are angled on the mess: you can look to the center of it and imagine a sickly underground discotheque.

Some of the nearby residents gather and are kept from the scene by yellow police tape. They look around aghast, clutching each other.

The local police chief approaches my mother.

"I'll have to take him in," he says, "just to be sure."

Another officer leads my father to one of the patrol cars. They pass us. My father pulls away slightly from the officer, who still easily holds him. "I had to do it," he says, his eyes twitchy and watery and bloodshot. "See here, it was a dirty place. All kinds of danger in there."

But I know in my blood that this isn't true. I can see that my father's affliction is a dangerous one, one that knows no boundaries, one that cannot be appeased or reasoned with or defeated by my childish marauders; its burn is beyond even him.

The officer tugs at my father. Ash flakes snow down on him, coating his hair and shoulders and the black leather vest that hangs off his bony frame.

The flakes tumble off him as the officer pushes his head down and into the patrol car. The door slams. I count to sixty and think: there is no end of earth. My mother and Junie and I huddle near the bench. My mother's arm is braced on the back of it, and supports us all. The police car pulls away but I know that my father will be back again, in some form, and that his true end is as far away as ether.

Navigations

It's a hot summer, and the fever lives. Its ancestry stretches back to the first bone and cell. Its technique is to enflame; unchecked, its signs kill.

It permutates countless times and now lives in Madison, inchoate, rising from a dormant millennium. He carries it with him as he drives the grain truck along a stretch of highway, concrete fumes roaring forth in the morning's ninety-degree heat. The humidity cuts off his oxygen supply, and the throb in his head passes from top to front, behind his eye sockets.

He pulls the truck over and steps out on the wide shoulder, his boots crunching gravel as he crouches to check whatever it is that rattles when he hits forty-five. Nothing. He straightens, waits a few seconds for the dizziness to pass. The problem will eat at him for the next sixty miles, all the way to Slinger and then east to Cheyenne, past the soybean fields he's known since he was a boy, past the alfalfa fields slated for gated-community development. The dark, tilled earth was once Sioux land, but now it's machined and sprayed, all its ghosts choked off; its voice can't be heard except by the coyotes that clip along the sloped edges of it, tails down, noses twitching.

His Uncle Ives's voice comes to him. You got nothing to lose here.

He can't dwell on this or on the long driving day ahead. He has to concentrate on staying awake, on keeping his mind sharp and active. Ives—weak-backed, mildly arthritic—is counting on him.

It was Madison's first season as a farm apprentice. Madison's mother made the arrangements, and what was Madison going to say? Was he going to make a case for his other options? He'd work on the farm, do what was needed, and move on.

Madison hops down in the bushes and crabgrass to take a piss, then climbs in the truck. These long stretches without human contact tighten his vocal cords. He tries them out now and then by singing along with the radio just to make sure they work, but today he finds that he cannot sing and that he cannot look at the parched fields and the white highway without squinting.

He knocks the truck into gear. It rocks as it climbs over the shoulder's thick concrete. He punches the accelerator. Around the bend, the landscape opens. The truck begins to rattle. He curses, knows he'll spend the night under this damn truck sorting out the breakage. He knows this as well as he knows the grasshoppers, in their frenzied swarm, rising from the rocky bluffs and bolting for water, pelting the windshield like hail.

In the morning, Madison can barely lift his head off the pillow. Ives knocks on the bedroom door. "Early bird gets the worm," he says.

Outside, near the feedstore's receiving area, Madison looks at the ground, his stomach turning, his breath short, sweat already forming at his hairline.

"Now listen," Ives says, checking out the storage shelves. "There's a delivery coming today. Get all this shit moved to the back. Up high, behind what's already there."

Ives was a common man in that he disregarded sickness. A day for tilling was a day for tilling. There were no days off, only off days. And plants, as he liked to say, don't take vacations.

Not that Madison was complaining. If his body wanted to collapse, then it would; Ives would just have to bring the forklift around, scoop him up, and put him somewhere. It was better to move through the heat, keep his sight on the next task. He was in a place between high school graduation and the rest of his life, but for the last two years his spirit was filled with lead and dangerous hopes. It was indecision that killed him, and it was the land stretching out in all directions that reminded him of how much catching up he needed to do, of how easily a future could set its eye on a friend or a neighbor or a damaged and restless brother and whisk that person away.

Madison loads pallets with hundred-pound bags of sweet feed and with boxes of power tools and garden implements, then starts the forklift and brings it around. He loads a pallet on the forklift and drives into the receiving area, then throws the bags up and over the existing ones. He knows his origins are modest; he feels this when he walks through town, when he smells the mildew of the farmhouse, when he goes to the bank to deposit the stipend his uncle pays him every two weeks. He knows he's the second, more responsible child of his mother's.

Ives was the one who taught him how to play poker and how to shave and how to remove an engine from a car. Years ago, Ives bought him and his brother, Russ, who was still around, mountain bikes and zoo passes. And now that Madison had lived here, walked the fields himself, watched the ledger unbalance itself after just one month of incorrect weather, he could see why a man would need company.

Before noon the work goes fast. He opens up the side doors and the big overhead doors, and a breeze keeps the spilled grains and dust blowing out. But in the afternoon the breeze quits and the air is yellow and heavy. Flecks of oat grains hang in the air, perpetually unsettled, penetrating his nostrils and sticking to his sweaty forehead and neck. Every time he bends at the waist, all the blood in his body seems to rush to his head. He drinks water by the gallon.

Ives walks in, wiping his brow with a rag. "Fan on the combine's down again. Damn thing's almost brand new. And I'm going to need you to pick up some scrap metal."

It's evening by the time Madison drives a couple towns over and fills the pickup. On the way home he thrusts his arm—the inner part covered with the hairline scratches he gets from stacking the bags, his palm snaked through with rash-red twine burns—out the open window, feeling the pressure of the wind. The sweetness of the air tells him what stage the alfalfa fields are in, their quality and likely yield. He had cut them himself for many years with his uncle's equipment, before he was an official apprentice.

He'd been starving his fever but now the smell of cooking beef coming from the highway entices him. He pulls into a family restaurant near the interstate and sits at a booth. A waitress dressed in a red T-shirt and black pants hands him a menu.

"I'm Jess," she says. "I'll be your waitress."

Madison scans the menu. "I'll have the Mexican omelet. And

an orange juice."

"Not serving eggs. Dinner menu is all he's cooking back there."

"The ham then? Can he do that?"

"Yeah, sure. Sandwich or the meal?"

"Meal's fine."

She goes behind the counter, where she clips a piece of paper on a rotating metal wheel. A hairy hand reaches around and snaps it off.

Madison leans back and puts his feet up. His half-brother, Russ, left for the first time even before graduating high school, and when he came back he was angry and quiet and his eyes drifted when you talked to him. But the day Russ left for good was one of those obscenely sunny ones, the kind where the piercing glare off tar and chrome made your eyes water no matter which way you looked. They had eaten roast beef and mashed potatoes at a place just like this, and after, Madison watched Russ get into his car, his long black hair curling at the ends, his tanned forearm hanging out the window. They had grown up swiftly, it seemed, like characters in movies, where years pass after a few seconds of blank screen. Russ pulled out of the lot, creating a giant dust cloud. After Russ disappeared, their mother, who had long since stopped praising God and angel, started praying again, nightly, by her bedside. Madison couldn't fall asleep until she was finished, and when she did finish, her mumbled incantations hung in his ears, haunting his sleep.

She said, *I have failed that boy time and again.*

She said, *He will eat me alive.*

Madison would watch her sitting at her dressing table, combing through her hair with her fingers, then her brush.

One day, she said, *How long have you been standing there?*

Just wondering what you're doing, he said.

I'm sitting here, is what I'm doing.

He'd make her a toasted cheese sandwich and coffee, and leave the meal on the table. Later, he'd hear the dishes on the counter, her silence, the flush of the toilet, her pacing, her nighttime hope.

And still Russ did not come home. The one letter Madison did receive was read and thrown away immediately, before he would be tempted to show his mother. Instead, he took the money that was in it and bought her a necklace for her birthday, helping her with it as she sat at her dresser, as he stood behind her, feeling her heat on his fingertips.

In self-defense, the body sets itself on fire. No two fevers look alike, but they all dance corpuscularly and disappear when the blood has done correct work. Madison's fever jumps bodies and now lives in his uncle. Ives comes in the store in a long shirt, chilled, sweating just the same. His teeth chatter. He says his joints feel like there's sandpaper wedged between them.

"Why don't you sit down. I'll get started on the blade," Madison says. He goes in back to get one of the two replacements. He finds them, still boxed, on a dusty shelf. He hears what sounds like a vehicle approaching and thinks he should go see what's going on, but of course his uncle is already heading that way, already lumbering toward two men who have gotten out of a navy blue sedan.

Though Madison has not seen these men before, he knows the car, which is from the nearby university. As far as Madison understood it, these men wanted to talk money with Ives.

Grief might have cleared the land, but it is maintained with sweat and metal as earth turns over auger blades, until the dirt is ready for oats and alfalfa and wheat and corn. Ives's first season had gone well, but the second saw leafhoppers and weevils and a second-generation corn-borer infestation. The third season's soybeans got thrips, turning the fields to mush. By the time Ives switched to organic methods, the farming community had become politically divided; he had been tempted to give in to the biopharming people, in this case two CEOs and the local university's chancellor, and was eager to pocket the six-hundred-dollar-an-acre payment for planting a test crop, for watching over it as it grew edible vaccines.

"Those guys'll never leave me alone," Ives says, later.

Madison sits on the workbench, facemask on, watching. Ives guides the arc welder. Madison hears the fusion clicks of molt and flame as the liquid metal pools at the blade's base. After a few minutes, Ives powers down and lifts his mask. "Look at that seam," he says, indicating the smooth joint.

Madison takes off his mask. "They know you know your shit."

"They don't want to know about all that." Ives had gone beyond the basics of seed strains and organic pest-control techniques. "They won't be happy until they see that what's mine is theirs, or until they pollute everything with their GMOs."

Later, after a dinner of grilled steaks, Madison gets out a deck of cards and shuffles. Ives throws the steak bones to the two stray dogs—a lab and some kind of spaniel—that have learned to hover at the back door at opportune moments. Ives throws the bones across the yard and lets the dogs sort out who gets what. His throw has no snap to it, and when Ives bends to untie his boots, he loses his balance.

At the table, Madison deals. "Sleep in tomorrow morning, why don't you," he says.

"We'll see." Ives gets a glass and pours in some whiskey, straight, the same way his mother drank it, except when she drank it, Madison would leave the room.

Madison wins three hands in a row. Ives says, "Well, beaten again by the whipper-snapper."

"Just a little luck," Madison says.

"Nope," Ives says, pushing his chair away. "You're in the receiving line."

Madison thinks of a funeral line snaking from the back of a stuffy room to the doors, of people awkward and overpolite and dressed up. He thought his own mother would be the next one in a casket, but instead it was his grandpa Harrison's funeral his memory showed him. He remembered rows of chairs, of men in suits talking and talking, of his mother's sweet perfume as she told him to sit still. He remembered how Ives looked that day: annoyed, distracted, tired.

It isn't until Ives turned out the lights and has gone to bed that Madison thinks to ask, what do you mean, receiving line?

The fever turns Ives into a zombie. He's a tall man, a man who can now barely see due to massive recurring headaches, so now he continually leans against walls, and if he's not leaning against them, he's running into them. There is too much to do, too many instructions, too much weather and daylight.

Madison looks out the feed store window. Ives is testing the combine. Madison has an image of the man falling like a cut tree into the newly welded blade, and vows to try to be the one running the heavy machinery for a while.

Ives's temperature is at a hundred and two with Tylenol, higher than Madison's was, and holding forth. Madison knows the maximum healing potential of whiskey and that Ives is far beyond it. This morning his eyes were bloodshot, and the coffee pot shook when he poured. His own mother wasted away in doorways, and after every recovery came a backslide. Madison brings gallons of water to his uncle. As his uncle drinks, Madison pictures a flood: water beating fire, the way it always would.

But still, Ives sways in the wind, too exhausted for evening cards, too pale for thought or for giving orders.

Madison thinks of calling his mother and asking her to plead with Ives. Ives would do anything for his baby sister, Bethany. He accepted her every time she came knocking, and would possibly even listen to her when she told him to go to a doctor, when she would no doubt tell him that fevers are demons in disguise but beatable if you attack on all fronts.

Out on errands one day, Madison stops at the diner, thinking to eat and bring home some soup for Ives. He sits at the same booth and has a dinner of meatloaf and fried potatoes. He gets chicken noodle soup to go. As he leaves the tip, he sees the waitresses talking and looking at him, so he adds another dollar.

Outside, a woman has the hood up on her car. Madison thinks she looks familiar. "Need help?" he asks.

"Got about as far as I can get with it," she says. When she turns to him, he sees that she's the waitress he had last time he was here.

"Won't start?" he asks.

"Nope."

"Did you just get off work?"

"Not really. How did you know I work here?"

"I remember you. You're Jess."

Madison runs to his truck, grabs a toolbox, then slides under the car. Even from under it he can smell her: detergent and something floral. She bends down, her hair brushing the ground. "Can I hand you something?"

"Nope," Madison says. "Main thing is your alternator."

"Pile of crap."

"Well, if you don't maintain it."

Jess sits on the curb bordering the landscaped front of the diner's lot. "Actually, I don't work here anymore," she says.

"Quit?" All Madison can see are her knees.

"Fired."

"You'll find something better."

"Maybe. Problem is that I'm not a very reliable person," she says.

Madison slides out and sits next to her. "I can call a tow truck for you. You're probably going to have to leave the car with the mechanic for a couple days."

"Shit." Jess's eyes dart around before she fishes around in her purse for a cigarette. "Sorry. Thanks. What do I owe you?"

"A swim."

They walk carefully down the steep gravel slope to a flat rock that sticks out over water the color of worn copper, and float out to the middle of the quarry on a couple of giant black inner tubes. Madison is soon completely wet, but somehow Jess stays dry despite carrying with her both an open beer can and a copy of *Cosmopolitan.* "You sure it's okay we're here?" she says.

Madison leans on his tube. "Positive. This is my friend's dad's place. He knows I come here."

They drift. The quarry hasn't changed. Even the narrow ridge on the far side, the ridge that Madison dived off of when he was younger, was still there. The branches of the giant willow tree, directly across the quarry, still skim the water's surface. When he was small, he floated underneath them, concealed in the giant foliage dome, stray water drops and twigs falling around him.

"There's a rumor about this quarry." Madison says. "Two kids stole a rowboat, rowed themselves out to the middle here, but there was an accident. They drowned."

"How long ago?"

"I don't know. Long time. I heard about it when I was a kid."

She paused. "Where?"

"Right about here, I think." Suddenly Madison clings to the tube as if something is grabbing at him, then slips through the center of it. After about a minute, he surfaces a few yards away from Jess. She lets out her breath. "Jesus Christ, I thought you drowned. Asshole."

Madison swims over to her, thrusting his elbows over the side of her tube. She sits in the middle of it, her beer can sticking up between her knees. Past her belly he sees the ghostly orange-yellow skin of his legs as they kick slightly to help him balance. "I found it," he says.

"Shut up."

"Yeah. Right down there." He points.

She looks past his arm. "A sunken boat."

"Yes."

"It must be pitch black down there."

"I have something for you." He opens his fist to reveal a quarter. *"You could've gotten that anywhere."*

"There's loads of cash down there, you know." He lets go of her tube, preparing to dive again.

"No, don't. It's too creepy," she says.

Jess pages through her magazine. Madison, back on his own tube, looks at her, raises a hand to his forehead to shield his eyes from the sunlight. "What's that?"

"Just a magazine." Her pink toenails glisten under the water.

"No, I mean what are you reading?" He reaches out for her foot and spins her over to him. "Give it here." Jess had dog-eared several pages: an article on breast cancer, one on self-esteem and depression, and one with a set of pictures of Madonna and Molly Ringwald.

Jess watches him skim the pages. "You seem like a really nice person."

"I suppose."

"I'm not who I might seem to be."

"What, a college girl who can't hold a job?"

She looks at him. "I have to try to get clean. You know, get my life together."

"Okay."

"What do you mean, 'okay'?"

"So get clean. My mother used to try that." He spins her inner tube, then stops it. Beer sloshes out of the can. "Maybe I'm not who I seem to be."

"What, a redneck who needs to shower more frequently?"

"Yes."

Jess grabs the magazine back from him and paddles the tube toward the giant rock.

She turns. "It's an ugly thing, all this fear," she says.

"Yes."

"I can't go on this way."

"Okay."

She climbs up on the flat rock. "I'm going to get wet now," she announces.

"It's about time."

She dives in and swims a few yards underwater, beneath him. Through the water he feels the strength of her kicks. She surfaces. Her eyelashes glisten; she looks ten years younger than her age, which Madison thinks must be about nineteen.

She says, "I'm the type of person who thinks about death. But I don't know why."

"It's okay."

"What, thinking about death?"

"Yeah, but I meant not having an explanation."

"I wonder, if more people did think about it, maybe they'd get along better. But people think I'm morbid." She smiles broadly. "Thanks for fixing my car, by the way."

Madison figures out how to use the grain mixer. He gets a few tips from Ives, who now is in bed a lot, and then pours whole, crimped, and crushed grains from the hopper into bags, biting into a grain now and then to make sure it is sweet rather than bitter, and piles the bags up in the back, where they will sit for seven or eight months before being moved to the front shelves. He measures out corn, oats, molasses, linseed, and minerals for sweet feed, which go into fifty-pound bags. Corncobs get tossed in a large bin, and bran goes into smaller bags.

Customers wanting diet recommendations for their animals stop Madison on his way from the storage units to the front of the store. Soon he is able to suggest rations for all types of horses: short-barreled, pleasure, hackers, hunters, jumpers, racers, foals, colts in training, ponies, saddlebreds, quarter horses, and western breeds, and is able to warn about such things as colic and founder, as they related to improper feeding. He suggests proper feed storage techniques, explains how cod liver oil helps animals stay healthy and how a grass diet aids in the healing of their wounds.

One day around noon, Madison goes in to check on Ives. The

side tables are crammed with medicine bottles, tissues, half-empty glasses, rubbing alcohol, thermometers. To Madison's surprise, his uncle is dressed, sitting on the bed.

"Feel clear-headed today," he says. "Considering." Still, he lies back to rest. "I was just out talking to Mike Ritchie and Darren. Says you got a real knack. Ever consider staying on?"

"Maybe."

"Should." Ives adjusts a pillow under his head. "You ought to think about it."

"Yeah, okay."

Ives sits up and pulls a pipe out of his pocket. He holds a match to the bowl. This body ain't gonna last much longer."

"Your fever's gonna break."

"No, I don't mean that."

Madison watches two flies mate on the window sill.

"Lemme tell you, Madison, you're a good kid. This here ain't heaven, but it's better than a poke in the eye." He pauses, looking hard at Madison. "It's the way the wind is blowing. There's only one thing I can teach you, and that's that nothing stays. Nothing at all." The pipe handle clacks on his teeth.

Madison turns toward the window. He looks out at the highway, the vast fields on the other side of it, the monotonous dip of telephone wires from pole to pole. A town that was disappearing from his vision like a mirage from a thirsty man.

"Well, anyway, give it some thought," Ives says.

Nights, Madison drives to campus and parks across from Jess's dorm. At ten Jess runs out, and they drive to the quarry, where they fuck madly in the cramped space of the truck.

After about a week they migrate to the back of the pickup, and from there to a white clapboard house off-campus, where some friend of a friend lives but is always out of town. Madison is inside of Jess one night, just about ready to fire, when cracking sounds join their moans. After a couple more thrusts, the top corner of the bed collapses.

"Oh! Goddamn," breathes Jess.

Madison grips the top of the mattress, pinning himself up and against Jess, and keeps moving. When they finish they roll uphill toward the safe side of the bed. "Don't worry, I'll fix it tomorrow,"

Madison says.

The next morning Madison repairs the bed frame and a host of other things: the leaky kitchen faucet, the sliding closet door, the sticky bureau drawers, the dryer, the ceiling fan, the window screens, the porch railings, even the little television set on the counter that hadn't been touched for years.

"I can't believe you fixed all this stuff," Jess says.

"Well, she's letting us use her house." To celebrate they watch some goofy new sitcom, then go out for pizza. They park at a turnoff and wander into the brush that borders protected state land. A small trail leads into the woods. They walk for a couple minutes. Dusk is just setting in, and Madison smells rain on the way. The trail tapers to almost nothing, so Madison turns now and then to keep an eye on a landmark: a giant misshapen boulder, situated where the main trail ends.

"Hey, I gotta pee," says Jess. "Don't look."

"Nothing I haven't seen."

"You've seen a woman pee."

"Yeah. A friend."

Jess looks at him.

"We were camping."

"Oh."

"Really, don't go too far."

"Just far enough to keep out of sight." She laughs. It's a laugh that has tease in it. It's a laugh that says *you're worrying about nothing.* It's a big brother laugh, Russ's laugh, a laugh that Madison, as a boy, dreaded because it meant Russ was going to leave him sitting somewhere, sometimes on a sidewalk in a bad neighborhood, sometimes in a woods, like this one, while he went in search of cigarettes. The cracks of leaves and sticks would fade and then there would be nothing. Madison was nearly sick with the thought of freezing or starving to death right where he was sitting.

Russ always came back, though, with candy or cards or poker chips, probably stolen, and Madison would follow him home for dinner. Russ was an expert navigator; he knew shortcuts, he knew where the freight tracks led. He could go anywhere, do anything. In a few miraculous minutes, it seemed, they were back in familiar territory.

It was only a year later when Madison, alone, bounded into the woods and found, to his surprise, that he knew the way, that he had stored the directions in some unknown part of his brain.

He hears Jess zip up, then rustling as she makes her way back to the trail. He looks up at the fluttering oak leaves, agitated by the brewing storm. He longs to wander around, to walk again on wooded paths, and to realize that all along he had known the secret turns and twists.

Several months after Russ left, Bethany lapsed again. They lived in an apartment by that time, and there weren't many places to run to or hide in. She no longer sat at her dresser combing her hair or admiring necklaces or catering to meditations; all of this was replaced by anything that moved quickly: nightmares, headlights on the living room walls, a dealer's quick steps out of sight.

Madison hid medication bottles and locked all the alcohol under the sink. He sat in parking lots and loitered in stores as long as he was able. He disappeared in other ways as his own mind betrayed him, told him to get into trouble in order to confirm his existence.

He was no good at listening to voices, and isn't now as he sweeps out the receiving area. He drops the broom and walks to the house. With Ives in bed all the time, it is impossible to watch the store and do all the other things that need to be done. He has it in his mind to see if Ives would hire another guy, a temporary addition, but that was the easy question. Madison walks to the house now for a different reason, and as soon as he enters the kitchen, he knows he made the right decision.

In the bedroom, Ives lies with the radio on, his position nearly unchanged from that morning. He seems to be asleep, but his head shakes and jerks, and his lips have a blue hue. Madison checks the bottles of painkillers, and figures that Ives has not overused them.

Ives can barely speak. Madison sees a body yellowed and deflated, beyond sweat and odor. This stillness is different. He thinks of the fever demons his mother once talked of, and this time picks up the phone.

He doesn't plan what to say. He just dials the number and tells her, as guilt sets in, that he's waited too long and that Ives needs her to come over. He can hear her gathering things as she talks, but can't answer her questions. It's Saturday, so there will be no doctor appointment. It'll have to be the emergency room.

Two minutes after he hangs up, he gets a call from Jess. She tells him "cold turkey," that she's a half a day into it and thinks she's going to die. She asks him to come over and he says he will, though it makes no sense, running from one crumpled-up body to another that will soon look much the same, but he goes.

Outside, the air haunts him. It rises in swirls around him, though there is barely a wind. He is deeply afraid. The note he leaves on the table for his mother says he has to go help a friend, but it's the faces of strangers that rise around him now—the people in cars he passes, the ones walking through town, the students on campus, the ones watching from second-floor porches—all of their failings and needs clawing at him.

In the house, Jess is in the bathroom vomiting. The door is closed.

"Jess, I'm here," Madison says. He can feel the subtle shaking of his knees. He knows she hears him, he knows she cannot move. He knows that at first, she will not want him to see her.

He sits in the hallway, across from the door.

"I have candy bars," he says.

He answers for her. *Thank you, Madison, you're a decent and kind person.*

He tries the bathroom door. It's locked. "Jess," he says. "I won't come in, but you need to unlock the door."

He hears her moving, then the door being unlocked. "Thanks," she says. "I'm sorry."

"I know. It's okay."

"I'm going to die."

"No, you're not. It'll be over soon."

"Don't go."

"I won't."

Thank you, Madison, you are an angel from the heavens.

It's dusk already. There will be no sleep, and her violence will come soon. He goes to the kitchen and opens drawers. He grabs the knives and anything else sharp and dumps everything under the sink. He locks the doors with a short chain and padlock he grabbed just before leaving. The key goes in the front pocket of his jeans.

He turns on the television, and in a few minutes Jess comes in. She drops towels on the floor and lies on them. "I have to be near the bathroom."

"Do you want a candy bar?"

"Yes." She sits up.

Madison unwraps one for her. She eats half of it. Her hair is stringy, her makeup already smeared.

"How are you?" he asks.

"Shut up," she says, and gets up. She goes to the bedroom.

The words will come, he knows this. He will not let her out of his sight for the next few days. There will be many words and no sleep. There is no doctor, and no antidote.

He wants to know why he stays. He wants to know what keeps him at the farm, what keeps him in this town, what keeps him here now, in this recliner, in this living room, with this woman.

He watches two programs in the evening lineup. He makes sandwiches. As he finishes the last one, Jess enters the kitchen. This time her eyes are bloodshot.

"I have to get out of here," she says.

"No."

"Come with me."

"Nope. It's against the rules."

"You're a jerk. You always think you know everything."

"I know more about this than you think."

"You're such an ass."

You are my savior.

"You're a bastard, let me go."

You are the only one who can help me.

She cries now, loud gasps bursting from her face. "You think you have everything under control."

Madison turns. "Sit your ass down and eat something. You're shaking."

Jess goes for the door but Madison blocks her. "Please let me go," she says.

"No."

She reaches for the doorknob but Madison catches her wrist. She fights him, pulling, but he twists her arm behind her.

"Ouch. Fuck you," she says.

"Are you going to behave?"

"Fuck you."

She pulls again, and this time Madison lets her break away. She goes into the living room and lies on the floor.

He brings her a glass of water. "Drink," he says.

She knocks the glass out of his hand. He goes for a towel, but when he returns, she's gone. The bedroom door is closed. He rushes to it, thinking of the window. He opens the door, thankful she hasn't locked it.

The room is sour and stuffy. Jess lies sweating on the bed. "Please, can I have water?" she says.

He brings her a new glass and watches her drink. Then he sits on the floor with his back against the wall.

Nervous exhaustion finally tires Jess out. As she sleeps, he calls home, but there's no answer. He leaves Jess's number on the answering machine. After he hangs up, he leans his head back, feels his arms twitch, his own body falling away from him.

When he wakes, his throat is thick. Jess sleeps, still. On the way to the kitchen, the hallway sways beneath him like a rope bridge. He drinks right from the tap. The moonlight scatters through the blinds and onto the kitchen's floor, creating long shadows on the Formica counter, a counter he now notices resembles that of the diner. He sees Jess's arm sweeping over it, her mouth smiling wide while the old men tease her, called her honey and girlie and sweetheart.

He had shown off that day at the quarry. It was silly what he did—bringing her coins, amassing his meager sum.

He looks out the window, past his truck to the shed. Its shingled roof is caved in, a small section missing because of the lightning that hit it a few years ago, and now the opening is spongy and rotting away. He imagines the glowing eyes of mice underneath the exposed floorboards. He thinks of himself living under there, peering out from the darkness, observing all human activity from the knees down, the way it had looked that day from under Jess's car. It strikes him that whole animal families—generations of them—exist and thrive beneath creak, rot, and stench.

He imagines a shapeless mother and father. The indigo night doesn't save them but rather melts them down deep into uneven ground. He imagines his uncle as he must have been twenty years ago.

I failed him time and again.

He waits with his mother's voice until dawn.

A day later, he gets a call. It's his mother wondering where the hell he is, telling him that Ives is in the emergency room. She says that Madison better get home fast.

Madison tells Jess he has to leave.

"Don't go," she says.

"I have to. I need you to finish this out. You're almost there."

"I don't trust myself."

"You have to. You have to right now."

He is not one to talk about trust. He packs a suitcase and locks the feed store before pulling out on the two-lane highway. This time, there's no one on it. If he died here among this thigh-high corn, among the hollow barley stems, people wouldn't think twice about what endless landscapes are capable of, despite their beauty. He understands only this much as he approaches the lone stop sign at an intersection that takes you either to town or away from it.

He's hungry but can't bear the thought of eating and all the decisions he'd have to make. He'll drive instead.

Nothing stays.

The day his brother left, the sun caught the truck's chrome and shot glares into his eyes. Minutes went by but still, when he closed his eyes, he saw the glare-spots flashing.

Madison picks up speed. He passes the Blackstone farm, the corner where strawberries are sold each June, and the town center, where mothers run errands with their children and where older, hooded kids hang out on corners.

He accelerates madly once on the interstate. As the sky swirls violet and magenta he senses spheres: the imprint of a crater or the soft places inside the body. A tumultuous wind pattern, maybe, blasting its way through the atmosphere. Or the path of a roaming bloodbrother pumping pedals and breathing in fumes, laughing on a long road winding through autumn sun.

He sees a hotel and takes the next exit, looping around to its wide entrance. In the room, he wonders how long he'll stay. He doesn't call home because he can imagine the news. He doesn't call home even though he loves and is dutiful. When he calls, he does because the distance from point A to point B is too long.

Ives is dead; this is another certain thing. There was liver damage and there was heart failure, all complications due to the fever, complications that in turn allowed the fever to do its work. He can see his mother in the hospital corridors, his aunt Angie probably there by now.

He leaves the hotel room even before unpacking. Jess would be okay by now, if she managed to last the final half day. She might wait for him.

If the fever ever circled back to him, he'd drown it, once and for all. The demons would scream their goodbye, and the earth would silence them.

Part IV: Water

Finding Women

Silences

Russ didn't start out mute. He didn't start out wandering through thorny underbrush and weeds, forgetting all of his temporary mothers by the time he made it to the swinging fence door, the edge of switchgrass, the wild blackberry bushes. Rather, the quiet years descended upon him with no warning and no explanation.

He can't remember when his speech returned. He can't remember much about not having had it or what was good about getting it back. What was speech in the face of disappearing women, of nights in suburban dumpsters that at least blocked the impossible North Dakota wind, of abandoned sheds with soggy walls that pushed in easily, even for a boy.

The women came and went, their colors spun and merged and separated, a maddening kaleidoscope. The women fed him and bathed him and sometimes talked to him. But he ran away because he didn't believe a word they said.

He stopped speaking.

One summer, in a woods that whispered to him, he dug a hole in the ground and formed the dirt into a tiny cavern that he could slip into, where he could string together his neverending moments free from sound and syllable.

Years later, it's the mud he remembers, its potential for sculpture, how it rewards with darkness and protection and silence.

Hitchhikers

Russ grows up, and women come to him again. He watches this new set of them from up in his semi. By now he is accustomed to the sight of so many—an entire transient community strung together with asphalt, electrical wires, and taut lies—walking the gravel, the crabgrass, the guard rails. They all have the same crooked step, they are all branded and wayward. They say, *I'm from Canada, originally.* They say, *Bite my neck when you fuck me.* They say, *I hustle because I never found a place for myself.* They say, *Not long ago, I became old.* All of them lost to the next town, the next stretch of buckled concrete.

The youngest hitchhiker Russ finds is not his first, but she's the one he drives the longest distance, all the way across three state lines. She is quiet and still in the seat next to him. She cries, then sleeps during the four hundred and forty-five miles she is with him. He hates to wake her every time he stops for fuel, and to make up for it, he buys her hot chocolate and a ham and cheese sandwich, which she eats sitting cross-legged and finishes by the time he gets back from the men's room. So he buys her another one, egg salad, plus fruit juice and potato chips. Later, on the road, she says, *Thanks for the food* and smiles a heartbreak straight under his skin.

He drops her off at five hundred and twelve miles, slips her twenty dollars, and realizes that he would have driven her across the country, had she asked.

Is it best to start with the most significant woman? Or is it better to blend them all together so as to see all of their riches at once?

He gets used to the road, to the way everything eventually becomes something else, to how there is no going back to anything. Years pass; there are just stretches of concrete, a future close by and tightly held. For years he listens to CB snippets of half-conversations put together between location updates or static or sex noise, all delivered to him endlessly from the same baked tar he drives, the same overnight stops he parks at to sleep, lulled into dreams by the highway's vibrations.

His vocal cords dry up like stale rubber bands. He is practically mute again.

One night after fueling up and heading for the on-ramp, he sees another stray. She has a new backpack strapped to her. He slows to a stop, and when she climbs in she says her name is Rita. His nineteenth. She's shaggy-haired and pierced, slightly pixie-eyed, hitching, she says, from LA.

She, too, has always been mobile—*always been*, she says, *a damned itinerant*. When they reach their seventy-sixth mile together, she tells him of her superstitions, of how she believes that similar life events bundle themselves together in specific groupings, and that these groupings are not accidental. She talks of what the sky is capable of delivering if you ask it enough, and in the right way. She tells him that her dreams are of a pit of children, and she stirs them around with a giant wooden paddle.

This woman's dreams make Russ fierce and calm. He understands this soup of thrown-away people. He pulls into a motel parking lot, stuffs the log book under the seat, sees her looking at him. She follows him to the room and turns the lock on the door. He is surprised when he kneels next to the bed and looks over her. He is surprised when she sits up, when his arms hang heavy at his sides, refusing to touch her. He is shocked at how difficult it is to undress and lie next to her when she holds the covers open for him. He is shocked by his shallow breathing, his dry mouth, his shoulders touching hers.

He is shocked by what he doesn't say, such as how unreal she looks, and by what he does say, such as, *Sometimes I worry that I always take things and never give them back*, such as, *I can't remember the first seven years of my life*, such as, *You're a good girl for going home*, such as, *You make my feet numb*.

He turns to her. He says, *I think I feel okay now.*

Okay how? she asks.

Who are you?

Never ask me that.

You should tell me.

I told you, she says, *I'm an itinerant.*

Her hand slides over his torso. *Damned to roaming the flattest land on earth,* she says.

Russ takes her hand, kisses the tip of each finger, is shocked. *Is this the flattest land on earth?*

Probably. Look how far you can see. Nothing gets in the way. I like it, but I don't. Sometimes I do.

He kisses her forearm. *Tell me about the place you're from.*

She tugs at her necklace. *A tragic place. My town is filled with three things: dust and big attics and men who can't see past their back doors. This necklace? Amethyst, for protection.*

Tell me about hills. Russ hoists himself up and over her, mounts her, shocked. *I'm going to take what I can get now.*

I know that already, she says. *Hills keep me honest.*

She says they should love each other raw before she changes her mind, and that's what they do in the Vista Motel, until the sheets, stretched and damp, twist around their crawling limbs, roping them together.

Russ wakes in the middle of the night with Rita's arm resting on his chest. Moonlight brightens a spot by her feet and cuts across her calf. The precise weight of her arm, the disheveled bed, the strange, slow hours: he has been in a room like this before. He feels a far-away woman seated next to him, remembers rolling toward her weight, how her hand stroked his chest, how the sound of the heartbeat in his ears subsided. There were tiny blue flowers on the curtains and they filled his vision before the lights went out.

This woman fed him and spoke to him. How old would she be now?

Russ takes Rita's limp arm and moves it along his body. She stirs, then is quiet.

He sits up in bed, desperate for flight. He forgets Rita and the moonlit room as he pulls out of the motel an hour before dawn.

After fifteen miles, he feels a weird knot in his stomach, which he attributes to hunger. He thinks of Rita's loose ties, the greedy ears she had for him, her dreams of a hot sibling soup. Twenty-four miles later he craves her skin and her heat and her stories, and by forty-nine miles he understands that he has found and lost his first love.

She is gone by the time he drives back to the motel to find her. He doesn't even know her last name. He wants to strangle the clerk, who remembers no one, who sits eating a cheese and tomato sandwich, who doesn't care that the cleaning lady now strips the bed, washing away all of Rita's traces.

Russ drives the same forty-nine miles again, then pulls over, drinks bourbon, and vomits until he can't breathe. He sleeps it off right where he falls, in a scrubby ditch, two feet away from a colony of red ants.

That night he wakes before morning and blinks hard, his chest warm from the weight of a woman's touch. The weight does not disappear. He rolls over on the ground and is a mute child again, rolling toward the warm spot on a moonlit bed. Toward a woman, one of his disappearing mothers, toward a person he couldn't believe in, toward his other first love.

Just a portion of those missing years comes rushing to him: chili cooking on the stove, the woods, a girl his age but noisier, a mud cave, a fire pit with hot stones intended for purification.

He asks the sky for memory. Rita would tell him how. She would tell him to go home.

He realizes what time it must be and climbs, dizzily, to his feet. He has always been late. He is late, now, again, with a delivery to an office-supply store in Wilmington. When he finally pulls up to the loading dock and goes inside, the receptionist gives him a look.

Russ doesn't bother waiting for the dispatcher to contact him or for the company to let him go. He finds his pickup in the lot and heads east with the same cracked-up heart that sent him roaming, and now would bring him home.

Locations

The day Russ arrives, Madison is out on the old Ford. Russ watches him, the younger brother who stuck around, the one who now lives in the farmhouse where they worked together years ago, for years drifting apart under the sweaty palm of their uncle Ives.

His foot sinks into the fluffed soil at the edge of a mounded bed, and he steps away, suddenly aware of his weight, of old ghosts rising from the earth. Russ hasn't seen his brother for six years, which doesn't seem like a long time until this moment, as he stands on the periphery of the neatly plowed field, as he motions toward him.

Russ' heartbeat quickens as Madison jumps off the stopped tractor. Russ had left this for a world of concrete and asphalt, but around him now are acres of dirt, miles of beds swirled over the ground like cake frosting.

Years ago, his returned speech fell on him too heavily. He hadn't known what to do with it so he launched words at people like boomerangs. When the words doubled back, they told him that he was a bastard child of uncertain origins. They said, *You have no father because you dared to be born.* They said, *Once a fuckup*, they crawled into every empty space inside him and took long, recalcitrant residence. Sometimes they skipped around in his brain like flat rocks on water.

He hadn't stolen the money from his uncle's cash register. He wasn't the one who left the truckload of grain outside to get rained on and spoiled. And it was his brutal, recurring non-sleep that made him walk in the night unaware of his own motion, of gates left tragically open, of switches turned on, of precious equipment parked outside, hidden, to rust.

He knew enough to know that any attempt to convey the truth would have fallen on ears trained to disbelieve him.

The nights in jail were his, this he acknowledges. It's not that he can't accept blame: he ran the streets before he rode them on eighteen wheels. In jail, in a cement cavern blocked off with bars, the boomerangs richocheted. They said, in the voice of his blood mother, *Why do you do this to me? Just leave.*

Russ stands in the dirt, back home now for the first time in his whole damned life. He watches Madison—grown up, a man, darker and more serious. A man with a farm and a store to run, a man with roots and firm ground beneath his feet.

When Madison is a few feet away, Russ looks at his face. They shake hands. They wait.

Russ says, *Can't believe you're still here.*

Can't believe you'd show your fucking face, Madison says.

For a week Russ sleeps in a room with a sloped ceiling and a bare mattress on a metal frame. One night Madison appears in the doorway. *I just want to know why you're here,* he says. *You need work?*

I can keep driving, Russ says.

Well, if not, I can use the help. One thing, though, this is for real. And the pay's not much.

Yeah, okay.

For the first few days Madison sends Russ on errands and sets him up at the farm stand at a corner near town. Russ learns the names of all the vegetable varieties. He rings up purchases, watches women sort through bins. He smiles when he bags their items. He keeps his mouth shut.

One morning Russ wakes to find a note taped to the kitchen table, telling him to pick up a rototiller blade in Cheyenne. As Russ nears the town, one grey cloud gathers in the sky. Three drops land on the windshield. *Tragedy comes in threes,* Rita said, *because God created all patterns, and every pattern holds numbers within it.* Ahead, parallel with the horizon, is a line that seems to hover above the ground. As Russ drives, he sees that the line is a set of railroad tracks.

Rita said, *Two tragedies have between them the energy of the third, already brewing. It is only a question of how much time you have to wait.*

Two old Soo Line cars are parked at the juncture, their red color faded to a light orange, their sides tendriled with graffiti and bird droppings. He approaches the tracks and stops. He looks both ways: left, the direction of the drops, and realizes he had once been at this very intersection, facing this very direction; right, and he feels her next to him, the woman of the moonlit room, her hand on the stick shift, a turquoise ring on her pinky finger.

This woman once took him to a pond, to a flat rock big enough to lie on, and with him watched frogs swimming. She fed him waffles, she said, *And you are discovered*, and she left a tiny light on in the bathroom for him.

Two tragedies, Russ thinks. Long ago this woman took him in, rubbed his chest in the night, and he fled. And Rita, who made him weep and never waited to be rediscovered.

Lists

Russ jots down the names of the women he remembers. These include a real mother, all temporary mothers, girlfriends, and highway strays. It's a game he cannot win. Over three days, he compiles a list of thirty-two, and as he runs though them, he comes up with three more. The list begins with his biological mother, the original mother: a sinful one, of course, who has babies without men and raises them without fathers. This original mother, stained and imperfect, one day lights a fire in the middle of the living room during an episode of *Days of Our Lives*, because she wants her past to become ash. The wind takes this fire and pushes it, tumbling over itself, to the other side of the room.

When Russ can't think of another woman, he heads out to the feed store's receiving area. He untangles irrigation tape and stacks it in piles along the wall. Madison grabs the grease gun and goes after the Ford's fittings. Russ asks him about the fire.

All I know, Madison says, *is that it was an accident.*

Russ imagines the rooms of that small house combusting. He

imagines high flames, curling cloth, the blackened legs of a coffee table. He imagines his mother, young, sitting at the table with a gin and tonic, cigarettes stubbed out in a cheap ashtray from Tijuana.

Russ pictures this woman's hair pulling the flames into her body, burning her from the inside out into a pile of carbon.

Mom's been put away again, Madison says.

How long?

Don't know. Aunt Angie has power of attorney.

Madison moves on to the carbeurator, fishing out the rust, then tipping it over to test the float. He says, *I went to Aunt Angela's for a year while Mom got her shit together.* He pauses, then looks at Russ. *That was in Minot, I think.*

At least it wasn't the foster system, Russ says. *And how do you know it was an accident?*

That night Russ goes upstairs and lies on his side, listening to the rain pound the wooden sill he knows is rotting—the other day he pushed his thumb through the moist spot where the frame meets the wall. He smelled mold, a century of heat.

He looks at the list and can't find the justice in it.

He dislikes this brother of his, steadfast and lucky, the one with a sound mind, the one people go to for help. And he has things to say now to these women on his list, such as, *Would you recognize my face?*, such as, *I never should have run away from you*, such as, *Why didn't you try to find me?*

The sky has no answers. It is clouded with tragic droplets.

Now it's Cheyenne that comes to him in the night. The town that wasn't Cheyenne, that maybe was Cheyenne. The place on the tracks where he saw her, lifelike and dead, a ring on her pinky finger.

Russ's first phone call is to the Division of Social Services, which directs him to the record office. The woman finds his name in the computer. Russ gives her the dates.

There are five women listed here, she says.

That many? Russ says. *Give me the first names.*

Nadja Wilkenson is the name Russ writes down. It is all the office can give out legally, but it doesn't matter, the name is golden and heavy and warm in his breast pocket.

He starts with the phone books—not the skinny ones in the farmhouse, but the whole range of them at the Bismarck library. Not a single "Nadja," but plenty of "Ns," which he lists on a sheet of notebook paper, along with addresses. He tapes this sheet, this forest of Ns, next to his bed and looks at it in the morning, thinks of it in the field and as he drives to the farm stand six miles away, his own feet growing roots as he watches new moms with their babies examine pints of strawberries. His patience shocks him, the sudden opening of his gut and throat, how his chest becomes overwhelmed with breath, so much so that he knows that Nadja lives and that she is near.

Strays

Castoffs know how to build a fire. Besides Russ, there were three other boys and one girl at the fire pit. Not so much a pit as just a space to huddle in, a place to refuse to leave, a place to return to. A fifty-gallon drum held the hot orb that kept them heated, that freed the smoke that reminded them of what they were: nothing children on the out.

There were the regulars and the strays, the ones who stumbled upon the gravel clearing in a patch of weedy field about a half-mile through bramble, if you knew where to look.

They dragged railroad ties sprouting mushrooms from the middle of a group of saplings and baby maples only as tall as they were, thriving despite the litter and junk thrown to them by the careless and the stupid. They stacked the ties into benches, wrapped themselves in blankets, and lay on them. One boy had a thermos, which astonished them all. It was filled, more astonishingly, with whisky or scotch. They all assumed he had at least one parent, a treasure trove from which to steal.

It's why Russ didn't mind his own thievery—the five-dollar bills, the cigarettes, the boxes of cereal or bags of potato chips, a toaster from somebody's barn that he could sell to somebody's brother for cash.

Here, there was sound. Here was a sky that was too black but that looked upon them as equals.

One day a girl turned up with a slab of breaded fish freshly discarded in the back of a restaurant. They all skewered chunks of it on thin twigs, felt their saliva prickle the backs of their mouths. If they swallowed bones, they didn't care.

Russ watched for Jasmine most days, but soon she disappeared. The thermos boy was replaced by an older kid, a bully with dried snot around his nose. The two other boys, who were cousins, showed up with bread and rotting fruit, and gave some to Russ before they left for good.

One night, Russ searched the jacket pockets of the sleeping bully and came away with two dollars, a lighter, and a pocket knife, which he thought of using to slice open the bully's arm—anything to make him run.

The next time Russ went to the fire pit, no one was there. No bully. But also no fire, newspapers all used up.

Russ followed the path through the bramble, then turned off it, making his way through untrampled flora. The woods got thinner, the sky brighter, and soon he could make out a farmhouse with a woman working in the yard. Russ crouched behind a boulder and watched. He ventured out into the yard, heart pounding, terrified of discovery, terrified of not being heard. He vowed silence to keep clean. The woman saw him. She fed him and bathed him and talked to him. She didn't mind that he didn't speak. One night he rolled toward her as she sat on the bed next to him.

Nightmares

Russ's sleep is not friendly to him. Sweat flows from stale pores driven by broken glands. He wakes with mud on his pants, leaves in his hair, insect bites on his neck. He wonders how far he went this time. A few days earlier, he traced his footprints all the way to the woods and back. He lost the prints at the gravel part of the driveway, then picked them up again in the garage, where they stopped well before the door but did not go back or loop around themselves. He scanned the walls and pallets, searching for a clue to his own disappearance.

He feels the remnants of burrs wadded in the hair around his ear: a sign of his new route, his expansion of nocturnal borders.

He hears Madison moving in the room down the hall, then the creak of the steps. These stairs are hollow, or they seem hollow. Every morning he wakes drawn to the specter of concavity, the lure of a deep crawl space.

After a while, Russ smells melted butter. Madison shouts up the stairs, *Russ, you want pancakes?*

Yeah, I'll be down.

He sees a muddy print a few feet from his mattress. There I am, he thinks, but then realizes that the print is an old one. He gets up and goes to the window. The rain that began weeks ago and never really stopped has come on strong again. It is the middle of summer, and the swirling clouds drop inches of water at a time, then clear out and bring a white sky raining slow and steady. First the vegetable beds compact with the flood, then puddles form in the middle of the pockmarked fields and overflow into narrow streams riveting through rows that are no longer distinguishable.

Madison calls up. *They ain't getting any hotter.*

The tractors are useless in the muck. Nothing but rows of yellowed stalks dropping leaves by the minute, nothing but stem rot and bloat. The galoshes Russ wears every day make his feet sweat and wrinkle.

After breakfast, Russ writes to seventeen N. Wilkensons. He drafts a letter, writes it out in his best hand, then goes to the library to make copies. He gets home and folds the sheets into thirds, then puts them all in envelopes, careful to avoid the gummy seals, which are sticky from the humidity.

He goes downstairs and outside, not bothering with a rain jacket. He starts the truck and turns on the radio, which broadcasts the names of the latest flooded streets. The rain is so loud on the roof that he reaches for the volume twice, but the noise is too much, so he turns the radio off.

The letters haunt him. They say, *It is fair for lost years to be returned to you.* He thinks of his migrating women, his lost Rita, her traveling sisters. If only he had stayed. He tells them all to get to where they are going. To move quickly. To stay.

He puts his seat back. He tells his women that he's here for them, will always be here for them. He reaches out his hand and helps them over the cracks and crumbled edges of highway shoulders that drop into gulleys and ravines. He watches them pass him by and not look back.

He doesn't remember closing his eyes, but when he opens them he sees a dark gray sky, a bolt of lightning cracking it in two. He's lying in a pool of water or maybe sweat. He tries to move but he is too heavy. The sky flashes, the wind picks up, the remains of a squash plant brush across his cheek.

His back is kinked from the hardened soil, and despite the heat, a chill runs through him. After a while, he's not sure how long, he hears his name. In moments, Madison is there, looking down at him.

What the hell are you doing? Madison says.

Russ blinks, his vision blurred by the thick drizzle.

Come on, Russ, get up.

Russ begins to pull his arms from the muck. *Why did she let them take me away?* he says. He bends his legs, shifts his body to the flat space between rows, sees the impatience in Madison's face.

You can't just run off like this, Madison says, extending an arm. Russ grabs it, then reaches for Madison's legs, tripping him.

They struggle, gripping each other, deadlocked.

So you haven't changed, Madison says.

Russ wants to say that if he's causing trouble, he'll leave, but instead he pictures a huge pot of water. He envisions himself jumping into it, simmering there with his past sisters and future brothers, spinning around in the hot current.

Okay, if you want to ask questions, Madison says. *Why did you leave me with her?*

Russ sees his brother as a kid, finishing his homework at a tiny desk in a bedroom that the flames didn't touch.

Madison says, *Let me tell you how it was with Ma. How I had to hide the kitchen knives, how I waited for her in the emergency room while she got her stomach pumped for the sixteenth time. How I found her lying in her own vomit and had to clean her up.*

Russ releases Madison's legs.

Years of my life, gone, Madison says. *Watching over her, feeding her, carrying her. And I'm not about to clean up after you.*

Russ has a fistful of mud ready to launch, the ease of the fight drawing him in. Damned itinerants, he thinks. Walking roads of glass that drop out from under them, roads that unwind and spiral down into bottomless canyons. Shivering in the gravel with soaked bones and spirits, tripping as they look back to catch the next ride.

Destined to roam these flat lands forever.

The clump of mud is just silt now, running over Russ's opened fist and into the ground.

Tell me about the place you're from, Russ wants to say, but Madison is gone. The rain pounds his forehead and he lets it go on and on because he's settling deeper into the earth now, marking it with his fleeting imprint.

A response

In a few weeks, even the mud has disappeared, submerged under a mass of standing water. There's time for the town: the new cineplex, family restaurants, and hair salons alongside the old hardware stores and the bar with the pool hall in back.

Russ plays a game there now with the townies. They have the faces of hoodlums gone almost good. When the game is over, Russ drives to a nearby restaurant and orders the roast beef special, then treats himself to an ice cream sundae. When he goes to pay the cashier, he sees a woman with Rita's long neck and messed-up hair go into the ladies room. Even though he's caught just a glimpse of her, he takes his time paying, then goes to the phone to pretend to make a call. He thinks maybe he actually will make a call, to Madison to see if he wants anything, but he fumbles too long for spare change—a woman can slip out of a room in that space of time and lose herself in the fog or the heat waves or the gravel or the masses.

Five minutes pass and still there is no sign of the woman. Russ is sure he missed her while digging for coins, and now can't bring himself to call Madison at all. He sits on a bench by the window, grabs a newspaper, and flips through it, keeping one eye on the bathroom door.

Five more minutes pass. She is gone.

The train tracks in Cheyenne are safely above the level of the nearby standing water. Russ stops his truck on them, looks right, then left, sees the two rails converge in the distance. *Rita is with her brother now*, he thinks. *She is happy.*

But he can't know this.

He heads home along the empty highways. The kitchen light is on when he pulls in. On the table is a letter addressed to him. The return address reads "N. Wilkenson." He looks at the envelope, then sits.

> *Dearest Russ,*
> *I remember you, my favorite runaway. I will call you soon.*
>
> *Love,*
> *Nadja*

They agree to meet in Cheyenne. It's Nadja's suggestion. On the phone, her voice could have been anybody's. His was what it was. *I can't believe you have one*, she said. *I thought maybe that's why you wrote to me instead of calling.*

As Russ pulls up, she emerges from her townhouse. She is dressed in khakis and a t-shirt, the clothes of any woman. Russ parks. As he approaches her, he can tell right away that his memory has been even meaner to him than he thought—protecting him only by erasing her. He shakes her hand, takes in her straight dark hair, a grey streak through the front. The lines on her face mean nothing.

There is the ring on her finger, still.

Little Claw, she says. *Your nickname, do you remember?*

Do you remember, he thinks. These three words kill him.

They go inside and sit in a small living room on a floral-patterned couch, which Nadja calls a davenport. She serves breakfast tea and cookies. Russ watches her walk, bend, pour, sit. The woman of his dreams, the woman who haunts him and makes him walk through burr patches in the night. Here, to touch.

He cannot speak.

Nadja moves to the floor and sits crosslegged near his feet. She pulls out a photo album and turns to a marked page.

You've come back, she says. *Most never do. I had twelve foster kids, do you know that?*

The photos help. There is the kitchen floor and the box of toys, the olive green carpet of the living room, the braided rugs, the Legos. Uno cards, and the girl with the flower crown. Had she been so blonde? So tiny? The backyard, *where you arrived*, the steps, *which you walked up as if you'd been born on them, but only after three days went by*, the low shelves, *your favorite corner, your safe place*, the woods, *where you wanted to live*, and the pile of dirt, *your escape.*

I remember piling up the dirt, Russ says.

How many times did I find you there? You were a strange boy.

His throat closed. *I remember you now. You saved my life.*

No, you charmed us.

How far did I run? Russ asks.

Which time?

Russ can remember only the one time.

The last time? Russ says.

The photo album closes and Nadja sits back. *About three miles,* she says.

Where?

And that's barefoot. Your feet were bloody when they found you.

Who found me?

Sky, with her chanting, but in theory, the police.

Your sister?

Yes.

I knew there was another woman.

It doesn't matter who found you.

Russ grabs a butterscotch candy, which he hates, from the bowl on the coffee table, and unwraps it.

I went crazy when you ran away, Nadja says. *You nearly killed me.*

I'm sorry.

I knew they found you, but that's it.

I know.

I think you knew you were going to go back to your mother. That's why they were coming to get you. I told you. You were playing in the dirt when I told you.

I know.

No, you don't. Maybe you ran because you couldn't sleep. You were having nightmares. Well, not nightmares, exactly.

What then?

Night scares. You ran and ran, even though you were sleeping. Kids do, sometimes. They grow out of it.

Nadja goes to the refrigerator and pulls out a tray of sandwiches. Russ gets up to help her. She hands him a bowl of fruit salad and they walk outside.

They picnic on the concrete porch, sitting against the wall with their knees up. Nadja tells him that her sister still works with the bureau, that she's still a healer, and that she still tries to keep the Lakota people on the map. *But you wouldn't remember any of this,* Nadja says.

You're Lakota?

She is more than I am. But yes. She tried to heal you with a ritual, but you bolted out of the hut.

How did I walk three miles?
It's good to hear you speak.
I didn't say anything?
Not a word. We had you checked out.

Russ tells her his life as he remembers it, ending with his arrival on the farm. The parts he leaves out are significant, and the parts he changes are unfair to her, but there it is, a beginning.

After lunch they look at more pictures, and when Russ can't bring himself to look at any more, he says he has to be going.

On the porch he kisses Nadja's hand, and is shocked. He holds it between his own hands, feels her warm palm, sees the dirt under her fingernails, the hairline scratches on the sides of her fingers—these, the fingers of this particular hand, the hand of all his women who came, who went away.

We'll see each other again, Nadja says, and then is gone.

One morning two weeks later, Nadja calls to say that she wants to take him to the farmhouse he wandered to all those years ago—they'll do a driveby and then go through the town, maybe have lunch. Russ tells her that he'd like that, then hangs up.

He goes downstairs to make pancakes. When they are close to being done, he calls for Madison. He hears his brother above him, then his steps on the hollow stairs, and is grateful for the sound.

Lake Effect

Love, incubating

It scratches at Danni in the evenings and itches her legs under the sheets at night. It pulls at the neckline of her pajama top. She dreams about it—one morning she wakes up moaning, the sweat of ecstasy slipping at her hairline and between her breasts. She sits up to cool off, thinks, *Whoever loves me will not be sorry.*

These dreams go on and on and on. Every night there is a man at the door, outside the window, under the carpet. She rolls up the carpet so he won't suffocate.

Her love does not have the glandular conviction of adolescence nor is it threatened by midlife realism. Rather, it is arched, elliptical, moonlike, slightly cracked; it is luminous, orange, crepuscular, and smells of roots and chicory, and it is this way because it is ready to be given.

There is a new man in her life now, a man who is here because some other woman is gone. He is a man who emerged out of loss and, as such, cannot be denied.

Sarah, dead

The lake Danni lives on holds many loves. It holds the love of tide and current and of all that flows into it. It holds love from the looks of those who have seen it and wish to be close to it. It holds the love of people with destructive secrets, of people who want to be swallowed.

Danni's friend Sarah used to teach at the university affiliated with Danni's and also in an anthropology department, which meant that the two of them went to the same out-of-town conferences and sometimes met in the same function halls on campus. But the lake swallowed her four months ago, in April. Sarah's spirit was egg-shaped, and the night it collapsed, she had been visiting her brother Ian, a furniture restorer from St. Paul, who lived almost directly across the lake from Danni. After they ate dinner, Sarah went outside. She crushed cinnamon ferns and slick moss as she made her way down the wooded slope to the pier. She swam out into the lake, swam some more, and then stopped swimming. She sank to the silty bottom and took with her all of her love, her loves, and her potential loves.

Years ago, Danni's own brother, Ryan, left this earth by his own skilled hands. He was young; perhaps because of this—and because of her particular spiritual beliefs—she couldn't understand the idea of a lost life. Rather, she liked to think of it as merely clipped off, like a trimmed plant stem, slowed down temporarily but storing potential in the form of shoot and bud.

The man

Danni pours herself some coffee and sits at a miraculous table. It is heavy but narrow, and for that it seems to go on forever, to have been wherever it is forever. She calls it her infinity table, a lofty name given that she discovered at a clothing store that was going out of business. It is constructed of heavy wooden slabs and thick, carved legs. The table top has one drawer on each side. Now, it is loaded with end-of-semester test booklets, a laptop, and stacks of articles she intends use for her next paper, which she hopes to present in fall at a conference.

Danni notices that one of the drawers is open. She checks to see if there's anything in it, anything she might have needed or looked for recently. But the drawer is empty. This is not the only trick her memory has played on her. Her memory, or her eyes. All are tricks, though, and after each one she is able to convince herself that what she remembers, and what she sees, are all subject to the revisionist impulse. Which means she is able to sleep at night and view these mini-narratives as not only not harmless but essential for imaginative, critical thought.

She closes the drawer, then goes to the kitchen for a grapefruit. The kitchen window has just been replaced, and she looks out of it while she loosens the pink sections. She imagines Sarah pale and naked, descending down to the lake, stepping onto the pier, then lowering herself into the frigid spring water. Was the moonlight shining or were what must have been the black sky and the black water indistinguishable? Earlier that week the two of them had flown back together from a conference in Buffalo, where Danni suggested they coauthor an article for an anthology. Danni remembers that Sarah hadn't been paying attention, had offered only a nonsequitur: *I should have done more with my mind.*

Since April, Danni has been in touch with Sarah's brother, Ian. Initially, she wrote to him out of a sisterly concern for his well-being, but now they communicate regularly. She writes him an email message one evening. *If you're going to talk about love, you have to talk about death.* A glass of cabernet sits at her elbow. They had been exchanging messages about how some people drift far away and can't come back. He replies: *And birth.*

Ian refurbishes antiques, particularly large pieces like bureaus and dining tables. He has written to her of his latest, a Marot-style armchair. She writes to him of his efforts to deconstruct, which she jokingly calls a postmodern endeavor. He writes, *Years ago, I would have been merely a craftsman peddling stuff that had immediate value. Now I'm a magician.*

Danni thinks the night air must have swallowed Sarah first, and it must have smelled of beeswax and varnish. Ian's workroom bleeds out in this way. On the night of Sarah's drowning, he had needed to get a final coat of varnish on a Welsh dresser before going to bed. He left the workroom momentarily to get away from the fumes. He went in the house. And that's when he saw Sarah's clothes on the living room floor. She would sometimes disrobe this way when they were growing up—not in front of anyone, but when she was alone and about to go into the shower.

The wine glasses from dinner were half full, the plates still on the table, the leftovers cold and crusted over. He said that only later did he understand the significance of the years of lost smiles he saw emerge on Sarah's face all through dinner and, in fact, from the very first day of her visit. *The smiles,* he wrote, *of a woman about to destroy herself. Should I have understood this farewell?*

Sarah, alive
Danni sits in the middle of the dead woman's kitchen. The house

is the very last one on a dead end road, and small by contemporary standards. The kitchen needs updating, but the blue-swirl splash tile and gray-blue countertops are both calming and humble. She had just made a run for Italian sub sandwiches and lays them out on the table. She calls up to Ian, who had finished sorting out the spare room and had moved on to Sarah's bedroom.

Danni feels not like an intruder but an excavator. What to make, for instance, of nearly twenty sets of turquoise jewelry, none of which Danni had seen Sarah wear? Ian doesn't think the jewelry is worth anything—the style of the settings and the luster of the stones are of good quality but not original or obscure. And what of the Hungarian ceramic figurines? Possibly Sarah was saving the items for a potential daughter. But Ian said, "No, she never mentioned having kids," to which Danni replied, "That means nothing."

A month earlier, the oldest sister came to start the cleanup and found in the medicine cabinet a sister that neither she nor Ian ever knew. Internet searches revealed that the prescriptions were for anti-depressants and that the dosages were high. Ian was the one who came upon the closet filled with shoes, some with the stickers still on the bottoms, some still in their boxes and stuffed with tissue paper and dessicant packets. In all, seventy-six pairs of shoes.

Danni knows that there is a certain kind of person who collects and hordes, and that a person like this never feels safe. Danni looks at her own unmanicured toes and wide instep that make only flip-flops truly comfortable to her, and tries to remember Sarah unpacking in the hotel room. She had noted nothing unusual; Sarah roamed hotels the way she seemed to roam the earth: freely, even a bit carelessly. And still, she had done plenty with her mind, despite—or perhaps because of—her regret.

Ian comes downstairs and sits. He's wearing work pants caked with polish and wood dust and paint. He goes to the sink to wash his hands, then takes a bite of his sandwich. He says, "The lawyer says the final amount will still be over a million and a half."

The biggest surprise was finding out that Sarah was one of those closet stock-market traders who knew how to sell short and play the odds. Ian said that when she was just four years old, she made a wallet out of the old-fashioned cloth wallpaper they had in the house they grew up in.

Ian sits down. "So why academia? Why anthropology?" he asks.

These discoveries have hurt him. He and Sarah were the closest of the siblings, and he always felt he understood her more than even their parents. Her secrets, to him, were small betrayals that, together, created a path leading to her equally secret death wish.

Danni watches his long fingers wrap around the sandwich and squeeze it as he tears off another mouthful. "You're a big brother," she says, "you will always have questions."

After the conference in Buffalo and before Sarah's last meal at Ian's was a discussion Danni and Sarah had about the things the body knows and when it knows them. They both believed that memories were stored not in the mind but in the cells of the body. They had always wanted to get to the bottom of the discussion, which was essentially about the hidden energy that courses through the body, energy that waits years, even lifetimes, for release. How the energy keeps telling us who we are, and how it lies to us. Danni's lost brother knew he would always be the way he was: a slave to his illness, tyrannized by biological compounds that mental health experts still didn't understand. If foresight lives anywhere in the body, it must be in bone marrow; it cannot, say, be transferred out of the body in a cancer operation.

Danni wanted to ask Sarah if she ever noticed that their discussions often strayed toward the idea of lost potential, but bringing this up would keep them going on even longer, forgetting about dinner or finishing the laundry. It was early April, a week before the conference, and possibly nothing Danni said during that conversation was taken seriously enough by a woman about to be dead.

The search crew found Sarah's body in ten hours. The discovery was instinctual despite all the equipment: a diver said he felt deep into the tangled weeds along a certain section of the lake for a second time, then a third, because he heard the voice of his daughter just as his flipper became caught in them.

Dead brother

When Danni envisions a population, she thinks of countless stalks growing up from the fertile bed of a bog. There are many bogs, each containing millions of stalks. Each stalk releases pollen. Some stalks, like the one representing her brother, Ryan, get cut off or are blunted somehow. The release of pollen stops. An aerial view would reveal the tiny gaps in the stalk-field, and you would see the system lagging. This is life and death construed as a closed system. But if the cut stalks continue to produce pollen or whatever substance it ultimately releases, this substance must go somewhere—perhaps back into the root system lodged into the bog's ever-shifting bed. This is life and death construed as an open system.

Danni had been home from college during Ryan's last bolt away from life and was the one to see him flatline. Danni saw him, at that moment, as a free soul. She called for a nurse, who called a doctor, but even several hits with the defibrillator did not alter Ryan's path.

Ryan's funeral had an open casket, which was their mother's wish. She believed in a final view. Everyone made remarks about how peaceful he looked, how peaceful he must be, now, finally.

Danni barely looked at her dead brother. She didn't want to remember him looking so prepared. She looked at the plush satin of the coffin. She thought of him alive with his illness, his lost mind, of his body moving compulsively, dangerously forward. She had seen this funeral before, many times, in her mind, but the real funeral parlor was filled with tulips, not lilies. In this funeral, there were rows of chairs in which to exchange pleasantries and speak of short lives and better worlds.

Danni said the eulogy. She said Ryan's death was his own. She used the word suicide and included some statistics. She talked about the institution Ryan was in, how it smelled, what Ryan saw the last years of his life. She spoke of this place as a terrain and praised Ryan for the ways he managed in it. She spoke of the nail-mural he pounded into his bedroom wall and of another nail pryed from an institutional wall filled with decades of mold and rust; she spoke of this nail and how it pierced him, how the sepsis was stronger than the original wound, how the slow poison finally found his heart.

She explained Ryan's violence as a manifestation of pain, as a sign of misguided imagination. She spoke of historical delinquents and literary delinquents and how the Oxford English Dictionary was compiled, in part, by a madman. Her point had been a larger one about all people who fall through the cracks, about the failure of signs and systems.

Danni explained how Ryan's death inspired her: not to do more with her life, not that life was short, but that to imagine one's own death releases all of one's potential.

She neglected to mention love in any way, but didn't realize it until many years later, after moving to a lake with a woman's spirit living on the bottom of it.

Ghosts

Danni decides that, for lack of a better explanation, her house has a ghost. The ghost has moved on from opening drawers to walking up and down the staircase. It's the third step from the top that creaks, and Danni hears this typically in the afternoon, although once she was awakened by it in the middle of the night.

She wonders if the ghost is Ryan's spirit, which brings up questions about the paranormal. One camp believes that spirits don't move around from place to place, that instead they are former inhabitants or have some connection to the area. Danni writes to Ian about this. *There is a ghost in my house. What should I do?* This is at 9:50 in the evening, while she drinks a gin and tonic. At midnight, she checks her messages. Ian has written, *Put out some cookies?* Danni writes, *Are ghosts always previous inhabitants?* Ian writes, *I watched too many crappy movies to answer this question.* Danni writes, *Do you think it's Sarah?* Ian doesn't reply. She calls him, but he doesn't pick up. She writes again: *I'm sorry if I upset you.*

The next day, Ian asks her to dinner. She changes into a silky dress and puts on extra makeup. Before leaving, she tears a piece of paper from a tablet and writes, *Tell me why you are here* and leaves it on the table. She also leaves a cup of Earl Grey tea.

At the restaurant, they take a seat by the window. There's a large party in the middle of the dining area, and by the time Danni and Ian order their meals, the conversation has grown louder. Everyone seems to be reaching over everyone; silver platters dot the table; one man has a chicken drumstick in his hand and shakes it at someone across the table.

Ian says, "It's like 'The Last Supper.'"

"Except for the women," Danni says.

"And the laughter," Ian says.

They sip their pinot grigio.

"I don't know," Danni says. "They might have laughed."

"Yes, maybe out of fear."

In the middle of their meal, Ian says, "Speaking of last suppers, do you think she thought of dinner at my house that night as notable, somehow? What would be the point of bothering to eat?"

"Maybe she didn't plan it out," Danni says.

Ian says that after dinner he had planned to ask Sarah something about her ring, the ring of dynastic origins. It was a black pearl surrounded by diamonds, all set in silver. It wasn't a family heirloom, but its history featured famous ships and moguls. It nearly went down with its owner—the wife of a mogul's friend—into the depths of the Atlantic but instead that wife sold the ring for unknown reasons. The insurance paper trail revealed that it had been an engagement ring for a woman in Edina, Minnesota, then an engagement ring for that woman's daughter-in-law. Then Ian's friend, a dealer in antique jewelry, acquired it. Sarah received it on her next birthday. The ring held, in all, ninety-seven years of love, and on Sarah's finger, the reasoning went, the potential for its release. Ian had wanted to ask her whether she found out where the pearl came from.

The divers pulled Sarah's body from the muck a half a day later. Ian said that the forensics person had to cut the flesh away on her finger to get the ring off.

Lost and secretive Sarah, mountains of shoes, a body that lied to her. In her wake, a man, another dinner, potential love. Danni thinks Sarah would approve but then isn't so sure. She watches the last-supper table with its half-drunk wine and platters of devoured meat. In a few moments, she feels sick, and begins to think maybe she ate something bad. She and Ian walk to the car, his long fingers now wrapped around her waist, and by the time they get there, she is feeling better. She gives Ian a long kiss on the cheek. She cannot thank him properly. She cannot believe in him, sitting there, now starting the car and pulling it out onto the two-lane highway. In the space of the short drive, he becomes a mystery to her, so by the time she walks in her house she is not only surprised but motivated by her anger. She has never thought to call it anger—doing so seemed childish—but she sees it now, clearly, this anger toward her friend, a woman who told her nothing. Years of nothing.

And yet, this man in that woman's imperceptible midnight wake, a man who holds Danni, whose hands work her skin with warmth and pressure.

There is a great bog filled with stems and reeds and long blades of thick grass, and one more stem is cut off but no one can tell the difference.

The note lies on the floor. Danni goes to retrieve it, already concluding that its new position could be attributed not to a ghost but to the gust of air the door had surely created when she came in. She had forgotten to enter more carefully.

Danni, alive

You, on your death bed: channel the future you want in order to live a fulfilled life. It's "you" as everyman, and "everyman" as every person. It's "channel" as in "summon," or "think about." She has written this to Ian, and calls up the message from the "sent mail" list. These were old words, words already scrambled into the ether and put back together again.

Her imaginary death bed comes to her as a pyre. She lies there on sticks, facing light-blue sky with pink and yellow in the clouds, dusk falling around her, the final riddle having hovered in the last seconds: Where is the evidence that a lifetime has passed by? Did her presence outweigh her absence?

She hasn't seen Ian in a week. He's been buried in work. He's finished the dresser, a jewelry box, and a Windsor rocking chair. His clients are upper middle class people or dedicated collectors. They sometimes call, or even stop in, to check on his progress. Ian explains all the steps involved, flashes his long fingers over a carved Chippendale panel or the fretted door of a secretaire cabinet, puts their minds at ease. His own home is filled with treasures—an Egyptian-style chiffonier, a hand-painted Tibetan chest with bamboo trim and inlaid mother-of-pearl, a red Japanese dressing table with an elaborate lotus motif applied with gold-flecked paint. His "museum"—an old breezeway with newly finished walls and pine flooring—contains pieces waiting for auction: a toboggan, still functional, and a mission-style cradle.

All evidence of death and survival, the passing of the torch. Danni once told Ian that he restores the evidence of life, not unlike the work of an anthropologist. But pride, for him, was in a job well done, in keeping his hands busy, in making people happy, and she has no argument with this.

She herself is not just interested in but smitten by these artifacts, the sweat in the wood, the tears in the hinges, ages of sunlight in long, unencumbered surfaces. She hears them talk; the toboggan says *rejoice in the moment*, the cradle says *I can promise you this*. All the secrets smeared away in oils and polishes and ultra-fine-grain sanders.

She has Ian come over to look at her table. The wood is oak; he determines that quickly. The construction, done with wooden pegs, is solid but unremarkable. It is fashioned after a stretcher table, which were early dining tables, but this one is made of oak, not pine. Its patina has no depth; the color variation and relatively light weight both signal reproduction. "Good thing I didn't waste my time going to *Antiques Roadshow*," she says. "But maybe this is why my ghost likes it."

Later they go to the Walker Art Center, first wandering the Minneapolis Sculpture Garden before moving on to the collections. They end at a temporary exhibit. There is water everywhere in these paintings, either overt or implied. Danni finds herself pausing in front of a work depicting Ophelia and her river—a stylized swamp with Ophelia standing at the brink, her dress made of real cloth sewn into the mount. The words "cover me green magic" fall around her in glitter and sliver thread painted over with laquer.

Sweet Ophelia in the swamp, catching her death, recognizing her own weary soul reflected back to her.

That evening, on the pier, Danni fills the pockets of her cargo pants and denim jacket first with pebbles, then small rocks, then the larger rocks closer to the pier, rocks left white and exposed from erosion. All of them go in pockets, then in her left fist. Her intention is to understand the weight of these rocks in water, the exact feel of their pull downward. She lowers herself into the water, her right hand on the pier's edge. She lets go of the pier, stops kicking her legs, and lets her head submerge.

She keeps her eyes closed, feeling the subtle draw downward. Then, she seems to stop. She cannot dream of opening her mouth, of drawing in the cold suffocation. Is the breath held until the last second, or is the water just gulped in, the body snapping into panic, the rocks now crucial in the equation? Danni is out of time; she claws at the water, refuses to open her eyes. She paddles upward, the water becoming warmer, the light beyond her lids brighter.

She surfaces, long since letting go of the rocks in her left hand. Rising through the water to the top seemed to take minutes, but now that she has caught her breath, she realizes that it was more like seconds. She couldn't have been more than six or seven feet under water.

It was the air in her lungs, she thinks, that kept her buoyant, that allowed her to get back to the surface easily. She puts her hands on the pier and hoists her body upward, catching the edge of the pier with her leg.

She lets the water drip from her. *This fucking lake*, she thinks.

As she walks up the slope to the house, along the path lined with ferns, she understands that it wasn't the air in her lungs that allowed her to surface so easily but simply a desire to live.

Lake effect

It is probably the last day of summer. Danni and Ian wander down to the lake, taking the path with the stairs that lead from Ian's back door to the pier. His side of the lake is so different: taller trees, more shade, a variety of mushrooms. The water, too, seems lighter and greenish. A family of geese hugs the shoreline, the little ones dipping underwater, throwing their feathered butts upward.

They are here to swim. They drop their towels and ease into the water. Danni has an inflatable dinosaur, lavender with red splotches, and they push the thing back and forth as they swim out farther.

It's an unusually cool day, but the water holds the heat of the last two weeks of humidity. The approaching dark-gray band of sky forms at the tree line. Danni mounts the dinosaur and kicks over to Ian.

"This was a good idea," he says.

"Thanks," Danni says. "I don't have very many."

"I love when you're self-effacing."

Earlier they had talked about this swim: revisiting the site of the trauma, consciously re-creating positive memories, even embracing the bad memories.

He holds her face. "You're amazing."

She knows now that Sarah couldn't have explained herself,

couldn't have confided when there was no urge.

"Plus," Ian says, "I'm sorta rich."

The lawyer finally had the details worked out. Ian and the oldest sister were to split the million dollars Sarah had accumulated.

"Feels like tainted dough," Ian says.

"What will you do with it?" Danni says.

"Invest it in my shop. Or save it for a rainy day." Ian points upward. "Which it is now."

The gray line over the trees had bled downward. The gray hangs over their heads, though the sky over the far shore is still white. The raindrops, which fall sporatically, are the largest Danni has ever seen. The lightning begins first as full-sky flashes, then as individual bolts chasing each other across the lake.

They climb onto the pier and run up the steps into the house. Immediately, it starts to pour. They race to close windows, but already the sills are soaked. Danni finds some towels in a closet and begins mopping up the water.

Ian has stopped asking questions, and doesn't now, as he leads her to the bedroom and undresses her, as he pulls off his trunks and lies on top of her.

"This was a very good idea," he says.

"I agree," says Danni.

His grief blankets her as the night swells, as her skin rises to his touch. There is no moon, only this man who smells of algae and mud, who traces lines on her back with his tongue.

"If you love me, you won't be sorry," Danni says.

He opens her legs and sucks her. She sweats, her back hot against the sheets. She pushes into him as he intensifies.

Outside, the wind carries the storm elsewhere. The light becomes yellow. She looks outside as Ian enters her.

Near the middle of the lake, where the mist has moved out, is a flash of light. The wind stops. Danni tells herself she will remember the flash as lightning, the last bolt of a sensuous, volatile thunderstorm, but she knows lightning doesn't emanate from the surface of standing water.

She turns to Ian, arched above her, pushing deeply. The light must have been that of a falling star, all the way from the heavens to the lake, burning right up until the last second, when the water pulled it under.

The lake spares nothing, Danni thinks, and squeezes the corner of the sheet in her fist.

Ryan, alive

Ryan flatlined on a rainy night, the water rushing down the hospital windows, about an hour after Danni arrived to visit. He was covered in a blanket. Mechanical beeps counted out the seconds, and the blue room settled on his face. Evening became night, Danni's vigil parenthetical to his passage.

A year earlier she had visited him in the musty institution located just a couple miles away. The building was a renovated monastery, moss-covered with nails buried in the walls, a relic from an assortment of earlier times but now a repository for the disturbed or deranged or possessed. Ryan sat in a chair, dazed, recently sedated. The nurse station across the hallway both soothed and angered Danni.

She imagined the hug a sister might give to a brother in such a circumstance, but found her arms too heavy. If she ever said *Ryan, how have you been*, she didn't remember.

The men in the TV room one door down were howling. A nurse ran through the station door and across the hall. The security guards stiffened.

"Those are the real crazies," Ryan said. "They take their pants off and then they laugh, like children. If I take mine off, they'll laugh and forget that I steal from them."

Now, after months of steady decline, after a year of visits, the machine's beeps lured Danni closer. She didn't know how to wake him, so she reached to touch his shoulder, and when she did she found that it was mush and that her hand passed through it—no more flesh, no more blood, no more haunted shell deflecting the world.

There would be no revival.

There would be attorneys, a negligence case, a year of mediation. There would be a settlement. There would be belongings distributed, recycled, trashed. There would be ghosts. There would be a mother, thinned out and forever changed. There would be a sister plagued first with fear, then guilt, then regret. There would be years of dates, advanced education, boxed meals, therapy, new apartments, old furniture, presentations. There would be a down payment on a lake house, a man, creamy pearls, and sudden storms. There would be a harboring of love and a cursing of water, a love of water and a curse on love.

Lake, alive

The lake holds ice patches that hold shades of white, patches with arched edgings showing gray shadow. Fine winter dust whorls in small cyclones over the numbed curves.

Below, there are lights ready to launch upward, to catch the eye of lucky onlookers.

Danni prepares for classes at the long, enchanted table, bereft now of ghostly manipulations. She has a black-pearl ring on her finger, a gift, fitted at a special store, especially for her. If the ring brings the water too close to her, she'll take it off. If water still gets too close, she'll drown the ring, finally and forever.

She dreams of curses lifted.

In winter, the lake is far away, all its life shuttered and glassed in.

In mid-December, she corrects the last exam of the semester. She pours herself the last of the wine, looks out the front window for Ian, who is picking her up for their bi-weekly dinner date. Tonight she will have salmon or cod, anything briney.

Ian will go home and finish a credenza for a customer who lives on a narrow, winding road in the nether regions of the county. He'll let it soak up the polish and then deliver it, newly finished and ready to gather the stories of those it serves, as soon as the path is clear.

Danni will come home and climb into her four-poster bed and feel hibernation in her bones.

Walking on Water

In fall the earth closes down but the bodies of children shoot up. These children run naked into the early morning chill screaming with delight. They find things that crawl, things that have fallen into their laps, and sculpt little bowls out of mud on the picnic table. They collect maple leaves for school projects. They rip open chrysanthemum buds, smell the mint leaves they grind up between rocks. They swing from tires hanging from thick oak branches. They marvel at dusk, at anything that is potentially containable, anything that interrupts.

The body of the girl who lives in the gray farmhouse is shooting up, is badly in need of school clothes, but the mother hasn't a sense for or the money to buy them, and so the girl goes without. Seams are split, threads trail. The mother cuts these off—no sense letting the girl go ratty—but they come back again, appear again like dust. And dust, resented for its ubiquity, becomes an analogy in the mother's mind for the existence of the girl. This feeling creeps up on the mother; she is surprised and afraid of it and ignores it when possible.

When November eats away at the ends of daylight, the father decides that life should be offering him more tantalizing opportunities. The mother thinks there is no telling what the fantasy of this insolent and intrinsically lazy man could be. But there it is. He and the mother bicker well into an unusually warm evening, right in front of the girl, and then he is gone.

The girl gets on with her active but clumsy existence. Her uncontrollable limbs get away from her. She shuffles through the leaves that have gathered along the road's edges and finally reaches the end of them, which is where she will catch the school bus. By afternoon the wind will have blown the leaves about, and she'll kick through them again on the way home.

The girl has no siblings, few friends. On the weekends when the mother is quiet, so is the girl, who eats licorice in front of the fireplace and puts together jigsaw puzzles that would stump most children her age. Spatial relationships come easy for her, but the talent goes unnoticed.

The inside of the house looks either halfway decorated or overdecorated. The hairy man, the mother's boyfriend, brings swatches of carpets from the store where he works as a salesman. Rectangles of every style lie in every room in the house, though there is no padding beneath them and the size is never right. When they're really awkward the mother cuts them down with razor blades and uses them for throw rugs, or piles them up and kneels on them when she's scrubbing the floors. The girl, always with bare feet, likes to hop from one rug to the other. She travels the house this way, leaping from the bedroom to the hallway, from hallway to bathroom, in a color-coded hopscotch. Sometimes the rugs are islands and she is a giant, able to walk a great archipelago in seconds, smashing with her jumps and thuds the homes and heads of the people who live in it. Sometimes she rolls up swatches for Hanna the Babysitter, who rolls her eyes but takes them home anyway.

In the backyard the girl assembles piles of dead leaves, faces away from them, and then lets herself fall. The crackle fills her ears. Then she lies still and examines the leaves that have fallen on her, the dead orange ones and the dried-up brown ones that are the color of rot.

The hairy man moves into the farmhouse. He clomps around the kitchen, his heavy boots waking the girl in the morning. He wears a green hat with earflaps and when he comes in after shoveling, snow is clotted in his beard and bushy eyebrows. When it begins to melt, which is instantly, water runs down his face and neck. He doesn't bother to wipe it away. One day he jokes that he is melting. Help me, I'm melting, he says, his hands clutching his head, his eyes rolled back and wide. Melting! The girl knows he is joking, he's doing this because they watched the *Wizard of Oz*, but still, to her he is a redfaced monster and she is frightened.

The mother has been more tired than usual the last two years. She sleeps on the weekends and doesn't stop in the girl's room and forgets to remind her of chores left unfinished or never started. From her bedroom, the girl sees flashes of her mother's red hair as she turns the corner to the bathroom. The mother doesn't bother shutting the door. Sometimes she's paralyzed on the toilet, her almond-shaped body slumped forward, eyes the color of ink staring blankly at the shower curtain. Mostly she looks confused, as if someone has just sworn at her. Her stiff fingers, worn from years of entering numerical data into an office computer, twitch like dead-spider legs.

The girl has to remind the mother about catechism class, but the mother is not listening, so Hanna drives the girl over—not Hanna, actually, but the boyfriend of Hanna, who is seventeen and drives a rusted Pinto. In class the girl learns of miracles and terrifying punishments, of women who turn into salt pillars. These stories seem to her not unlike fairy tales, like King Midas's touch of gold, which is, she is told, a gift that seems good but is really evil. Like Eve, the religion teacher says, smiling sweetly. She learns the significance of holy water and that Heaven is far away, very high above, and that Hell is forever. She learns that she is blessed, that there is both a god and a man who cannot be seen and who are everywhere, who are everywhere watching. She learns that the god is angry and vengeful but also tolerant and forgiving. When vengeful and when tolerant? She does not know. She does not understand these words or the origins of the man, or where he comes from or lives, but nevertheless turns the pages of her communion Bible.

When class is over, the girl runs outside, where the Pinto is parked in the same place as when she was dropped off. Hanna and the boyfriend are inside, but the air is stale and the windows are foggy. So on the way home the girl draws pictures in the moisture.

At school the girl is quiet. The other children do not know what to make of her old clothes and snarled hair. The girls don't talk to her and the boys tease her wickedly. They try to trip her and on the bus they launch gobs of spit at the back of her hood, gooey clots that meander and slide until they are dry and flaky.

She is scolded in class for not speaking loud enough during show and tell. She has brought a small octopus, which her grandfather found washed up on the beach one day, preserved in a jar of alcohol. The small beady eyes look huge if you look at them through the liquid. She can't expand on this and no one has told her where or how the creature was captured. No one has ever explained saltwater or longitude or waves or driftwood.

On the weekends the girl watches Hanna weave cloth into her hair. The girl wants her hair twisted with cloth, so Hanna does it. The gentle pulls are soothing; she nearly falls asleep. The girl admires Hanna's skirts and long necklaces and pierced ears and nose and lip. When Hanna untucks a shirt, the girl sees that there are drawings on her, which so mystify her that she takes a black marker to her own belly; after the lines fade she wipes them off and begins again, pushing harder this time, but the marks are rough and clumsy and are not pictures at all but only ugly black masses.

Winter officially sets in with a whiteout, quick and unpredictable as a bank holdup. It takes everyone by surprise, sobers even the most seasoned old-timers, the most effervescent middle-agers. They have lived in this town their entire lives but all winters begin anew; the cold snaps thin the blood and jar the bones into memory. The nights pass, and in the morning only portions of windows are still exposed.

Hanna sings the praises of American winters because, despite the cold, she continues to earn lots of money on the weekends from babysitting—loafing around, talking on the phone, and making lunches for the girl. Sometimes she tells the girl and the mother about Germany. About how back in Germany her father died and about how her family's house—the house she has lived in since she was born —burned down, taking her poor mother with it and leaving eight siblings who are now destitute. When Hanna says these things she lets her shoulders go limp and her face drops but then she straightens up and breathes in quickly to show, as the mother says, her spirit and resistance in the face of hardship. The mother wipes a tear from her eye and says yes, I know something about destitution. The mother explains her own life as a wanderer, an itinerant, a redeemed hitchhiker, a woman who, luckily, stopped moving long enough to understand the trouble she was in. The mother is eager to believe in toil and the honesty it presumably fosters, and insists on paying Hanna an extra dollar an hour and even on letting her stay for dinner once in a while, on the nights when the hairy man works into the evening.

Hanna has the eyes of an eagle. One day the girl gets her boots and coat and mittens on and reaches for the latch on the storm door, but then Hanna is behind her saying, what, you go like this you will catch the cold, and makes the girl add snowpants, hat, and scarf.

The snow crunches beneath the girl's feet. Except for the few spots of asphalt on the driveway, the land is forever white. From this distance the trees around the pond seem to wind up from the snow like crooked twigs. The sun's glare makes her squint. She makes her way through drifts taller than she is, sometimes lunging, sometimes rolling, crawling, swimming as if in a sea. When she stops moving the silence invades. The girl doesn't have the words, they lie still and dormant, tender meat inside a hard nut's shell. The technicalities of winter escape her—what happens to grass? where do fish go?—but with wet snow comes the possibility of sculpture. There are echoes, too, there is the tingle in the eyes when they are fixed upon the blinding white shine, there are animal prints revealing life, there is the flash of gray fur or the edge of a charcoal-colored wing, there are dimples under trees where clots of snow have weakened and fallen from branches. She looks back at her tracks, the loose snow around them like the shavings from bored holes.

She spends nearly an hour walking, looking back, walking. Each time the house gets smaller. When she is finally too cold to wander any farther she makes her way back to the porch and into the house. She strips off layers, hair wild with static, and looks in at Hanna, who is in the living room talking on the phone and performing fantastic stretches, bony limbs jutting out in all directions. When she pins both legs behind her own neck, the girl cries out.

The girl's unfulfilled biological father would call the toilet the shitter or the crapper, and sometimes the girl tries the words out, says them to herself under her breath. She tries them out on Hanna, who doesn't understand, and then on her mother, who stares at her but says nothing. Shitter, crapper, the girl blurts.

The father comes back stumbling and tattered and reeking of booze but has theories about who is at fault for what, who owes him and how much. He stands swaying outside the back door. His index finger draws sloppy circles in the air. The girl watches him. The mother doesn't know what he's talking about. What is this, now? she says.

Another time he comes by and shouts that he's heading for Las

Vegas, where he says he's going to make his own future. But the future doesn't pan out and he's back yet again, banging on the door with sunken eyes and empty pockets. The mother slides the bolt. After the banging stops the mother takes pills. The painkillers for her migraine have not yet kicked in but logic seeps through the pounding membranes in her head. Where he get money for a plane ticket to Vegas, she says with flattened eyes.

The restraining order has no effect; the father stops by in the middle of the night, waking up the whole house with the sound of trash cans being kicked, with his noisy spurting car, with his deranged-cowboy enlightenments. They hear a popping along the front of the house and see that he's got a couple shutters ripped off and is going for another. The hairy man has had enough. The mother pleads and pulls at his arms but there's no stopping him. He walks barefoot out the backdoor. The mother's knees buckle and she sits at the bottom of the stairs with her ears covered. The girl rushes to the front window to see the father going at the siding with a hammer until the hairy man yanks him from the house. The hairy man towers over the father but the father rushes the hairy man anyway. They roll and struggle, then are out of sight.

In a few minutes the hairy man comes in the back door, his jaw hanging crooked and dripping red. He stumbles to the sink. The girl runs upstairs. After a while, she's not sure how long, a car pulls away.

The mother begins to have accidents. She falls down stairs while transferring batches of canned preserves, she falls off ladders while retrieving winter equipment from the high shelves in the garage, she falls over on the way to the car. She wakes up later with no memory of the falls, secure in the belief that the father is behind this. "You'll go to hell for fibbing, you will," she says to no one, to the eternally bolted back door, her face like a flat stone, her mouth drawn tight, ready to spit.

The girl comes back from school with drawings that lack detail, even a sun or a tree. They are just partial outlines. They are put on the refrigerator one after another. Soon the magnet cannot hold them and they slide to the floor.

In January the girl learns to check the roofline on the side of the house for icicles, which she knocks down with the handle of a broom. She digs for them in the snow and carries them in her mitten and eats them one by one until her teeth ache.

She forges a path beyond the small woods to the pond, now a glassy frosted disk. Where the snow has melted are large black holes, in the distance dark slivers of rim and arc.

She walks the pond's perimeter. In some places she can walk unimpeded on the tops of solid snowdrifts. She follows the warped and leaning snow fence; only a few inches of the top of it are visible. It winds and she follows.

She builds elaborate cavernous snow forts with several chambers. On hands and knees she is an Eskimo, she is in the Great White North, she lies on her back in the dark fort as dusk falls, listening to her breathing, to the wind, to the sound her mouth makes as she wets her lips.

The mother and the hairy man get married. They go away for a couple of days and it is done. The girl has a new father; she is to call him Dad. One day Grandma stands at the stove stirring tomato soup and says to the girl, how do you feel about that, about having a new daddy, to which the girl has no reply. She stares at Grandma. Who is this woman? People are becoming expendable to her. Her hold on them is tentative.

The tomato soup is warm and sweet but the girl eats too slowly and suddenly it is crusted over.

The girl shows Hanna the icicles and the fort and the secret places she finds in the woods. They make snow angels, stepping out of them carefully to preserve the images. They make them all along the pond's border, so that from a distance they look connected, like paper dolls.

Sometimes they go sledding. The girl pulls a toboggan out of the garage and drags it to the top of a bank. The downward slope of the land will carry them across the backyard and along the entire length of the field, puttering out just before it meets up with the road. Hanna gives her a push and down the girl goes. The girl imagines that a force is pulling her, that she is light, she is the air, she will cross miles of tundra, glide over the ice and snow until she reaches the edge of the earth perhaps, an arctic peninsula jutting out into black water. But what is after water?

They go to the abandoned treehouse, the one that the older kids took over. There are sets of initials carved in the walls, frosty rotted knotholes, bits of clumped mud and animal droppings, magazines with naked people in them. Snow covers half the floor, so they sit along the other wall. Hanna tells the girl wild stories about Germany, about when she was a child. Hanna asks the girl if she knows where Germany is. The girl does not. Later, when they unfold the map the girl is confused; her state is on one side of the map and Germany is on the other, away in a long lost world. Hanna points to a black dot, the place where she is from, but the name means nothing to the girl, nor do the rivers and lines and borders and colors she sees mixed together.

They make hot chocolate and Hanna talks of how she longs to go back and of how much she misses her boyfriend. The boyfriend who's waiting for her. The girl's mouth is open and she is staring. The girl has not yet dreamed of other lands but now longs to know a secret language and mysterious people.

The winter stretches out, goes on and on and on. The farmers are taking extra precautions; they have to worry about how to get to the animals in the winter and keep them alive. But the regular house pets have it bad too. They are let out one day and never come back; they are found later, eyes like marbles, perfectly preserved in a snowdrift. One day the boys down the road set their frozen cat against a birch tree, the sister looking on, howling, face glistening with tears and snot.

The mother now lives in complete darkness. The shades are pulled most of the day, and she wears the same purple bathrobe and the white slippers that are falling apart. She doesn't bother getting up with the hairy man in the mornings. She loses her job. One day around dinnertime she is up humming and dancing around the kitchen, but there is no food and when she speaks her voice is harsh. She says strange things to the girl, fragments, gibberish that the girl can't make out. She talks of what the Virgin Mary has said to her, how the rosary works, what messages her dreams hold. When she leans close, her breath is sour. Objects are misplaced; nail polish remover is in the refrigerator, cotton balls in the freezer; throw rugs have been switched around or removed entirely. When the girl finds Aqua Net in the pantry she moves it back to the closet in the bathroom. She knows she has not made these small but telling mistakes but does not ask about them. Her moist breath seals her mouth like the lid of a pot.

The hairy man doesn't know how to talk to children. He is polite and formal and overcautious, as if someone is watching him. He ties the girl's hood too tight and doesn't wait for her to answer his questions.

They go riding on a snowmobile one day. The girl is both terrified and fearless sitting behind the hulking man, on this powerful machine. They do not speak.

Suddenly they are doing everything together. For her birthday he takes her to a local pizza place, where he stands over her while she plays skee-ball. She wants a stuffed animal but her tickets buy her only a plastic comb, which she ends up leaving behind.

He shows her how to hold a rifle, which she can't do properly because of its weight, but he doesn't care. There she is, his daughter! he tells his friends at the bars. She'll shoot better than you pencil-dicks when she's older, he tells them. He shows her how to set metal raccoon traps. He buys a pair of used ice skates for her to take to the pond. He clears off a log to sit on and watches her, smiling away. He skips work and takes her for rides in his sky-blue Oldsmobile. He whistles and talks to her about the truck he's going to own one day, a black Chevy pickup. He calls her pumpkin. He takes her to bars on the weekends to watch football games. He makes her pick teams, which she does according to color. If there is a blue team, she picks it because blue is the color of his car and she thinks this will help. He wants her to sit on his lap, to sip his beer. She remembers that it tastes horrible but each time she tries it she decides it is not too bad. He wants her to share his basket of fries, to partake of what he partakes, to speak his language, to hold him in her mind, to hold him up in her mind, to think the best of him. He is practically alone in this world now, he tells the girl, who looks at him and blinks. He might as well throw in the towel. He orders the girl another Coke. Does she like Coke? What else does she like? What else can he get for her? He is offering the false, overbearing generosity of the drunk man, the blind camaraderie of a whiskey soul.

He goes on and on. He had a chance at owning land, he says, except that his evil brother stole it. You're lucky, he says to the girl, you don't got any brothers or sisters, can't be no favoring then. He's a carpet salesman, for chrissakes, does she know how completely idiotic that is? The problem is that people's sense of equality is all messed up. Just look at the courts. Look at God! The girl squirms away to use the bathroom but she does not come back; she wanders outside in the snow along the side of the building. He does not go after her.

Hanna pulls out a flowered case full of makeup. She is sitting cross-legged on the living room floor, holding up a small mirror with one hand and brushing her cheek with the other. She notices the girl staring and calls her over. She pats the floor; the girl sits down. Hanna tells her to close her eyes. The girl likes the feel of the short little swipes the tiny brush makes. She opens her eyes. Now look straight ahead and don't move, Hanna says. The girl's head moves everywhere. No, you cannot move, Hanna says, and steadies the girl's forehead with her hand. The girl doesn't understand what this brush is doing, so she giggles. She giggles more and then can't stop. She giggles so much she begins to cough. Hanna laughs too, then lies down beside the girl and smooths her hair. There is, on Hanna's face, the type of smile the girl hasn't seen in a long time. Hanna pulls out a tube of lipstick and says now part your lips just a little. The girl likes the waxy rub of it. The lipstick smells like her mother's purse.

The girl knows on some level that if the lake can hold a snowmobile, then it can hold her. She can wander out at will. At first she doesn't bring her ice skates, she just slides around in her boots. She is a feather, she is wind. She walks on water.

One morning the girl wakes to screams. She thinks it is a dream but then the screams come again. She hears heavy footsteps and then the back door slamming. She looks out the window to see her mother in the backyard, nearly naked, grasping her own hand and rubbing it, as if to get something off. By the time the hairy man drags her to the house, she has practically collapsed. Her lips are blue and her eyes are bloodshot and sunken. In February the mother disappears.

Grandma comes. She strips the girl down first thing and gives her a bath. The girl's head is washed with vinegar to get rid of the lice. The vinegar will ooze out of her pores for days. The hairy man has left. Just for a short time, Grandma says, but her tone is decisive.

A postcard comes from Hanna, who is in Germany over spring break. The girl tapes it up by her mirror but takes it down every day to examine it. The corners get soft and worn.

Grandma doesn't walk well, so the girl brings her tea and cough drops, and is the one on the receiving end of the UPS deliveries, the repair people, the Jehovah's Witnesses. She nods or shakes her head to respond to questions. She feels there is something to hide and so tries to; she has learned how to fumble her way through formal situations with adults, she has learned when to bother them and when to shut the door quietly, or hang up the phone quietly, and wander off to a different room. She has instinctually learned the art of silence.

The snow is melting. Drifts are crumbly and the snow seems almost dry. The girl runs outside without a coat—no one runs after her, now, or calls her name. Tracks appear in the mud around the pond—claw marks and rounded hooves and the forked prints of bird feet. She sits in the tree house for hours reading books that are too hard for her. She looks up "abyss" in the dictionary but the definition is "bottomless pit," which she doesn't understand. She cannot yet conceptualize a starting point without a destination, a beginning without an end, a story without a resolution. She opens a map but cannot find Germany and begins to cry.

In a month the mother is back. The mother who does not know life without a cloud hanging over her. She can hardly look at the girl. Children's faces rip her apart. The people she speaks to about her insecurity and guilt have said there is still time. If it's one thing people don't often get, it's time. Consider yourself lucky, they say. Your child has not forgotten you. Not yet.

The mother feels loss nevertheless and so indulges the girl, buys her too many sweets and toys. And clothes; clothes for once. The girl senses the desperation and is wary, but follows the mother everywhere, all the time. She hears the exaggerated excitement in the mother's voice but holds her hand anyway.

In spring the bodies of children are aimless, like the seeds that flutter down from trees. The magic is maddening; it is too fast for their eyes. Magnolia blossoms blow off, cover the grass like frosting. Time stretches out, the sun hangs lower in the sky. The children cannot sit still or walk in a straight line; they have the energy of winter stored in their bones.

They have grown. They don't realize how many generations have passed this way, how endless it is. But they know routine: what is there should be there again.

The hairy man is not living in the house yet but he is a presence. The mother talks to him on the phone every night.

The day comes when he shows up. He parks the blue Oldsmobile in the middle of the driveway. The girl is on the porch, waiting for the mother to get sandals on and lock the door. They are going for ice cream, a treat the girl knows the mother can't afford despite her new job with the state. Or can she? There is the hairy man, anyway.

What do the heavens mean by this—a mother, suddenly full of smiles on a warm spring day, an almost absent man and his blue car, polished and shining, a barefoot girl standing on the concrete, dirtying her feet, hedging her bets?

Tara Mantel's work has appeared in many literary journals, including *TriQuarterly, The Missouri Review, Quarterly West, Confrontations*, and *The Alaska Review*. Her work has earned a Pushcart Prize honorable mention, and she was a finalist in the John Gardner Memorial Prize. During her residency at the Vermont Studio Center, she began to collect the stories for *Elemental*. She is a graduate of the University of Minnesota and the University of Southern Maine.